Praise for C█████

"J.S. Breukelaar's new collection, *Collision* will punch your breath out, slam you sideways and hit you by surprise, leaving you exquisitely bruised and wanting for more. One of the major voices of our times, J.S. Breukelaar is a writer who fears nothing and takes you along her amazing narrative rides that defy genre and conventions, a reckless driver that only notices the signs on the side of the road in order to run them down."
—Seb Doubinsky, author of The Babylonian Trilogy,
The Song of Synth, and *Missing Signal*

"Strange and unflinchingly surreal, Breukelaar's stories read like dispatches from a fever dream."
—Keith Rosson, author of *The Mercy of the Tide*
and *Smoke City*

"I immediately felt captivated by J.S. Breukelaar's evocatively descriptive style, her convincing observations of human behavior and the incisive quality of her dialogue. At times it felt as though her characters, and the worlds they inhabited, were leaping off the page, demanding my full attention. Although each of the stories is very different, what remains constant throughout the collection is the author's skill in drawing her readers into the fantastical worlds she is describing. Yet these are worlds which, albeit in slightly distorted ways, are often all too easily recognizable, possibly because there is always an element of people struggling to make sense of, and adjust to, the world they are inhabiting."
—Linda Hepworth, *Nudge-Books Magazine* (5 stars)

"The stories are ruthless, nothing is safe—even the child who offers a lollipop and loses a wrist to the Clint Eastwood dog. Breukelaar experiments with the Gothic and queries the queer. Bedded within the tales is a voluptuous energy that turns pages. Tables pirouette in a blink and, before you know it, the story is eleven shades grimmer."
—Eugen Bacon, *Breach Magazine*

"Breukelaar tackles rejection and misunderstanding head-on by harnessing her wonderfully weird prose and creating an imaginarium from it, one that holds things you've never dreamt could—or should—exist."
—*Fangoria Magazine*

"Each of these stories stylishly investigates an encounter between characters and forces of otherworldly, or in some cases off-world, hues. But Breukelaar accomplishes much more than that. She delves into how such contacts—which range from the merely glancing to the traumatically concussive—lead to altered perspectives and transformations of the mind, a literary feat of the first order."
—Alvaro Zinos-Amaro
Orson Scott Card's Intergalactic Medicine Show

"*Collision* is a wonderful collection of complex tales that cross genres in ways that are never fully expected at the beginning but always fully realized by the end. The boundaries between different styles are as porous as the boundaries between worlds, but each aspect is precisely organized and elevated by Breukelaar's versatile and vital techniques. It's no stretch to say there's something for everyone here, but we can go further and say there's something for every version of everyone, even as they shift and change."
—*Hellnotes*

"Breukelaar's delectable prose draws in the reader, and I frequently found myself in that perfect hypnotic state where I forgot I was reading—the highest honor one can bestow on an author, in my opinion."
—Kris Ashton, *Andromeda Spaceways Magazine*

"Breukelaar's stories are fueled with gorgeous darkness, often thematically heartbreaking and always nothing short of amazing."
—Shane Douglas Keene, *Inkheist*

ALSO BY J.S. BREUKELAAR

American Monster
Aletheia

COLLISION

STORIES

J.S. BREUKELAAR

Meerkat Press
Atlanta

"Union Falls" originally published in *Fantasy Magazine* (July 2011)
"Lion Man" originally published in *Women Writing the Weird*, edited by Deb Hoag, Dog Horn Publishing, (November 2011)
"The Box" originally published in *Juked* (November 2012)
"War Wounds" originally published as "Field Manual" in *States of Terror Volume 2*, edited by Matt E. Lewis and Keith McCleary, Ayahuasca Publishing (October 2015)
"Fairy Tale" originally published in *LampLight* (March 2016)
"Rogues Bay" originally published in *Gamut Magazine* (July 2017)
"Glow" originally published in *Welcome to Dystopia: 45 Visions of What Lies Ahead*, edited by Gordon Van Gelder, Or Books (July 2018)
"Raining Street" originally published in *Black Static #63* (May 2018)

Title of "Like Ripples on a Blank Shore" based on lyrics from RECKONER, Words and Music by THOMAS YORKE, JONATHAN GREENWOOD, COLIN GREENWOOD, EDWARD O'BRIEN and PHILIP SELWAY
© 2007 WARNER/CHAPPELL MUSIC LTD
All Rights in the U.S. and Canada Administered by WB MUSIC CORP.
All Rights Reserved
Used By Permission of ALFRED MUSIC

Illustrations by Keith Rosson
Author Photo by Guy Bailey
Cover Design by Tricia Reeks

ISBN-13 978-1-946154-17-0 (Paperback)
ISBN-13 978-1-946154-18-7 (eBook)

Library of Congress Control Number: 2018963109

Printed in the United States of America

Published in the United States of America by
Meerkat Press, LLC, Atlanta, Georgia
www.meerkatpress.com

For Jack and Isabella

Contents

Angela Slatter's Brisbane-set debut novel, *Vigil*, was released by Jo Fletcher Books in 2016 and was shortlisted for the Aurealis Award for Best Fantasy Novel, the Locus Award for Best Debut Novel, and nominated for the Dublin Literary Award. The sequel *Corpselight* followed in 2017 and *Restoration*, the concluding volume will be launched in August 2018. Angela is the author of nine short story collections, including *The Girl with No Hands and Other Tales*, *Sourdough and Other Stories*, *The Bitterwood Bible and Other Recountings*, *Black-Winged Angels*, *Winter Children and Other Chilling Tales* and *A Feast of Sorrows: Stories*. Her work has been adapted for the screen, and translated into Japanese, Spanish, French, Chinese, Russian, and Bulgarian. Angela has won a World Fantasy Award, a British Fantasy Award, one Ditmar Award, and six Aurealis Awards.

Introduction

by Angela Slatter

Weird fiction can be a blend of ghost story, myth, and something that (from a distance and in very dim light) might well bear a passing resemblance to science. Sure, that's a messy description, a bit like trying to pour whiskey into a thimble, but that hold-all of 'weird' is just about capacious enough to cover what's offered by the works of J.S. Breukelaar.

It's supernatural and it's macabre. It's strange and it's bewildering. These tales shake you and stir you, all at the same time because J.S. is leaving her footprints on a path blazed by luminaries such as M.R. James, Robert Aickman, Tanith Lee, Kelly Link, Charlotte Perkins Gillman, Jeff VanderMeer, Gustave Flaubert, Edgar Allan Poe, Daphne DuMaurier, Leonora Carrington and Charlotte Brontë, to name but a few.

The first thing I ever read of hers was an old incarnation of a story called "Morningtown Ride," a kind of space opera horror. About three years ago I critiqued it and it's changed shape since that initial iteration, but the thing that *hasn't* changed at all is the very thing that struck me back then: the power of the tale. It was so bold, so out-there, there were some wobbles, sure, but the command of the language was clear . . . and the craftsmanship in her work has only deepened in the intervening years.

What I love about finding writers early in their careers and following along is the chance to see what they do next, how they evolve, and my big reward last year was to read her novel *Aletheia*. I felt that my breath had been, quite literally, snatched away. The short works I'd read before then had given but a hint of what might one day be produced: *Aletheia* was *that* thing; it was *that* moment. The narrative threads were masterfully interwoven, the style was elegant, the story a fugue to be lost in, to dream in, to surrender to nightmares in . . . in short it was a beautiful terror of a thing.

Which brings me back to this collection, *Collision*. Twelve stories old and new, some with the sense of a fairy tale, some feel like old school science fiction, yet others are entirely neoteric hybrids. When I think of J.S.'s work, I'm reminded of Kelly Link's pocket universes infested by mermaids . . . J.S.'s writing, like Kelly's, makes you believe such places could exist . . . and that you might like to visit there for a while . . . or, on second thoughts, maybe just reading about them is enough . . .

"Union Falls" is a tale of blue June days, an armless maiden, and a devil's own beat. In "The Box" life intersects with keystrokes to hide all our scars—for a time. You'll hear in "Ava Rune" the echoes of Norse mythology meeting Stephen King's *Carrie* in a bar to discuss what mischief might be done, what revenges taken. The homes and families in "Lion Man" bear more than a passing resemblance to prisons. In "Fairy Tale" the present and the ever-nipping-at-one's heels past collide. In "Fixed" there are house wolves and lessons about finding our lost parts.

In "War Wounds" monsters and memories are made, for better or worse. All I need to say about "Rogue's Bay 3013" is "strange angels" and leave it at that.

"Collision" is about loving where we cannot help and destroying what we must. "Glow" is a metaphor for displacement and diaspora in an increasingly compassionless world. "Raining Street" is one of the most original takes on Orpheus and Eurydice I've ever read. "Ripples on a Blank Shore" meditates on Fate's leprous power and the crumbs of dreams it throws us, and it's a fitting finish for the collection, this novella, because it shows yet again the next step, the evolution of a writer—and frankly, all stories involving a wedding should contain the line "How many dead?"

What more could you want?

There's a spark of magnificent strangeness and a strange spark of magnificence in each and every one. Herein you'll find skeins of horror, science fiction, literature, fantasy and, above all things, weirdness. Such weirdness! To paraphrase Pinhead the Cenobite, "Oh, she has such weirdness to show you!"

There's something very Alice in Wonderland about J.S.'s heroines, no matter their age or situation in life . . . some are ingénues about to get the rudest shocks of their lives; some are care-worn and lined, the roadmap of their lives carved deeply into their faces. They may well be surprised by the turns in the road, but they lean into the skid and hang on. Her heroes are grizzled or fresh-cheeked, they smell like too much aftershave or the kind of sweat only true fear can produce. Sometimes they're better than they should be . . . sometimes they try, sometimes they don't . . . sometimes they fail.

What I would say all these stories have in common, no matter their outcome, is *hope*. Hope for something better beyond our time in this place—and by that I don't mean something better for us in the beyond, but leaving something better behind for whoever— whatever—comes next. There is beauty here and pain, grief and joy, wonder and devastation, seamlessly brought together by a deft hand and an astonishing imagination.

Collision is the entrance to a psychedelic rabbit's hole; I urge you to make the journey, but don't forget to pack some snake beans (go on, trust me, you'll see what I mean).

Union Falls

When the girl turned up for the job in her black jeans and cute haircut and no arms, Deel just shook her head, no. Girl wiggled her shoulders and flicked her hair in that way.

"Just give me a listen," she said.

Selwyn at the bar stared at her out of his good eye, pushed his glasses up on his nose even though they were already up as far as they could go, and Deel waited but he just kept staring. And then Henry trotted out from behind the bar with beer stuck to his whiskers because he'd been drinking the slops again and went right up to the girl and sat on her shoes. Black Van sneakers with pink trim. No laces.

"Are you wet?" Deel said, looking at the water seeping out from under the girl's soles.

It was one of those blue June days, the air heavy with the smell of overheating asphalt and baked pollen. Deel yanked at the neck of her tank top, sucked hot hair in through her mouth and felt like she was choking.

"I had a dip in the lake," the girl said. "Water's so clear you can see right down to the stones."

And Deel noticed fine strands of hair stuck to the wide, pale forehead, but whether from sweat or lake water, Deel could not tell. The girl was wearing a T-shirt and the sleeves hung out over the smooth nubs of her shoulders and flapped empty against her torso.

"You do realize that the gig's for a piano player?" Deel said.

"So do I get an audition or what?" The girl shrugged out of her satchel strap, stepping out of one shoe and catching the satchel in her lifted foot all in one motion. Deel caught a glimpse of a challenge deep below the surface of the girl's whetstone eyes, and she didn't like it. Fast-forward to an interior shot of Deel's mailbox, a letter stamped from the antidiscrimination board vying for room with all the bills and notices and empty offers.

"Henry's drunk again," Deel said to Selwyn. "Those slop trays don't empty themselves."

The girl—whose name, according to her crumpled CV, was Ame—flicked her eyes between Selwyn and Deel as if to gauge what ran between them. Satisfied, she acknowledged the listing, slobbering dog at her feet with a nudge of her sneaker and turned her pale head finally to the unused Casio keyboard in the corner of the small room, wavering in reflected light from the bottles and glasses behind the bar.

"Guess we better give her a listen." Selwyn kind of shook himself like he just woke up and Deel glared.

"Cain't hurt," said Pete, his Carolina vowels making Deel's flesh crawl at this ungodly hour. She could barely cope with his *cain'ts* and *ain'ts* and *gee mahnour sayvenths* after sundown with a couple of beers under her belt, much less in the hard daylight of a Saturday afternoon. But Pete was the bassist and Deel's daddy had played bass in a college band so she let it lie. The girl, who'd left out the bit about having no arms, was the only one who'd replied to the small ad that Selwyn had placed in the Pennysaver. They'd all agreed that the whole band had to be there for the interview, Jake the drummer a no-show as usual.

Deel caught the girl's hard smile and regretted not wearing lipstick for godsakes. She sipped from her cold coffee for something to do with her hands, but she had a slight hangover and what she really needed was a drink.

"Okay," she said. "But . . ."

But the girl was kicking off her other shoe and at the keys before Deel had worked out but what. And what she pounded out with her

feet was Meatloaf's "Bat Out of Hell." Crashing chords and swarming riffs. Her smooth feet and long, black-varnished toes were stark
against the keys, and every so often her head would shake to the side
or nod back and forth. Because the instrument was so high relative
to the reach of her legs, she played slightly hunched and looked to be
levitating on the stool, her torso motionless and her legs, impossibly
limber, dancing up and down the keyboard.

Afterward, she swiveled around to face them. No one said anything. Henry furtively lapped at a pool of his own vomit and no one
stopped him. Selwyn's good eye, the color of rain, just stared at the
silent keys which seemed to have taken on a kind of conspiratorial
nakedness, privates unfairly flaunted. Deel looked away. Beams of
dirty light fell on the bottles, and a cell phone bleated from downstairs, the smell of oil and exhaust sharp and cold from the no-name
Gas and Lube.

"What?" The girl looked from one to the other. "You did say it
was an eighties band."

The girl put her shoes back on and waited downstairs while they
talked it over. Deel pointed out how you can't have an amputee
keyboard player in a town like Union Falls.

"I don't need this," Deel said.

And Selwyn said, calmly returning her affronted gaze, that no
one did. "But the Lake View's taken all our trade with that open grill
and fresh charr and so-called music, is the thing."

And in Selwyn's good eye Deel caught a glimpse of her own fero-
cious ponytail and worried mouth, but Pete just kept saying, "chick
is hot, chick is smokin'." So she said, "Well better ask Jake about it,"
but Selwyn just shrugged. So, in the end, Deel said she'd give it a
month and hadn't they better go wake up their so-called drummer
and start rehearsing?

After the boys left, she called the girl back in but when Deel said
her name, the girl interrupted.

"Ay-mee," she said. "It's spelled Ame, but you say it like Amy."

Deel asked for references, which Ame pulled out of the satchel
with her teeth and which Deel gingerly removed from her mouth.

Deel didn't like this. Shadows sliced across the girl's face and fell like a mask across her dark eyes and Deel noticed tiny scars hatched on her jaw and one on her chin. In the wrong light she could be just standing there with her arms held behind her back as if hiding something in her hands.

"Boo!" she said.

Deel flinched, a cold knot of rage tightening in her chest.

"You were looking at me like you'd seen a ghost," said the girl, a wide white smile instantly enlivening her features. "The scars are from falling on my face. When I was a kid."

Deel swallowed and started leafing through the references. She saw that the girl was from Albany, was twenty-two and had dropped out of music school but had been playing in bands since she was thirteen.

"If you're looking for the section that says how I lost my arms," Ame said. "You won't find it there."

Deel put down the references. The girl's lips curved in that joker grin that did not quite extend to her eyes. An insolence to her affliction. For the second time this morning Deel felt her flesh crawl, but this time she hated herself for it. She felt momentarily frightened and wanted to call Selwyn back in but stopped herself. She needed time to think of a way to fob the girl off, no matter what the guys said. It was her bar, in the end, and her call.

"Can I get you a cup of coffee?"

The girl shrugged like she didn't care one way or another, so Deel went behind the bar and poured the coffee, telling herself that the whole thing was a bad idea, not just the girl, but the whole band thing, and maybe even the whole bar, just taking it over when she did, and what she should have done was sell the house and move on like everyone in Union Falls told her to. Move on, yes, but then Selwyn turned up for the bar job, not a college boy, too old for that, but not a farm boy either, not exactly. Guitar in a muddy case on his back. And things just moved along from there.

"How do you take it?" she called into the shadows, Ame hidden from her at this angle. "Your coffee."

There was no answer, and Deel thought—hoped—that maybe the girl had gone, but then her voice cut across the shadows, an effortful croak.

"With a straw," she said.

* * *

Deel put Ame on a one-month trial. She explained that the band played every Friday and Saturday night and the pay was ten percent of the takings, so she better rustle herself up a day job. But Ame never got around to that, and she seemed to get by, mainly it seemed on leftovers Deel brought her from home. Deel would soon learn that the straw thing was just for show, give people a chance to get used to her—what she was capable of. Ame could hold a coffee cup in her feet, put her contact lenses in with her toes, even ride a motorbike with one foot on the throttle and the other on the brake, as they were to discover. But back then she held back and looked for all the world to Deel like a kid playing look-ma-no-hands. Enjoying herself.

Deel asked where she was staying, and Ame said she didn't know and what about the Village Inn down the road?

"Parents and visiting alumni." Deel hesitated. "Pretty pricey."

And this time it was her own voice that sounded strange and disconnected to Deel when she heard herself offering Ame the room above the garage. It had been shut up since the previous manager, Randy "Raccoon" Helmstetter, his scrawny arms and legs crosshatched in self-inflicted knife wounds, had locked himself in with his precious raccoons, cuffed himself to the bed and eaten the key. When they finally busted down the door, Randy was not quite dead, his entrails flung around the room like silly string, and a raccoon sitting on the floor chewing on one of Randy's osteoporotic finger bones.

"Room's in the back," Deel said. "So you can't see the lake, but at least you don't get the fumes from downstairs."

"I don't need to see the lake," Ame said. "I know where it is."

* * *

They rehearsed through the week. As Friday approached word got out about the keyboardist who wailed with her feet. Deel knew what they were saying in the town, at the IGA and the Post Office—how she'd really lost it this time, and maybe she had. There were plenty of people who thought she should have moved on. Her daddy had been a successful songwriter and session musician. She could have moved back to Jersey or New York, started a new life for herself instead of reopening the Pump Bar, which should never have been reopened, folks said, and especially not by her after what happened. She knew nothing about money, they said, and they were right. Look at her house, a three-story Georgian ruin slid into disrepair—there was a pulpiness to the floor beneath certain rugs, and a strange smell from the basement. Only one burner worked on the stove, and water pressure from the faucets was nonexistent. The back porch hung off the house by rusty nails and splintered beams, and Deel was sure that any day now it would end up in the lake. The head of the HOA, pushing for a condemnation order on the place, stopped Deel on the street and said she'd heard about the amputee keyboard player.

"A gimmick, Delia? Are you really that desperate?"

No, Deel thought, not a gimmick. That wasn't how any of them would describe Ame in rehearsal. Selwyn had lowered the keyboard for her and shook his head in wonder at the new sound she gave the band with her lush keyboard strokes. And how she got him to move in closer to the mic and told Pete to add in some slaps for a funkier rhythm. There was too much flesh on her for a gimmick and more blood in her melody line than the whole band put together. Not to mention how she drove Pete's Honda 300 up and down Cherry Tree Lane behind the bar, with her feet.

But Deel knew that the HOA had a point. It would take more than a gimmick to fix her house.

Over the next week the band rehearsed a bunch of new songs and Deel heard Ame running some synth riffs that she'd rearranged for the keyboard just to update the sound. When Pete, in a fit of jealousy, maybe, drawled that maybe the sound didn't need updatin', she drawled back, "No, but Delia's porch needs fixin' and whinin' won't pay the bills, so one more time from the top, boys—a week to go before shit gets real."

Deel felt her legs go cold and she wondered how Ame knew about her porch.

* * *

Opening night the place was more than half full. The band opened with "Rock Lobster" and by the time they closed with "Bat Out of Hell," which would become their signature encore, there were more than thirty pairs of sneakers, steel-toed boots, and high heels stomping on the worn linoleum. Deel ran out of beer. She barely had time to look up from the taps, but when she did there was Ame to the left behind the band—she'd wanted it that way, she told Selwyn, this was no pity party—in a circle of blue light with her pretty feet snaking up and down the keyboard. Selwyn singing his heart out and all but swallowing the mic every time he looked over his shoulder at Ame, smitten, Deel supposed, from day one.

* * *

At first the crowds came out of curiosity.

"Everyone loves a creature feature," said Ame, her wide mouth twisted up in that same grin that never seemed to reach her hard, dark eyes.

And Deel conceded that it was true. Just like how at first everyone, especially the college kids, came because of what happened to Randy—drawn, maybe, to the making of an urban myth. And then it was Deel herself, the unmerry widow intent on making a fool of herself. Well that got old quick, and then all that was left at the bar were the grease monkeys from downstairs and the occasional seasonal worker or farmhand intimidated by the Village Inn or the Lake View, which in the end, took all the college kids.

So what with Randy and Deel, the Pump had had its share of freak shows.

"Three times the charm," Deel warned Selwyn, and she was right. At first the crowds mainly returned there to see the amputee at the keyboard. But what they saw, instead, was Ame. Sitting there in the blue shadows with her phantom arms tied behind her back, she seemed totally in the flesh, riding the keys with her feet so agile and free that you forgot they weren't hands, forgot her affliction and forgot your own. The Pump Bar got so crowded on Friday and Saturday nights that the band started up on Thursdays too. They'd all—Deel, Selwyn, Ame and the boys—stay back sometimes to unwind and Deel noticed how Selwyn bought himself new glasses and Ame beat Jake at pool playing with one end of the cue stick on the bridge and the other between the varnished toes of her right foot. One night, over tequila, they played Truth or Dare, and Ame said dare because the truth about her was more boring than you'd think, and Deel said dare because she didn't know the truth anymore, so Pete, who could neither forgive Deel for hiring Ame, nor himself for wanting her to, dared Deel to let Ame give her another ear piercing.

"Kill two birds with one brick, so to speak," he drawled.

Selwyn said no, but Deel waved him off. As Ame moved in close to Deel's ear with the needle, brushing Deel's hair with her toes, the boys grew silent with maybe a last titter from Pete when the needle pierced Deel's skin. Deel felt the prick. She met the girl's dark, depthless eyes, smelled the liquor on her breath and the lotion on her skin, and felt a tight sweet lick between her legs that reminded her of her husband Larry, of breastfeeding the boys. Of any number of caresses she'd known, for the past five years only in her dreams.

* * *

Randy's room had stayed closed off even after Deel took over the bar. She went in it once and felt herself surrounded by something that shouldn't be but was. It was as if whatever part of Randy had seen himself eaten from the inside out, was still there and was still hungry. But Ame settled in just fine. Deel brought her blankets and pots and pans and helped her clean it—the walls slick with fungus, a strange sandy debris across the linoleum—but still she felt ashamed of keeping the girl there.

One Sunday morning a few weeks after Ame started with the band, Deel was in the bar stocking the fridges and when she looked up, the girl in her bathrobe was standing in the storeroom doorway. The sleeves of the short robe hung empty, like some kind of prank, and without makeup and her hair wet from the shower, Ame looked like just the kid to play it.

"You want some coffee?" She was smiling, but she looked unusually pale.

Deel wiped her hands and smoothed down her hair, followed Ame into the narrow hallway between the storeroom and Randy's tiny studio in the back. The hallway canted down and oddly to the left as if knocked out of kilter by some subterranean event so that the front did not line up with the back. The little studio was bereft of decoration. No photographs or posters or knickknacks, nor even, surprisingly, any music. No computer, or speakers, at least that Deel could see. Just scattered souvenirs from the long walks in the woods and by the lake—fossils, lake stones and dead wood, a squirrel skull the color of vanilla ice cream. Deel watched Ame move around the kitchenette taking things down and putting them away with one foot, her black nail polish gleaming and defiant in the morning gloom. After a while she pointed to Deel's cooling coffee with her toe.

"Too strong?" said Ame. "I can boil some water."

Deel shook her head, her throat bunched in a painful lump. She would move Ame into the lake house, she thought, after the weekend. Three floors of emptiness by the shore—the girl could have the second floor all to herself. Deel was amazed she hadn't thought of it before; she could practically see Ame in the big corner room, the one with windows looking out onto her precious lake.

Ame often came to rehearsal damp although Deel never saw her swim, never saw her hanging out on the dock with all the other college kids, and she guessed that Ame was more self-conscious than she let on. Deel sometimes saw her down at the rocky shore, mostly with Henry, and from a distance with those long smooth legs of hers, she'd look just like any other beautiful young girl in cutoffs. Sometimes Ame and Henry would take off into the woods and Deel would watch them go and wait for them until they returned, falling all too easily into those old habits of secret care, imagining the girl groveling in the dirt with her teeth, digging with her toes for treasure. It would be dark when they returned, Ame damp and exhausted and starving for the supper Deel left wrapped in foil for her, and for which the girl's return was thanks enough.

∗ ∗ ∗

The crowds at the Pump Bar kept up over the summer. The band got a write-up in the Falls Post, and Deel introduced a basic snack menu—burgers and sandwiches and small pizzas. She was a good cook and they never had to throw anything away. And Selwyn invented the Happy Hour Special—some poor excuse for a cocktail he cobbled together out of cheap vodka and tropical fruit punch. It all helped, but it was mainly the music, and the music was mainly Ame. She sped some songs up, slowed others down, lowered the key by a half tone, added bells or looped Selwyn's vocals. And although she stayed in the shadows, backstage at left behind Selwyn, everyone knew she was there with her look-ma-no-hands stance and the blue lights playing across her varnished toes.

But then, a couple of weeks before Labor Day, they were playing their final set and Selwyn changed the order of the playlist. It wasn't the first time of course—he had always been good at reading a crowd—but what happened next had nothing to do with changing the order of the songs. It was just after midnight. Deel watched him step up to the mic and felt a queasy tightening in her belly.

"Folks, before we bow out for the night, and I know I've already introduced the band"—rowdy applause—"but I'd like to close with a specially-arranged number from our keyboard wonder here, Ame,"—tumultuous stomping—"who rocks the eighties, rocks the night, and rocks the freakin' world!" Roars from the crowd, a flock of white hands in the air.

Selwyn stepped back from the mic with a strange smile on his face and picked up his guitar. Deel froze, icy panic needling up her spine. The blue spotlight penciled in on Ame. Jake counted them in, and Ame hit the piano intro—a famous riff from a song Deel had never heard them play.

What the hell? Deel said under her breath, but what it was, was "Bette Davis Eyes" and what the hell, was that after the intro, Ame took her feet off the keys and put them on the floor and began to sing. Her voice began in a whisper, swelled to a croak then to an off-key keening, but it wasn't that. Not her voice, or that she was off-key or out of time—it wasn't the what of anything. It was the how—how her sitting there so in-the-flesh, so naked and far from home—how it spoke to needs and hurts that could not be spoken and could not be sung except badly. How it made everyone think about everything that had been amputated from their lives. How Pete's head lowered in shame, and how he began to drool. How Selwyn's backup vocals degenerated to a flat *ooohh,* and Deel knew that he was thinking about the fight with his army brother that had cost him his eye. And how what Deel was thinking, beer from the tap waterfalling over the mug and down her knuckles, was about Larry and the children gone in the blink of another eye.

The band shambled on, their faces blurred by tears, everyone in the audience lost down some private hallway knocked out of true, dancing alone or vomiting tropical fruit punch into the bathroom sinks. And still Ame kept singing, that terrible, needful croak, sitting there with her hands tied behind her back like a human sacrifice, a virgin led to the slaughter.

By the end of the song the bar was empty. No more hands in the air. The band packed up and finally it was just Deel and Selwyn left. He offered to lock up, but Deel said no. She started to shake and then it was her turn to throw up into the sink.

Selwyn came around and held her ponytail away from her face. He knew, of course, what she was thinking, what she always thought about this time of the year. She finished and stood up. He swooped down to offer her one of those hugs she'd never from day one known how to take or what to give in return.

"I'll be fine," she said, wiping her mouth with the bar towel. "What the hell happened?"

"She'd asked," Selwyn plucked at a loose thread on his sleeve. "Said she wanted to do a song and that it was one of her favorites."

Deel put down the towel and glared at him. Anger had been her cloak for so long now that she slipped into it without even thinking.

"Unrehearsed?" she said. "I should fire your ass."

He shook his head, miserable but not for himself.

"We rehearsed," he said, gently. "I may be a sucker but I'm no amateur."

She looked down at her shaking hands. All the lights were off, and there was only the dull glow of the fridges. The edge of her wedding band was a circle of fire in the darkness.

"I know. So what happened?"

"She sounded okay in rehearsals. Not brilliant, but okay, and we figured after everything she'd done for us—"

"For us?"

"For the band." Selwyn's voice was rough. "And for you."

Henry's paws clicked across the floor from the stairs where he'd been waiting.

"I don't know." Selwyn took off his glasses, wiped them on a corner of his shirt. "She seemed to need it."

Deel felt her mouth quiver. "Have you seen her?"

Selwyn shook his head. He looked scared. Scared not for the absence of the girl, but of it. And Deel too, suddenly terrified of the stranger whose references she never checked, whose police record she had never verified. Scared she'd gone and scared she hadn't. They both looked across at the storeroom door and Selwyn said he'd check but Deel said no. She said he should go home. He looked hurt at being shut out but it wasn't the first time, and Deel was surprised to hope that it wouldn't be the last. He picked up his guitar, tucked his hair behind his ears, and walked out.

She waited until his footsteps had died away and then she waited some more. Then she got up and went into the storeroom and down the zigzag hallway, its walls almost brushing her shoulders. She knocked on Ame's door, waited, and then let herself in with the spare key.

Moonlight slanted in and shimmered on the surfaces of the kitchenette, on all the dead souvenirs on shelves and on the windowsill beside the bed. Deel picked up a flat silver skipping stone. Her hand closed around it, cold as night, smooth as bone. She looked through the window at the woods up on the hill, at the moon thrown up from the lake, and when she turned around, Ame stood in the doorway. Deel's heart hammered. The wavering smear of the girl seemed formed out of the darkness itself.

"I was born this way," Ame said. She didn't move.

"I guessed." A cold drop of perspiration wormed down Deel's ribs.

"I'm sorry about tonight," Ame said. "It won't happen again."

Deel swallowed, didn't think she was going to cry and was ashamed when she did.

"I know," she said. "I'm sorry too."

Only the gleam of Ame's eyes and the flash of the buckle on her satchel broke the darkness of the form in the doorway.

Deel's legs gave way and she sat down on the bed. Ame didn't move, waiting.

"They were coming home from camp," Deel began. "The week before Labor Day. Larry and the boys. They were ten. Twins. I hadn't wanted them to go so young. I knew it was a bad idea. A Dodge pickup with a dead doe in the back and four drunk hunters in the cab hit them head-on at ninety miles an hour on Route 90. Larry and Lucas died instantly. Sam lived for a week in the hospital. But he never woke up. His eyes opened once or twice, though, and I never left his side, just waited for his eyes to open so I could wave. Stupid. I thought . . . I hoped . . ."

Still the girl didn't say anything, her form motionless as a lake pile, the night washing in all around her.

"He'd be fifteen this year," said Deel, through her teeth. "What does that make me?"

Ame then came over to the bed and as she came closer, Deel was struck by her pallor. She sat down beside Deel. There were dark patches of water on her jeans. Her skin looked damp. She leaned her head into Deel's neck, and Deel froze. Then slowly, awkwardly, she reached an arm around the poor, abbreviated torso and pulled her close. She could smell lake weed and the woods in the soft-cropped hair, felt it tickle her chin. She hadn't touched a soul since her family was killed, not really. Oh, Selwyn tried to give her one of his awkward smooches every New Year's Eve, his arms out like windmills, and she'd shared a few stunted couplings with truckers over the years, but nothing like this. This melting one being into another. Deel tried to give the girl some of her warmth, and Ame inched in closer. The moon shone through the window, and they spoke occasionally and in torrents broken by long silences. It seemed once to Deel that Ame had fallen asleep, a subtle decline in the weight against her, and later she must have dozed herself, curled up freezing on the bed and dimly aware of Ame getting up and moving around the room, collecting her belongings and packing them into the satchel.

When Deel woke again just before dawn, a blanket had been thrown over her, and the girl was gone. Apart from the stone she still clutched in her hand the room was empty, empty of Ame, of the ghost of Randy Raccoon, of all the dead souvenirs.

Deel ordered a keyboard book and began to teach herself how to play. The guys joked about how they might even let her join the band one day, just don't expect a mic. Business wasn't as good as it was when Ame was there, but better than it was before she came, and Deel found a handyman to help with the heavy lifting on her porch. One late night after closing, Deel offered Selwyn a partnership in the business and his attention returned from wherever it had wandered—listening for a wet footfall up the back steps, maybe.

"What on earth for?" he said.

"It's a living." She smoothed down her hair. "That's something, isn't it?"

He gave her a half-smile that said he knew there was more and that he hoped she'd tell him one day. How that night in Randy's room when Ame turned back once from the doorway, Deel had sat up on the bed to wave.

And Ame had waved back.

Raining Street

Our neighbor, Marie, waves me down with those square hands of hers, flapping like fleshy wings. I have just dropped the kids off at school and consider pretending I haven't seen her, turning blindly up the path to our own front door. But she would know I'm lying. She peers at me from beneath bushy eyebrows, like steel wool—a sign, she assures me, that she is really much better now. Nailed to the spot, I watch her wind a long strand of silver hair around her fingers, give it a tug. It pulls away from the scalp, leaving a bald patch flecked with blood. She opens her fingers, letting the autumn breeze snatch the hair away to get snagged on the clothesline. What is there to say? She grins wickedly, eyes disappearing behind tidal folds of flesh.

I make myself smile. The trick is to think of some excuse to escape her unsettling jabber, go inside and try to balance my books, work out where or how I'll make ends meet. But tearing myself away from Marie—it all seems too hard. Loneliness is exhausting. Worst case scenario, it's one hour I'll never get back again, and one thing I have plenty of these days is hours. The curtains at our windows twitch—could be the wind, or Jules, doing a terrible job of spying on me. But Jules, I remember, isn't home. Not anymore.

Marie's husband Donald appears between the two houses, lugging a laundry basket. An ancient, gnarled oak tree in their backyard (you can see the dark branches over the pitched roof) keeps the place in perpetual twilight, so Marie and Donald have been forced to string their clothesline at the front of the house. He fusses with the pegs, his hands customarily gloved, according to Marie, for his arthritis. The silvery filaments of his wife's hair flail on the line above him.

"Cold's coming," Donald says in his womanly voice, and there is something ominous to the way he adds: "Heating bill's through the roof."

Marie billows out as usual across the sidewalk but there is a new set to her smile, a waxy gleam in her eyes. Behind her, Donald's stoop over the laundry basket is even more precarious than usual, and there are lakes of sweat under his armpits despite the chill. I wonder if they've had a fight. New angles in his hands poke beneath yellow rubber kitchen gloves, sharp hints of bone.

My mind races, trips over itself. The children clung to me this morning like monkeys—maybe I should try and rustle up some fun for them, but with what? A video and pizza won't break the bank—maybe—but thinking about it saps my strength. I've nothing left, no reservoir to fight the exhaustion with either sleep or will. Besides there is that worry, buzzing like a fly in a dream, that I'll offend Marie. Jules would say the woman was too thick-skinned to offend, but I'm not convinced. I have seen something hurt move and retreat behind her deep-set eyes. A knowingness that makes my skin burn in shame. Her chins quiver a little and I hate to think that, to her, I'm just like everyone else in this cold and unfeeling place.

Jules was in my dreams last night, slyly erotic—and as secretive as ever—so I must have slept some, but I woke exhausted and with a cold weight in my gut. Jules could still scare me a little.

There is a *louche* quality to Marie's fleshiness that I find both repulsive and irresistible (the writer in me, Jules would say, not without tenderness), allusions beneath the unkempt *hausfrau* drag, to a glamorously disrespectable past. I can't help but think about her having sex even though she's out of shape and possibly not very clean. When she prattles on, I imagine those eyes sparkling before they faded and sank beneath the fleshy folds, her face framed by golden curls before they silvered and thinned. Now she is That Woman—the one in every neighborhood who talks your ear off beside the mailboxes, no chance to get a word in edgeways, like she has you under a spell and before you know it, there's time out of your life gone forever. Disappeared along with everything else.

Jules never had time for Marie, not even an hour. "Would it kill the witch to throw that old housecoat in the wash once in a while? Or to put on a bra?"

But I saw a great fall behind Marie's stinky defiance. I suspected financial ruin, or some monumental disappointment in love.

"You think?" Jules had laughed, meaning Donald.

I had tried to ignore the sneer in her voice. I was glad to make her laugh.

And anyway, she'd had a point. Looking at Donald awkwardly pinning laundry to the line, I can't see him having sex with anyone—my imagination won't stretch that far. There is something *missing* about him, and it's not just the way he habitually coughs into those gloved hands. His limbs don't quite communicate with each other, making him rush at you one minute, back off slowly the next, looking into the distance as if searching for a lost opinion, or the grown children he seemed to have misplaced, or his own life, traded in now for someone else's. You can't help feeling sorry for Donald, Jules would say, more like a shadow than a man.

Two cats, a tabby and a black tom with an orange ear, have found a patch of sun on their quaint, sagging porch, and the tabby squawks at me as if to say, *Stay*. Or maybe, *Go?* Warning or welcome, I can't work out which. Marie squats down, surprisingly agile, to yank a weed at the foot of the mailbox—plainly a purpose to her loitering, and although I'm not sure what it is, I feel caught up in her unruly web, this *presence* bordering on obsession. She stands up to ask after the kids, which leads to some more dogged waffle about their own long-gone brood and then to the disappointing ending of the TV series she and Donald have been binging on, and then . . .

I guiltily lean against the fence, so overtaken by the need to sleep that the drift away from Marie's operatic chatter is sensual, almost erotic in its surrender—and when I return minutes, or it could be hours later, she is saying something about a little-known shopping precinct way across town where you get the best—and cheapest—groceries. I shake myself awake, straighten up and push away from the fence, weirdly refreshed.

"It's because of the immigrants over there." She brings me back, chopping her arm threateningly in the direction of the intricate city skyline across the water, three bridges from our quiet, leafy neighborhood with its restored old homes and inclusive schools. "Refugees and what not. They look at the prices over *here* and go, no way."

"No way," echoes Donald.

"Beans," I weakly concur, "were nine dollars a kilo at the supermarket yesterday."

"Nine dollars a kilo," she shrieks. "Over there, you could get a whole box of beans for that, I imagine. Snake beans too, which are much tastier, although they go bad quicker. And other magical temptations—all the exotic stuff *they* keep for themselves."

We, too, were immigrants once. Country girls, young and in love. Jules had applied for a head chef position in the capital, asked me to come with her. With the freelance work I could do from anywhere, I had nothing to lose. It was an adventure, after all. Two kids later and with a restaurant of our own in a neighborhood we couldn't afford or still hadn't adjusted to (or that maybe after all had not adjusted to *us*), we began to feel less and less like adventurers, and more like unwelcome strangers in someone else's idea of Eden.

It made Jules uncomfortable when I talked like that. She said to save it for the novel when I could get to it, which wasn't often. Paid copywriting work came first, and there were always those evenings when Jules needed help at the restaurant, or with the accounts. My skin tingles with the memory of delivery drivers unloading trays of meat and vegetables from belching trucks that looked like monochrome cutouts taped onto the vivid colors of the upscale avenue. You'd never know the trucks had been there after they'd gone—they left no sign that I could see, or maybe I just wasn't looking hard enough. I tried once or twice to offer the drivers a drink—fresh-squeezed juice or ice tea—but they always refused, said they'd get something once they were home. "Home," they'd say, making drinking motions in the direction of that jagged skyline. Like they knew they didn't belong where we were and feared to eat or drink anything of this place.

* * *

Marie says, "Who can afford beans at nine dollars a kilo?"

Donald shakes his head sadly in agreement. There is a grim validation behind her eyes again, as if to say, *Not a single mother like you.* I flush because it's true. I can't afford fresh fruit and vegetables in the city, but I don't want to return to the country. The children have friends here at school. I feel close to Jules in this place, her slim figure at the edge of my eye, that scent of her on the sheets, the voice in my head.

But for how much longer?

Marie plants both hands on her hips, the housecoat buttons gaping to expose broken capillaries and belly fat. I look away, my brimming eyes making a blur of Donald, a blur of the oak tree with its dark arms enclosed around their gingerbread house.

"It's so hard, being alone." A gust of wind tugs Marie's hair free of the sagging clothesline, and it disappears into the sky. "I know you're hurting, Rebel." There's a croon to her voice now. "But an adventure . . . a day for yourself . . ."

An adventure . . . and yet. The children at school, the long drive to the city and back, not to mention what it will cost in gas. I should forget it—just have a nap, write that review for some electronics magazine and carry on as always. Maybe try and scrimp even more than I already do. No more of those packaged snacks for their lunch boxes, maybe. Less wine. Less meat . . .

Less everything.

I think of the spicy soups Jules would make from bone broth. Thick with noodles and tender beans, vegetables she ordered in wholesale from that distant market across the three bridges. Those trucks filled with fragrant bunches of herbs and all the special cuts of meat that Jules knew about, sourced from hidden suppliers deep in the civic heart, just *three bri⋅ges away*. Why had she never taken me there? Why had I never taken myself?

"It's a wonderland, truly. Nothing like the supermarkets over here," Marie leans in, her breath clovey. "Do you know that most of the so-called fresh vegetables on the local shelves have been sitting around in cool-rooms for days, or have been genetically modified. And the chicken is gray—you ever noticed that?"

I have.

"Go and see for yourself. The kids can come here after school. It'll only be for the afternoon. Donald will make his world-famous crepes."

Donald grins from the clothesline, scratches his ear with a rubber-gloved finger. The children did go over there once or twice when I had to help at the restaurant, and Toby told me about the delicate crepes Donald made with lemon and sugar—so bad for them, Jules said. But what choice did we have, with no family of our own here to help out? When I think about it, *Marie an⋅ Donal⋅* are the closest thing to that. To family. I look one more time over Marie's shoulder toward that magical place that Jules kept to herself. I repress the anger—it's to be expected, I'm told. One of the stages. It's not real, I'm told. Jules would be proud of me for following in her footsteps, for trying to get the finances under control. For not giving up.

I think about that nap, about sleeping forever.

But then a cold whiff of Marie's unwashed housecoat brings something unexpected with it—the scent of possibility. Not only in the world, but in myself. Where is that possibility now? Heat washes over me. That chance? Not here, I imagine, not in this prim soulless suburb, but *over there.*

Beyond the bridges.

A faraway spire needles a patch of blue. Donald has finished hanging up Marie's stained dishcloths and his undershirts and announces he's going inside to make the batter for the crepes, clapping his gloves together, as excited as a child himself.

"You never know what's around the corner," Marie says briskly. She smiles at the distant skyline as if at a long-lost friend. "Or who. *Over there.*"

I nod yes, yes, pushing my uncertainty aside. I tell her that I'll text the children and call their teachers. All business now, Marie draws out detailed directions on the back of an envelope she fishes out of the mailbox.

"You'll need one of those folding trolley-bags," she tells me, offering hers. But I have one in the car, and without even going inside the house (what if I see Jules there—what if she's somehow able to talk me out of it?) I drive across three bridges to check out the prices in the forgotten streets of the city.

* * *

Marie is right. In the shadows of the graceful towers and glittering hotels, there's a whole other world. I wander up and down the dirty, noisy alleys and byways lined with fruit stands, or huge wooden crates on wheels from which vegetables spill; behind shuttered doors at half-mast, hooded vendors preside over nostril-tickling mounds of spices and teas. Racks of cheap pastel sweatshirts clack on plastic hangers, and women with their hair tucked into white caps slice bloody hunks off plucked or flayed carcasses to be weighed on creaking scales. I treat myself to a sweet buttery coffee brewed from behind a hole in the wall. From a discount store that smells of residual monomers and incense, I buy the children magic markers and a Fairy Tale coloring book—I think of how Jules would love the way Little Red Riding Hood looks like a Kardashian and Prince Charming more like a Korean alcoholic.

Thinking about Jules here feels different than missing her back in our neighborhood, when there is both too much that reminds me of her and not enough. Here I feel her near. There I only felt her gone.

I buy a huge tray of strawberries for dessert, enough to share with Marie as a way of saying thank you.

I owe you, Marie, I think, half delirious. *I owe you big time!*

I decide to wait until I'm closer to home to buy the cream for the strawberries, my mouth watering, the children's smiles getting ever wider in my mind. I pick over fruit that looks like human hands, or is covered in horns; peer into cages crawling with scaled insects that smell like a cross between urine and chocolate. I make reckless attempts to bargain as Jules might if she were here. I chastise her with fond irritation for not taking me here herself.

"Better late than never," I say out loud. And no one looks askance as they would in our neighborhood where talking to oneself is like littering, or wearing pajamas to the store. *Remember, Jules, that's where we met—we'* *both gone to the 7-Eleven in our pj's—you to buy milk for your flat an* *me to get cigs for my mom.*

Remember?

I'm mainlining those dueling sensations of freedom and reassembly like a new drug, connections proliferating, old ties cut. I try to imagine which store she ordered the restaurant meat from, or the vegetables that were her specialty, the hot sweet soup whose name I could never pronounce. And there surely . . . there she is ahead of me! No mistaking those slight, determined shoulders (she was so thin in the end) lost in the crowd but always right around the next bend . . .

"Jules!" I call.

One wheel on my trolley-bag snaps under the weight of groceries—boxes of tiny eggs and bunches of herbs and sacks bulging with beef, pork and ground lamb. I gape at the hobbled bag under its weight of exotic—and even better, *affor* *able* loot. I have gone, as Toby would say, from zero to hero, escaped finally from paradise, left behind the big empty house where I write empty words while the kids are at school learning nothing if not to forget. Learning to smile again, moving away from me.

But it can't be Jules up ahead, because she doesn't look back.

Reality washes in. But it's a version that makes my skin itch. My eyes sting. I grab onto a stand of beans for support, feeling as though I might fall. Snake beans and runner beans and yellow beans. Beans the size of kidneys and as long as arms, or beans as small as grains of rice that look like tiny eyes, beans as black as tar and blue as veins. Dried beans and tinned beans and marinated beans, stewed beans in sticky crocks floating with fatty flesh, and jars of rainbow-colored jelly beans. I am suddenly ravenous. Shaking with a needful, nagging hunger.

Deep in the valleys cast by the shadows of the towering buildings, I drag the broken trolley-bag to the car, the straps of grocery sacks digging welts into my arms. An oasis of one tribe gives way to an island of a different one. Calls to prayer, an impromptu football game in a mud-churned field. Disorientated by the cacophony—hawkers advertising their wares, bell towers pealing the hour, funeral processions of chattering transvestites—I notice, with a twist of renewed panic, that the sun is getting low. I load the trunk and get in behind the wheel with a groan of relief. I'll be home soon, and although I'll catch the commuter traffic crossing the bridges, I hang onto that thought. Home. I steer past the thronging shops and hawkers, which takes longer than I want to in the traffic, until eventually I get to a winding boulevard called Raining Street. The car feels heavy beneath me, sluggish as if reluctant to move in that direction. The road twists on and on.

I reach for Marie's envelope, but Raining Street is not on her hastily drawn map. I peer down the lanes, searching for a familiar sign. Smoking food stalls obscure my view, make my stomach growl. I brake to avoid a stray cat, black with one orange ear. I strain to hear my own thoughts over the loud music coming from busy corners around which crowds swell. The rattail braids and knit caps of the musicians register at the edge of my eye. It's getting later. The children will be getting hungry too.

I pull over, consider buying something from one of those smoking stalls, but I've already spent too much. Instead I get out, go to the trunk and loosen a few snake beans from a bunch tightly bound in a rubber band. I bite off the tip. It's delicious, surprisingly nutty with a peppery aftertaste. I look around me one last time for a road sign and finding none, get back in the car.

I drive slowly through Raining Street which seems to go on forever but which empties out eventually into intermittent strip bars and boarded-up banks. I have chewed to the bottom of the half-yard-long bean and spit the slender stem into my sweating hand. I slowly take a steep descent, trying to work out where I am, take a turn I think will put me onto the first bridge toward home . . . and then another one, and soon I am unarguably lost. I pull over next to a dusty costume store to check the GPS, beginning to wonder about the state of the meat in the trunk. Why had I bought so much? Will it even fit into the freezer? My stomach sours. I step outside again to check the bags of lukewarm meat and already wilting vegetables jammed amidst the beach towels and library books. An empty bus rattles past up the hill, the driver in wraparound shades. Traffic is sparse. The street lamp above me fails to turn on. A whiff of blood and strawberries stings my nostrils. Beyond a closed door in one of the unlit apartment buildings, a couple begins to argue in a language I don't know, urgent and hopeless. Starving, I grab a bundle of snake beans and hurriedly get back in. I lock the car, check the rearview. My eyes stare back at something just over my shoulder.

I crunch through the last of another bean, extract the inedible stunted stem from between my lips. My mind circles again to whether the children have eaten. I steer through the dusk, shift gears and turn down the winding hill. According to the GPS, I need to take a right-hand turn at the bottom of the switchback, which I navigate too quickly in the deceptive light, the descent steeper than I thought.

I am sure that this will get me to the old highway that leads to the first of the five (or is it three) bridges back to the affluent neighborhood that I can no longer afford and to the children who have lately been dressed for school and spreading peanut butter on their sandwiches before I've managed to wake up in the mornings. I thank God, again, for Marie, and for Donald's crepes, remember too late that the last time Madeline ate them, she complained afterwards of a stomachache. She said that they were slimy and reminded her of skin. Sweat pools at my spine.

Don't eat the skin. Whatever you •o.

On the map, Marie has marked out the cheapest butcher, the freshest fruit stand, the best place to sit for *kopi*. But now with the car filling up with the smell of dead flesh, I can't bring any landmarks to mind in the teeming neighborhoods, and all I can recall from Raining Street are instruments lowered at the end of the song.

* * *

I keep driving. The raw beans sit heavy in my gut. I toss the tough, yet fragile-looking stems, with dirt still clinging to some of them, out the open window. When we'd just come in from the country, I'd been conscious of how people stared at Jules for tossing even an apple core into the bushes—and much later, we'd both tried not to smile when Toby insisted that his banana peel was biodegradable. But the car reeks of blood and overripe fruit, making it hard enough to concentrate without a pile of half-digested green waste on my lap. Better out than in, Jules would say, or maybe that was me.

I spit one straight out the window.

The setting sun fills the car with rusty light. Even with the window open, the smell of the meat is overwhelming. I drive past vacant lots and abandoned self-storage buildings. The pedals feel sticky underfoot. Liquid runs into my shoes, between my toes. Eventually, I pull over and dial Marie's number, fumble it once, but reach her machine on the second go.

"Rebel?" the machine says in Marie's quavery voice. "What kind of a name is that? The child of hippies, right . . . or drunks. Wait, didn't you say your parents had a band? A country band?" She stops to clear phlegm from her throat. "Was that it? Well, I imagine that you never saw yourself as the type to run off, like your mama did, but maybe you just need to get your head on straight, girl? That's the kind of thing she'd say, isn't it? How grief's a bitch and parenting's a motherfucker and all that? Well you should've thought long and hard, Ms. Rebel, because if living was easy, everyone would do it. Now what you need to do, child, is keep driving as long as you can. The redness filling up your car? It's not the setting sun, is it? But I expect you know that by now. Madeline and Toby will be fine. They tell me they love you. I'm sure that's true, for now. But memory's a tricky thing, child, a devilish thing . . . I expect you know that too . . ."

The phone drops from my hands; Marie's tinny voice rasps from the mic. My throat closes around the scream. I manage to stumble, gasping for breath, onto the curb. Blood sloshes onto the pavement from a rising red pool on the floor of the car. I back away, leaving red footprints. The road stretches empty in both directions. All is still, dead still, and utterly silent. Above me is no longer the sky but a watermark, slowly spinning, of the whole city I'd left behind . . . the tall glass towers rooted in place by the random scrawl of dirty streets and forgotten people . . . the lacy bridges connecting the bland affluent neighborhoods one to another. The air shifts behind me.

"I always hated that freakin' harpy." A sigh. "You wouldn't listen, though—you big old softie."

I close my burning eyes. I don't have to turn to know who it is.

"I miss you too," I say.

I'm afraid of what she'll look like after all this time. I'm afraid she won't be there when I turn around. So I don't.

"Marie's full of shit," she says. "The kids will always love us. They need you."

"Where are you?" I ask. "Why have you never brought me here before?"

"You're not ready for it yet, Rebel."

"Marie said—"

"I told you not to listen to that lying crone."

I half-sob, half-giggle. "Don't be a misogynist, Jules."

"And how exactly," her laughter is warm, full of love, "can a woman be a misogynist?"

I reach for her hand. "Cold."

"You can look at me, you know. I'm not covered in worms or anything. What's that smell?"

"Strawberries." I angle my head toward the voice, keeping the high flat planes of those cheekbones—her pride—just out of focus. "I bought them for the kids."

She groans theatrically—always. "They were the only thing I could eat in the hospital, remember? In the end. And that sinful heavy cream you brought in to help wash them down."

I bring her icy fingers to my lips—the wedding ring reflecting the russet glare of the blood-filled car. Jules takes me into her arms. She feels the same. Her mouth and tongue are as warm as my tears, and when we separate, I tell her she looks the same. Almost. Filmier. Less substantial. Still Jules though. She smooths the hair off my damp face.

Then she spits something into her hand. It's a shred of bean flesh from my mouth.

"*Vigna unguiculata*," she says. "Snake beans?"

"I bought a whole box. I've been munching on them, tossing the stems out the window. Sorry."

"We used these all the time at the restaurant, remember? For the soup."

She'd fallen in love with Southeast Asia as a backpacker, and we'd planned to go there together as a family. Thailand, Vietnam, Singapore . . . I reach for her but she's walking away from me toward the rear of the car—it seems like miles, as if we've been on a travelator while we've been talking, like at the airport. The nausea is overwhelming, the snake-ball in my stomach, time wound around itself like that thick tangled vine of silver hair wound around the clothesline—not past, not present but both and neither—the restaurant, my job, the children we raised together in the neighborhood that spat us out in the end.

But we were never free.

I can just see Jules crouching down behind the car. She comes up with something in the palm of her hand—one of the bean stems I'd tossed out the window.

"When did you start eating these?" she calls.

"Raining Street," I say. "I know I shouldn't have littered but I just wasn't thinking. What the hell, Jules, the birds'll eat them and if not—"

We look at each other across the empty length of road, half smiling. "They're biodegradable," we say simultaneously. What she doesn't ask out loud, since I hear her thoughts like my own, is what made me toss the (non-biodegradable) snake beans outside the window in the first place. What made me leave a trail? What makes any of us?

"Well, let's *hope* the birds haven't gotten them all," she says almost to herself. "Listen, I reckon these will get you home if you hurry, at least to Raining Street. It's at the edge of a kind of gorge, a trench. Did you notice how it got steep after that?"

The descent.

"It's the boundary," she says. "The border . . ."

She slumps. I don't have to ask between what and what.

"If you'd waited until you were here"—she clicks her chin at the empty road beneath the spinning sky—"it would have been different. You might not have a chance. Once you eat something from this place, it's harder to leave."

I look around. What is there to eat here, I wonder, and who is there to eat it?

"Those kids need you, Rebel. Don't ever give up. Promise? That old witch'll do them no good. Look at what she's done to Donald."

"But what about her disease?"

"There isn't a name for what she's got." Jules's eyes go straight inside her. Her lip pulls up in a grimace, chunks of gelid green bean flesh between her teeth. "The only one sick was me."

I feel a prickle of dread, the same unease I'd known after the restaurant was a success, and then when she'd finally come to bed at the end of a long night, fuming about a difficult customer or a bungling apprentice. I never blamed her for the booze I could sometimes smell on her breath, or the lateness of the hour—I never wanted Jules to know how fearful I was that the restaurant was asking too much of her, or that we were.

"And her real children?" I say, thinking about Marie and Donald rattling around in their gingerbread house, all those empty rooms. "The ones all grown up?"

I'm shaking. My feet squelch in the blood-filled shoes.

"Or not." Her voice is barely a whisper, too soft for me to hear, but I do. Like a voice at the bottom of a well that is my heart.

"She knew that as soon as I saw you I wouldn't want to leave," I say. I'm tired from the long drive. I think about that nap again. "Marie knows everything." The twilight flows like a river over the car. I feel like I'm asleep even though I'm awake. I think about kicking off my shoes and finding a soft spot in the ditch and spooning with Jules, until we both drift off.

"Rebel! Wait. She doesn't know everything. She just thinks she does. She sent you here sure that I'd make you stay. That I'd cook you something, maybe with the beans. But she forgot about Raining Street." She lowers her voice to a stage whisper. "Or maybe she doesn't know."

She smiles and jiggles the bean stem at me. "She doesn't know us. She thought I'd want you to stay. But I don't. I want you to go home, to try and live without me. You'll do that, won't you? For me?"

Crimson lights flicker on and off in the sprawling ceaseless city.

"You want me to go back?" I say. "Even if it kills me?"

"Don't let it." She stumbles toward me, feeling her way around the car. "Don't give that old witch the satisfaction."

She's wearing the embroidered silk slippers I buried her in. We bought ourselves matching pairs for our first Christmas together. Her face ripples.

"What about you coming with me?" I say through the tears. "If I can leave, so can you."

"I've been here too long." Her skin looks too small for her skull. "You better get a move on. It's uphill all the way to Raining Street, and the trail will be hard to follow."

"Raining Street," I say.

"Once you get there, you'll be fine."

I tell her I love her, and I always will.

"You better," she says. And then she is gone.

I return the way I came, inching along and stopping wherever I think I see a fragile, curling stem by the side of the road. When I do, I put it in my pocket. Sometimes I get it right. Other times, it's not a bean stem, but something else. A creature in the shape of a human hand with blind, seeking fingers tapered at the end. They claw at me, because they can.

Eventually I run out of gas, leave the car at the curb, open the trunk with all the stinking meat in it for whatever still eats down here. I find a piece of rebar for the hand-shaped creatures, some of them as big as dogs, pointed teeth sunk into a cavity just beneath the tapered middle finger. I get lucky sometimes. I must have thrown out the occasional seed too when I was leaving my trail, and some have taken root in the barren soil of empty lots and front lawns strewn with bicycle frames and rubber gloves floppy with time. When that happens, I carefully pull the long, snaking fruit from the young plant—a foreigner in this place, like me—and I keep walking. I chew the sweet young bean carefully, see it taking root in my stomach, sending out tendrils, carving a path back to that secret place. The street whose name Marie could never know.

I wonder what other people call it. Other lovers. Sons, daughters and other lost mothers. That borderline between lost and found, under and over. Forgetting and not. I wonder why Jules called it Raining Street. Or maybe that was me.

It is dark here at the bottom of the hill, and mostly empty, wind-blown with dumpsters and burned-out cars, behind which *another* waits. He's been with me for a while, his uneven cowering footsteps now ahead of me, now behind.

"Donald," I call. "Come out, come out, wherever you are!" When he finally emerges—his rushing gait even more twitchy than before, his sclera meaty and red—his flayed hands are on me in seconds. He gets at my face, rending the flesh from my jaw with his broken finger bones, the jagged shards of his wrist—going for my tongue, I suppose. I beat him off eventually with the bar, but it slows me down. I spend the winter between the walls of a derelict store, mashing snake beans with some Advil I find in my pocket. When the frost thaws, I come out, catch my face in a smashed car mirror. I keep away from reflective surfaces after that.

I learn to spot his syncopated trail in the dust, and one day, I find the skull of some poor creature as displaced as me. It's human-like but smaller, with jagged fangs and a distended snout. I spear the rebar through the nostrils, use a shard of glass to cut strips off an old tire to lash the skull onto the end like a mace. I manage to get the Donald-thing in the groin finally, matter spurting and his screams echoing along the windblown ways; no sign of Marie coming to his aid. Poor Donald. I'm sure she has other familiars to send my way, and I'll be ready. But Jules was right. It's a big damn hill. Freezing in winter, burning in summer—and always tinged with that crimson dark. Come spring, the smell of May lifts my heart a little, and I kneel down to touch a brave dandelion daring to grow in the cracks. But then autumn hits with a shriek and that dread gust blows straight from her cold heart. Half blinded by driving rains and swirling leaves, I feel my way along the steep path. I hold the mace in one hand, the other seeking out bean stems—knowing in my heart that I'll get to the top one day, back to my children, and back to you, Marie—memory being a tricky thing, and devilish too.

The Box

Getting her in the box was one thing. Keeping her there was another. It took all his expertise, all his care. She'd said they should do more things together, so he wrote a running program (she loved to run) and in the program, unlike reality, he was the better runner. Well, faster. She still had better form. He'd give her that.

"I love it when we run together," she said when they turned off the path and emerged at the railway crossing. Over the unseen shore the sun was a yellow ooze. The lights of the neon palm tree from Wiley's Juice Bar played across her face. She'd order a kiwi lime frappe. He'd have an iced mocha. She cocked her head, panting, at the distant drone of the ocean. Her hands were on her hips, her nipples erect. She smiled at him.

"You really push me," she said. "It's all I can do to keep up with you."

He said, "Really? Keep up with me? You were so far behind that I thought I'd lost you at one point. Did you decide to stop and take a nap?"

For a moment she looked aggrieved. Then an arch, sly look came over her. It was something that he hadn't written in, and his fingers were a blur over the console as he tried to correct it. She scared him sometimes, even now.

"Just kidding," he said. "You kept up, pretty much."

"I could hear the ocean," she said. "I can still hear it."

"And you've got great form. I'll give you that."

Confusion darkened her brow. Her head was tilted at an odd angle. His hands froze over the console—what was it? She could be hard to read, sometimes. Even now.

"How could you see my form," she said, "if you were ahead of me most of the time?"

In the dark, Adam smiled and shook his head. He'd walked right into that one. He wiggled his fingers (like an orchestra conductor, he thought, or a surgeon) and began to type, sparing the briefest of glances across at the girl lying in the dark. Wires waved like tentacles from her head, flowing into the box.

"Not all the time, Lu. Once or twice there, I slowed down enough to let you pass, and you looked good. Poetry in motion, love, and best ass in the business, by the way."

The ugly new furrows on her brow cleared. She liked it when he called her love. It was a new thing with him, a British mannerism she said was sexy. She beamed. Took a step closer. He could smell her shampoo (verbena). Sweat pooled at her throat, and he could taste it at the back of his eyeballs and it tasted like tears.

Smells and tastes were a bitch to code.

* * *

Lucy remembered the impact. They had been fighting. She was at the wheel, so technically it was her fault but she would have been given (or taken) the blame even if Adam had been driving. But this time he wasn't. It was her. This would not make her cry.

At first it was always dark. She did things in the dark. She was running, it seemed, which she liked. Or fucking. The dark was sexy. She was naked. But she wanted to see the ocean. It was always just around the corner. She could hear it, almost smell the damp sand and sweet kelp in the rock pools. But she couldn't see it, and wanting to made her tired.

The dark lifted a little and they were together again. He seemed different, a changed man. They did more things together now. Like, they ran together, which was sweet of him but weird; she had always liked to run alone. And he talked a lot more, much of which sounded to Lucy like noise, like the whisper of a seashell.

✳ ✳ ✳

They were sitting at a booth in Wiley's Bar. It was nighttime now. The ocean drummed from the distant shore. She was talking about her work, about the boss who bullied her because she was hot for her. Everyone was hot for Lucy, even her boss, Kate, who was married to Katie, at home raising their second child. Kate and Katie had been to their place for dinner. Kate's hungry eyes had followed Lucy around their small kitchen, and by the end of the night, Katie was very drunk.

Adam wrung his hands over the keyboard, remembering. He shook his head and reached for the Japanese canned coffee on his desk. A colleague, when he still had colleagues, had told him how to pronounce it—*kan kohi*. The little apartment was in darkness. Outside the freeway roared. Was it day or night? He had one cupboard filled with kan kohi and another filled with cans of Bacardi rum and cola. When his supplies ran out he ordered more and the boxes arrived at the front door to their apartment. In the beginning it was easy to tell whether it was Bacardi time or coffee time. But somewhere along the line he got the cans mixed up and started drinking rum in the day and coffee at night. It didn't matter. The canned coffee tasted like Cuba libre now and vice versa. The mind was a strange thing.

Lucy looked tired. She had bold red rings under her eyes, and her lips were cracked. In the booth, Adam pointed as politely as he could to the blood oozing from her ear.

"Oh no," she said, "I'll be right back."

She got up to go to the restroom. After she was gone, Adam brushed shards of glass off the seat. When she came back, she'd freshened up some. Lucy wrote publicity copy for a cable TV station. He put a hand on her thigh while he talked.

"That promotion I was telling you about," he said, "is in the bag.

Pretty much. Then you can quit your job and go back to your dissertation. Would you like that?"

Adam worked for an engineering firm in the Valley.

"I'd like that," she said. "I love you."

Lucy leaned against him in the dark. The table in front of them was strewn with kan kohi and crunched cans of Bacardi and cola. Adam took a swig. In the beginning he had ordered cases of Snapple for Lucy. But when the Snapple ran out he didn't order that anymore. One less cupboard to worry about.

Before he could tell her he loved her too, a swarm of her friends pushed through the front door of the bar, letting in a gust of cold sea air. Lucy sat up straighter in her chair, looked past her friends and out through the closing door of the café. Adam felt a headache twinge. He hadn't written her friends in. Why would he? He made an angry right-to-left swipe across the bottom of the console and the friends hesitated and a few of them turned around and went back, but some of the others kept coming. They mobbed the booth and squeezed in around Adam and Lucy, reaching for the cans of rum and passing them round. One of her friends started talking about film theory and then someone chimed in about individualism and modernity and then the split subject came up and the mind-body problem, and Adam, who was an engineer and worked for a firm in the Valley designing bus stations, and who had no idea of who Fassbinder was, or Deleuze or Horkheimer, huddled over the console in the dark with a crumpled can of rum between his naked thighs and flicked at the console with the back of a bitten fingernail. Across the room at the center of a swirling system of colored lights and buttons, the box hummed and Lucy lay there with her wild mane of wires and behind her closed eyelids, pulsed worlds within worlds.

He'd created them all.

* * *

Her friends seemed different somehow. She felt cut off from them since she and Adam had decided it would be better for her to drop out and get a job. They needed money to pay for the wedding and after that, Adam had been sure she would go back to school. But Lucy didn't know anymore. The wedding, a modest affair in the Gaslight district (all the hotels on the beach had been too expensive) had been four years ago. Her friends from school talked over her, as if she wasn't there, yet she felt exposed somehow. Naked. Her flesh tingled and she tried to cover herself. She tried to follow their arguments, found she couldn't place some of the papers they referenced or films they'd seen. They'd been her friends forever, some of them since high school, and now here they were, with their beards and thrift store glasses and dog-eared books on Horkheimer they pulled from the pockets of stained corduroy jackets. Adam loved them too, he told her. So why was he pulling away, and trying to pull her away too? He had her under both arms and was pulling her out of the wreck and her friends recoiled in horror, hugged each other and wept. Lucy waved back tentatively, glancing up at Adam's unshaven chin, his blistering neck.

Now they were alone again at the table and his hand was hot and sticky on her thigh. She gently removed it, got up and weaved through the joint to the restroom. She looked like hell. Maybe that was why her friends had gone. She lifted her head to the ceiling to stop her nose bleeding (it bled all the time these days) and, as a distraction, she tried to decipher the bleeding cracks on the ceiling.

I love you, the cracks read.

The blood seeped from the cracks and dripped down onto her upturned face, so it must be true.

They were driving to the coast. Adam knew it was what she wanted.

"What I really want . . ." she had started to say (he wished she'd keep both hands on the wheel). He would give her everything. The boss bullied her but Adam would rescue her from all that as soon as he could. She would finish her degree so she could teach, and they'd move away from here. Her friends were bad for her. They made her feel inadequate, as if she'd failed, and she hadn't yet. He was sure the Horkheimer dude had a thing for her still. They'd dated for a while in college before Adam came along. Lucy said she loved how Adam was different than her friends (dumber?) but got along with them all so well. He wondered where she got that from. Had she ever even noticed that he hardly said a word when they were around?

When her friends called after the accident, he told them she was resting. His colleagues sent a card. Adam's hands slid over the console. After a while people stopped calling. He told the hospice nurse that his insurance no longer covered her visits. She said that he would know what to do. He and Lucy were all to themselves now and for the first time, Adam felt that she was truly his. He gave her whatever she wanted. If he didn't know what she wanted, he made it up. He could hear her tapping at a keyboard and he smiled in the dark. He'd written that in for her. He wrote a scenario in which Katie fired her, which would never have happened in reality because the cable station was lucky to have Lucy and everyone knew it, but he wrote it in anyway. She was upset for a while but cheered up when Adam told her how he was put in charge of a meaty new robotics project that supported them both (dreams were easy to code).

The typing had stopped and in its place was a ceaseless pacing, like a tiger in a cage. A strange musk began to emanate from the coils and cords around her head. It was almost time for her morning coffee. He checked his watch—was that a.m. or p.m.? He heard a noise behind him, or in front of him, it was difficult to tell. Directions were hard to code. He adjusted his iWare and there she was in the dark, at the door to the office he'd coded for her. She was naked. She had an athlete's body. A flat stomach, high full breasts. Naked was easy.

"Would you like to play chess?" she said. They'd learned together, studied the moves and strategies from the Internet.

"The movie is in an hour," he said. "Don't you have to get ready?"

She liked to watch movies—documentaries or art films mainly that involved ominous silhouettes at the end of narrow hallways. He downloaded whatever she wanted. She wrinkled her forehead again. One of her eyes had come loose from its socket in the accident. The left side of her face had blistered down to the bone. Adam frantically worked the keyboard, trying to overwrite the insistent memories—but hers or his, it was hard to tell.

"You're right," she said. "I need to get cleaned up. I look like hell."

She turned away. Closed the door behind her and Adam shivered and rocked back and forth over the keyboard. A jagged piece of steel from the accident pierced the base of her neck. Adam's knees banged together. He was naked too, his body wasted away on a diet of rum and microwave pizza.

* * *

He looked great to her now, better than before. His body rippled with muscle, health bloomed in his face. It must be all the running they were doing together these days. She'd gotten faster, though, or he'd gotten slower, dropping further and further behind. She could smell the ocean, hear the hungry caw of the seagulls.

"Come here," she said.

"I can't." His voice boomed in her ear. "I don't know where you are."

He panicked to keep up with her. She fingered the volume down on her control.

"I'm here," she said. "Where you put me."

He came toward her, his face a little blurred, like a face in the rain. She peered around the bar at the flickering walls. Where was the door? The people—she could hear movement and murmurs in the dark.

"Where?" he said. She could see him look up from his console, confused. "I can't find you."

"Over here," she said. "In the box."

His head slowly turned to look at her. He hinged up the lens. A collapsed, stunned look came over him. His jaw hung open and he had coffee on his chin. He was naked. A cord flowed from some-where behind his ear and he dragged it behind him as he stood up and approached her. He stank of rum; his eyes were wet and puffy. Above his sunken belly, his chest was still scarred from the accident.

He reached out a hand to her twitching fingers but drew back before she could grasp it.

"Let me out," she said. "You can't keep me here forever."

"Please," he said.

"If I'm in the box then so are you. But you don't have to be."

"Lu . . . I don't want you to be alone."

"I'll be okay. It's what I want."

He smeared the dribble across his chin with a trembling knuckle and drew the black lens back down with a snap. Then he turned and went back to the console. Standing over the keyboard, he began to type.

"Adam?"

He shook his head. She could tell he was crying. She wriggled into her sneakers. The neon light reflected off his bony ass. Behind him she could see the beach and, breaking away from the bruised horizon, a single wave, vast and unending. Adam typed faster and the wave grew bigger. Closer. She turned away and began to run.

Ava Rune

At the edge of town lives Ava Rune and her stepuncle or half-something-or-other, Willard Rune. Tires tower in the front yard and engine blocks litter the rear. Beside the farmhouse is Willard's work shed where he does wheel alignments and repairs and sells tires, same as all the other Rune boys until they got married and moved away, or stayed on and were eventually buried beneath the engine blocks scattered amongst the wheat grass. For Willard Rune, the last of the line, at five-feet-three with a bad knee and a scalp condition, marriage does not loom as a distinct possibility. But then neither, at only thirty-nine years old and with an iron constitution, does death.

Ava keeps out of Willard's way as much as she can. School days are fine, but over the long still summer weeks, with her friends overseas or away at camp—and to be truthful, Ava can count her friends on a few fingers—keeping out of Willard's way is easier said than done. At going-on fifteen years old, she's learned to take no notice of his bad moods, his quick heavy hands, his table manners, the weeping sores on his scalp. Ava keeps herself busy with the cooking and the chores, and every summer evening until dark, she sits by her mother's grave, a headstone set beneath a bloodwood tree at the edge of the property, and writes stories. Sometimes the stories come easily, like they did for her mother, sometimes they come urgently, and she can feel them low down in her body, like something trying to push out, and sometimes they don't come at all, and Ava sits with her back against the headstone, listening to the sad warble of the birds and wishing she had a cigarette.

Willard would kill her if he caught her smoking, even if he was the one who taught her how to roll her own. "Better me than one of those donkeys she goes to school with," he'd said even after Ava's mother had protested, shaming him by reverting to the Icelandic pronunciation of his name, *Villar*, how it was meant to be said.

But ever since Ava's mother, Madlen, died, no one is allowed to light up within sniffing distance of the property, not even Willard's customers. Willard taught Ava a lot of things, like how to fry a perfect egg, shoot a fox with the .303, patch a tire, fix a fence. But one thing he didn't teach her, was how to tell stories. That she learned from her mother, from the notebooks she filled with tales of magic and vengeance. Ava uses just plain lined exercise books leftover from the school term. She writes her stories in the margins around algebra equations and spelling tests and passages carefully copied from geography textbooks ("nitrogen and phosphorous pollution from the North Sea is causing . . ."). When it's time to go in to make Willard's supper, Ava carefully puts the notebooks in a tin box she found in his shed and locks it with a brass padlock. Ava keeps the key around her neck. She hides the box in a gummy hollow of the tree that drops white flowers down on her mother's grave.

* * *

One day the telephone rings and Ava picks it up, thinking that as usual it is someone wanting to book their car in, and she gets ready to write down their details on the pad beside the phone. But instead, the voice on the other end of the line asks for her.

When she says, "This is Ava?" it comes out like a question.

There is a dead silence on the other end, during which Ava senses the caller has their hand over the mouthpiece. Then the hand comes away and Ava hears breathing and the voice returns.

"Hey, Ava. This is Pete."

Ava doesn't say anything. She feels that a response is required of her, but she doesn't know what that is. Finally she says, "Pete who?"

"Peter Reid from school."

Ava blinks in the dim hallway with the telephone receiver growing damp in her hands. The red and green glass panels in the door at the end of the hallway throw prisms of light through the shadows like knives.

Ava says, "Hi."

After another short silence during which Ava senses the hand pressed against the mouthpiece again, Peter Reid asks her what she's been doing.

"Not much," Ava says.

Peter Reid's father owns a discount carpet warehouse and Peter lives in a big house in town. On hot afternoons when Ava walks home from her part-time job at Subway, she can hear splashing and yelling from the Reid's swimming pool.

Peter tells Ava that he just got back from Byron and it was really boring.

And again, Ava doesn't know what to say.

"I'm having a party tomorrow," Peter finally says.

Tomorrow, Ava remembers, is Friday.

"At my place," Peter says.

"What kind of a party?" Ava hears herself saying, as if it makes a difference.

Peter pauses. "It's, like, a barbecue, I guess. But you don't have to bring meat or anything. Just your swimmers."

Ava wishes her heart would stop beating so fast. She tries to sound bored. "What, like the whole class?"

Maybe his mother told him to invite Ava, out of pity. The only time he or any of his friends ever looked at Ava was once in history class when the teacher explained to the class about all the people from places like Norway who came to Australia during the gold years. Someone stuck his foot out into the aisle, and Ava tripped on her way back from the blackboard, where the teacher had made her write out the Icelandic spelling of her name. *Aava.*

Peter says, "Yeah, so not the whole class. Just, like everyone who hasn't gone away. It's so boring being stuck here. And hot. Seriously, the pool is the only place to be. I'll pick you up."

Peter is talking quickly now, like he's trying to get it all out while he can. Ava can hear other people in the room with him, and once, Peter tells them to shut up. Peter is probably sixteen but he had to repeat because of a year his family spent overseas. He says he and his older brother will pick her up tomorrow at twelve. His older brother needs to come with him because Peter doesn't have his full license yet.

"I don't think I can," Ava says.

There is another pause, and Peter says, "Why not?"

"I have things to do."

There is a new silence on the other end which sounds different than the previous one, because she can hear him breathing. Ava wonders for a moment if Peter is actually disappointed. Now she feels bad for saying no.

"Bummer," Peter says. "Are you sure? It's so fucking hot. Sorry. I've got beer. Lots of beer."

"Beer?"

"Yeah," he laughs. "My parents are in Europe. Everyone's coming. Like Paige and Jimmy and Lou and Callan. You know them, right?"

"Not really."

"They're cool, you'd like them." And then he says, something else, in a lower voice. "I like that story you wrote for English class. The one about the tree and the dragon, Nid-something."

"Níðhöggr." It was Ava's mother who taught her about the lying dragon trapped gnawing at the roots of the world-tree that bleeds for it.

"That was pretty cool," Peter says.

Ava tries to think of an excuse. But then she hears the screen door slam behind the kitchen, and Willard's voice demanding lunch.

"So can you come?"

"I can ride my bike," says Ava. "You don't have to pick me up."

"All the way into town?" Peter says. "It'll be too hot We'll definitely come get you. The gold Monaro?"

Ava knows that gold Monaro. Peter Reid's brother brought it in for an alignment once. Ava knows that Willard won't let her go anywhere near that car.

"Don't come to the house." Ava licks her dry lips. "It's a dead end, hard to turn around. There's a place up near the turnoff to town. There's a tree and a broken white fence. I'll wait there. If I'm coming."

"Awesome," Peter says. "That's great."

"What if I'm not there?" she says. "I don't want you to waste a trip."

"Don't worry about it. It's a good road to go for a spin, anyway. Nice and straight." Peter says. "But hope you'll be there."

And then he hangs up.

Willard's shape in the kitchen doorway at the end of the hall is like a dwarf's, sharp and dark and watchful.

"Who was that?"

"Wrong number," Ava says.

Willard shakes his head. "Second one today."

She can smell the ointment he puts on his infected scalp.

Ava goes to the kitchen and takes out meat and cheese for Willard's lunch. She wonders why Peter Reid invited her to his pool party along with Paige and Jimmy and all those kids who look right through her in their rush to get off the bus and into his swimming pool after school. Sometimes, instead of getting the bus, they all pile into that gold Monaro, with its blunt reptilian nose and sun glinting off the side skirt. The car fishtails out of the school parking lot, the smell of its exhaust hanging in the air and a wake of dust in its trail.

Ava doesn't have a swimsuit. After she brings Willard his lunch, she cleans up, and peels the potatoes for dinner, then puts them in a pot to soak. When he's gone back out into the shop, Ava goes upstairs and lowers the steps to the attic. She climbs up slowly and opens a trunk and starts pulling out her mother's clothes. Tight black dresses with shoulder pads and skimpy halter neck tops and concert T-shirts. Pressed bloodwood flowers that spill from notebooks. Finally Ava finds a faded string bikini, the Lycra worn bald in patches and the strings with barely any stretch left in them. There is a dusty mirror in the attic and Ava quickly undresses and tries the bikini on. Ava's mother was smaller than her, a tiny size 8. Ava is a size ten when her period isn't due, but—partly because it is a little stretched out—the bikini just fits. Ava looks at herself in the bikini, her eyeliner and mascara plentiful and black. Ava thinks she can get away with wearing some cutoff shorts over the bottom anyway, and maybe not even taking them off when she gets to the party. The party—just thinking about it makes it hard to breathe. The attic is stifling in the afternoon heat and she begins to feel dizzy. She takes the bikini off so she doesn't stretch it anymore and goes to close the trunk, her arms rubbery.

"Ava?" it is Willard at the foot of the attic ladder.

Ava is naked. She grabs her jeans and tries to step into them, but instead, falls face first against the corner of trunk, splitting her forehead above the temple. She lies on the planks naked with her jeans around her ankles, warm blood running into her eye, listening to her uncle putting his steel-toed boot on the bottom slate of the ladder.

"Ava, you up there? You know you're not allowed." He puts his other boot on the next rung.

Ava is not allowed into the attic because of the possums, Willard says. But she knows it's because this is where he put her mother's things. It is Madlen's place, not hers.

Ava kicks weakly at the crumpled jeans around her ankles. The attic spins, a blur of cobwebs and possum traps and broken chairs. And suddenly, her mother sitting there on the top of the trunk with her legs crossed, an unlit cigarette between her fingers.

Her mother smiles.

"It's too hot up there. I told you," Willard says from the bottom of the ladder.

Ava lifts her head to get a better look at her mother, but the room spins again when she does that, so she blinks furiously through the blood in her eye. Her mother is still there. She picks up Ava's T-shirt and tosses it over.

Willard takes another step up the ladder. "You're not going through Madlen's things, are you? Ava?" He says it like that: Ah-vah.

Ava's grandmother on her mother's side was Icelandic. She brought Madlen with her when she married Ava's Rune grandfather, who had already sired a bunch of boys with his first wife, an English woman who pronounced *Villare*, Willard. Madlen was just a teenager when Ava was born in this very house to a father Madlen would not talk about. And after a while, Ava stopped asking. Her mother bounces her crossed leg up and down and lights her cigarette. She blows a perfect smoke ring.

And then the phone rings.

Ava listens to the *brrring, brrring* of the phone, gooseflesh rippling along her bare legs, and watches her mother blow smoke rings.

"Goddammit," Willard says. "I bet that's the wrong number again."

"I'll get it," Ava manages to call out. "I just came up to check the traps."

"Why? I just baited them." The phone rings again. "What's to check?" Willard calls up the ladder, his voice taut with pain.

"The possums kept me up all night," Ava whimpers in the heat. "And the bait's gone."

"You should have got me." His boot on the next step. "I smell smoke."

The phone rings again. Ava's mother points to her knee.

"Your knee," Ava says. "I'm coming down. The phone . . ."

Her mother nods approvingly. If there's anything Willard hates, it's being reminded about his knee, and the operation he tells himself he'll get every year.

"Fuck my knee," Willard says and steps down the ladder to answer the phone.

Ava's mother blows another smoke ring. It hovers in the air for a moment, before taking, briefly, the shape of a heart, and then it is gone.

"Nice tits," Ava's mother says, and then she's gone too.

When Ava gets down from the attic, with the possums' fruit from the traps hidden in her jeans pockets, Willard is standing in the hallway, cut by prisms of light, and the smoky perfume of Ava's mother hangs thick in the air.

"Wrong number?" Ava says, keeping her head angled away so he can't see the cut.

Willard shakes his head and his eyes are damp, and he limps off into the shop without saying a word.

* * *

The next day Ava tells Willard she's walking to the bus stop to go into town and work on a project at the library. When he asks about the Band-Aid on her temple, she says she cut it on a low branch on her way to the pigs.

"Look where you're going next time," he says.

She makes him a shepherd's pie, and she puts extra meat in it because of how he had his head lifted to the air in the wake of Ava's mother's scent. It's early when she gets to the broken fence at the crossroads. The heat of the day has not yet settled over the paddocks. The neighbor's gray horse swishes his tail at her as she walks past. Ava is wearing her mother's bikini under her T-shirt and shorts. The cut on her temple stings and she spent the morning Googling "concussion." When she offered to help Willard reset the traps in the attic, he'd told her to shut up and leave him alone.

Ava feels self-conscious about the Band-Aid, and she applied extra makeup to compensate for it, but on a positive note, it gives her an excuse to stay out of Peter Reid's pool. No one wants blood in their pool.

A pool. Ava has never been in a home swimming pool. The last time she's swum in any pool was last summer when she had a babysitting job that required her to take two kids to swimming lessons after school. Ava sits on the broken fence. The birds have gone quiet ahead of the heat. The sun crawls up the hard, blue dome of the sky like a yellow spider. Ava's temple throbs. She flushes when she thinks about her mother and looks down at her breasts swelling under her T-shirt. In the only picture that Ava has of her mother, she and Willard are in high school and all dressed up for the Year 12 formal. When Ava had asked why Willard, Madlen's own stepbrother (gross), had to take her, he'd said that Jim Reid, Peter's old man, had asked her first, said he'd fight any other man who got in his way. Madlen said she wasn't a piece of cod to be fought over, and that they could all go to hell. Willard grinned crookedly, remembering how she'd already bought the dress—why didn't Willard take her instead, she'd said, like it was no big thing. But Jim Reid didn't take it so well. And there is nothing so bad for a woman's reputation, her mother had warned Ava, as a humiliated man.

In the picture a tuxedoed Willard is a half a head shorter than Ava's mother, who wasn't tall. She was dark-haired with blue eyes like Ava's, but unlike Ava, her chest was flat as a board. Sitting on the fence, and crossing her legs as her mother had done, Ava lights a cig and practices her smoke rings.

At 12:30, Ava stands up and crosses the country road. There has not been a car this way for over two hours, never mind a gold Monaro. There is only this road to her house, the dirt-colored farmhouse at a dead end with its tires stacked in the front yard, and a sign hand-painted by Ava's mother on a rusted white car hood, saying, "Rune and Sons, Tire Sales and Repair." Ava's mother had painted two flowers and two crude wrenches beside the letters.

At two o'clock, Ava is lightheaded and sinks to the base of the ghost gum beside the road. The gum offers little shade, but Ava is too weak to move. She is drenched in sweat and her belly is cramping. She has a tampon in her bag, but she doesn't want to risk squatting behind the tree to change it in case that's when Peter decides to show up in his brother's gold Monaro.

And then, at three o'clock Willard drives past in his truck on his way to the pub, and Ava quickly crawls behind the tree and into the scrub behind it so he won't see her. She gets red dust in her hair and the cut above her eye begins to sting. A raven caws, its silhouette on the branch malformed and watchful. When she returns to sit on the white fence a bull ant bites her on her toe.

At four o'clock, she starts the slow walk back to the house, weaving along the edge of the road. She hears a distant throb of an engine and the lazy bleat of the raven flapping overhead. The rumble gets louder and Ava hugs the side of the road. She doesn't look at the Monaro as it flashes past and spins to a stop a hundred meters ahead of her. She doesn't stop walking. She brushes a fly off her face and her fingers come away smeared with sweat and makeup. The Monaro idles sideways across the blacktop, throbbing. Its gold paint hurts Ava's eyes. The window slides open and Peter nods at her from behind the wheel, his brother laughing and bringing a can of beer to his lips. There are other boys in the back seat and one girl. They lean forward to take a look at Ava as if they can't believe what they're seeing and they are breathless with laughter. Ava smells weed. The raven's cry sounds like a baby goat being led to the slaughter. *"Waaaaaah, waaaaaah!"*

One of the boys makes crying eyes with his fists. Ava keeps walking. Exhaust from the car rises and winds around the pale branches beside the road. One of the girls takes a drag on a cigarette and spits out some gossip about Madlen Rune, nothing that Ava hasn't heard a million times before. But this time it makes her stop in her tracks. It makes her eye a rock lying to the side of the road, and wonder how far she could throw it.

But then Ava buckles over in a sudden cramp and feels something loosen. Warmth spreads between her legs. The faces in the car turn from mirth to disbelief. Peter stares at her crotch. When Ava looks down at the red patch on her shorts, it is as big as a saucer. She straightens up and keeps walking, holding her head high, her back straight. Peter's eyes widen but his mouth is grim with revulsion. He reverses in a tight turn, spraying dust, and straightens up pointing back the way they came. They are laughing inside the car, and yelling but Ava can't make out many of their words. They keep saying, "Oh my God," and "disgusting" and they keep saying "loser," and the raven, closer now, calls, *"waa-aaah,"* so that Ava can barely hear the lies they're spinning about her and her family. She keeps walking. The blood trickles down under her shorts and all she can think about is how it's ruining her mother's bikini. The Monaro rears back one more time, like a dragon, and its gold scales cut the rays of the sun. It surges forward, belching fire, clawing at the road. She doesn't look back until she hears it scream.

Ava stops, swaying. She turns to see the dragon nose to nose with Willard's truck. Willard inches it forward slowly, so slowly that the tinkle of the Monaro's headlights as they shatter is almost musical. Willard then backs off a couple of meters and kills the engine. There is someone beside him, a woman, who opens the door and gets out. She moves to the front of the truck and she raises Willard's .303. Peter screams, not because of the gun, but because the woman is Ava's mother. She is beautiful, like the *Vølva* at the beginning of time, when the tree-world was just a sapling, and its roots were strong and free. Her skin is as white as the moon and her hair is black as the night. Her eyes are an icy blue. She wears the dress she was buried in, a belted pink sheath from some Japanese designer that shows off her figure—the high small breasts and curve of her belly. Her feet are bare.

"Liar," she says and shoots a hole in the front tire of the Monaro.

Peter screams again. A boy in the backseat—Callan—is crying like a raven.

"I'm sorry!" cries Peter.

"Liar," Ava's mother says again, and shoots the other front tire. The dragon hisses in rage, and lurches to its knees. The girl, Paige, screams and puts her hands over her ears. Peter's big brother puts a hand over his mouth and vomits through his fingers.

"Pants," says Ava's mother, stepping out to the side of the truck to get a better shot at the rear right tire. Birds burst from a paddock. Peter's mouth is moving, Ava realizes, in a silent prayer. Because by the time Ava's mother comes back to the front of the dragon and trains the gun on Peter, the skin on her smooth forehead has thickened and dropped like candle wax over her left eye. One half of her face is melting. Her other eye is a cold blue flame. Her flowing black hair has grown patchy and something moves in it. Tiny bones. Her lips are black and pulled back from yellow teeth—her pink dress faded to translucence, and roped in a dripping, living lichen. Worms seethe between her toes. Peter squeezes his eyes shut, whimpers, "Ohgodohgodohgod."

"On fire," Ava's mother says. Her voice is wind through scrap metal. She lowers the gun and gets back in the truck.

The Monaro hobbles down the road on three shot-out tires that will all require brand new rims by the time they make it back to town. Ava watches the trail of dust left in its wake. Then she climbs up onto the tray of Willard's truck, not because her mother is in the front, but because Ava's shorts are soaked in blood and she doesn't want it to get all over the front seat. Besides, she knows that by the time they get back to the house, her mother will be gone.

"You're just lucky I left some shepherd's pie for you," Willard calls out of the window.

The engine starts up on the second go and he drives toward home. It is late afternoon. The sun hangs low over a bank of clouds and the brown fields are slanted in shade.

"Yes, Dad," Ava whispers. "I guess I am."

Lion Man

When Turner blinked in the glare of the afternoon, the hand was still there. It lay on the leaf-strewn pine bark, where Clint Eastwood had bitten it off at the wrist. The child whose hand it was, stood staring at it, a bubble of spit between her lips. Turner shuffled forward and then back and glanced around. The playground looked as empty as ever at this slant-shadowed time of day, except for the mother (he guessed), talking on the phone over by the basketball hoops. Well, she had her back to them, to her child. To the pale little hand lying amongst the scattered leaves, camouflaged you could say, if not for the bright bracelet of blood still clinging to the severed edge.

The child blowing spit bubbles and Clint Eastwood muttering to himself behind the roundabout.

"Try eBay," the mother said into the phone, picking at a thread on her jacket. "Or Craig's List. The one you have's an old model."

She was twitchy and thin, but rounded in the shoulders. She wore black leggings and a short jacket that rode above her skinny ass. She stood in boots with a crack in one heel with her back to the child who was probably in shock but not yet bleeding to death. Turner watched blood pour from the grimy edge of her parka sleeve. The fist of her other hand was tightly clenched. He heard a *thwok-thwok* building in his temples like a chopper and wanted to duck, wanted to pick up the hand and throw it into the bushes or screw it back on, hey presto, but all he could do below the runaway hammering of his heart was say, *Fuuuuuuuhhhhhhkkkkkk*, or think it.

The mother thumbed a green shopping bag higher on her shoul-

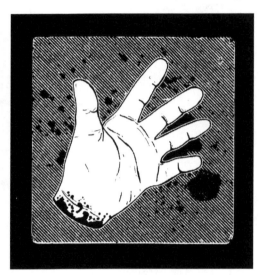

der and hunched against the winter chill with her back to Turner. Her fine dark hair stormed around the phone grafted to her face. Turner pulled off his belt and took a step toward the child. He bent down and wound the belt around her right arm over her parka and he lifted the arm up so the blood would flow back to her heart. She stood there with her arm above her head. Look, ma, no hand. But the mother didn't look. The child's face as white as paper. From one small nostril an icicle of snot bungeeing up and down in time to the spit bubble from between her lips. Her eyes flicked behind him to Clint Eastwood, his ears down and loping off out of the playground, past the tennis court and through the parking lot and over to Turner's truck. Turner followed, looking back once at the child. He drove carefully, with a dry mouth and knifing bowel, to the apartment, where he threw his possessions into a duffel bag, and an hour later they were on the road.

The world was no longer a safe place for them. They put dogs down for mauling kids, he was sure of it. Turner felt too small in this world to live without Clint Eastwood, he was sure as hell of that. Pain helped, gave him something to expand into, but not enough. He'd had his tragus pierced the day before at Industrial Art in Harrison and the whole side of his face throbbed like a sonofabitch. Advil didn't help but he chewed it anyway because that was his process. Chewing and hurting, he listened to Clint Eastwood snore in the backseat. They'd be coming for them both, he just knew it. Turner's heart labored like a moth emerging from its cocoon. He tried to burp but all it did was set fire to the back of his throat. Ridgebacks weren't all that common in the state, at least he hadn't seen too many of them. He checked both mirrors again to see if anyone was following him. The traffic was good. Road signs sliding in and out of the dusk as if they knew where he was going, even if he did not.

It was a four-hour trip but he made it last for twelve. He stopped at the Falls and for a late supper at the old diner just like when they were kids, before he'd ever even heard of Rhodesian Ridgebacks. Speedy, Gran's poodle-terrier-dachshund-whatever, wetly farting in the backseat beside him in Granddad's green Vista Cruiser. His brother, Wheeler, in the front next to Granddad depending on who called shotgun, which was usually Wheeler and even when it wasn't, the old man would call it for him. And Turner in the back with Speedy. And sometimes Gran who liked to shop at Alexanders down in Hoboken. The cancer was probably already at work on her even then, and on Speedy too, Turner thought. The journey, or exhaustion maybe, dropping down on him like a plank and making him feel like crying. He kept seeing that hand there, pale as a lemon on the winter leaves.

Night fell just outside Utica. Turner fiddled with the radio. He found a news report about a nine-year-old girl who had her hand bitten off by a savage pit bull in a Paterson playground. She was now in a stable condition in the hospital, awaiting reattachment surgery. Her mother had seen the whole thing, the report said.

"Not even half," Turner objected.

The mother claimed she had been unable to stop the dog that lunged unprovoked—"She offered me her Chupa Chup," said Clint Eastwood, "blueberry apple"—and pushed the girl to the ground. This, said a hospital official, would explain the bruising and lacerations on her back.

"You never lacerated anyone," said Turner finding Clint Eastwood in the rear mirror, incredulous behind his black mask.

The girl had struggled, the report continued. She flailed out with her hand, so the dog, allegedly tore it off. Just the one hand. The mother reportedly screamed for help—"she never looked up from her phone," Turner said—which is when the "attack" dog dropped the hand and ran off.

"Bullsheeet," said Turner. "You never run from anything in your whole life."

"What do you call this?" said Clint Eastwood, his worried eyes flaring momentarily red in the rearview.

"Listen," said Turner, twiddling with the radio dial even though the volume was fine, but the last thing he felt like now was a lecture from the dog about courage and facing your demons. Clint Eastwood could go on about such things but this was real. This was really happening. On the radio, it was the mother talking now.

"I was prepared to pull it off with my bare hands," the mother's voice was high-pitched, a careful voice. "You just find the strength when you need to."

The mother described the dog that attacked her child as a "monster." She said it was a white pit bull with yellow fangs and red eyes. It bothered Turner that the mother called Clint Eastwood an "it"—he was easily offended.

"You're a Ridgeback. So it can't have been you," said Turner, because that's the kind of thing Wheeler would have said. Clint Eastwood shivered. Turner wished he'd just settle back down to sleep again.

But the mother was just trying to cover her skinny ass, Turner knew, like the rest of us, just trying to cover our tracks. He wasn't sure whether to be disgusted or sympathetic or just plain relieved. Authorities praised the mother's presence of mind in retrieving the hand and pulling off her belt and tying it around the child's arm. The report said the child was too traumatized to be interviewed at this time.

Clint Eastwood was listening to the report with his ears cocked and his brow creased in that strange vertical frown. Turner's heart swelled with the pain of his love.

"A pit bull?" said Clint Eastwood, the world's greatest director.

"Doesn't matter," said Turner. "They can round up all the pit bulls from Paterson to Poughkeepsie. Once that kid IDs you, we're sunk."

"Coward," said Clint Eastwood, with his characteristic growl.

"Fine," said Turner. "What would *you* do if they tried to put *me* down?"

Wrrooogh wrrroooogh, Clint Eastwood said, springing up from the jump seat and leaning on his front legs over the front, then lifting his right paw with the white sock up to scrape at the air just in case Turner missed something. Like the fact that the white paw was the right one, same side as the one he bit off the girl, and that they were in deep shit.

"I get it," Turner said, shaking off the prickles on the back of his neck. Clint Eastwood was scary sometimes, he had to admit.

The dog yowled.

"Case closed," said Turner, softly. "Now get down before someone sees you."

Dawn was breaking when he turned off the freeway and onto the long pink stretch of the country road between the ghostly farm-houses and clumped silos. He drove past the familiar white rail guard that told him the next bend was the last. A gabled ruin stood close to the road behind leggy hydrangeas growing above a broken picket fence. Turner pulled into the rutted gravel driveway beside it and drove around to the garage. He parked on the grass behind it unseen from the road. Then he let Clint Eastwood out and pulled up the wooden garage door. The Vista Cruiser was up on blocks. The garage was dark and bone-cold. He heard a scuttling from above. He could smell leaf-rot and taste the cold, stale air on his tongue, foul and foreign.

He let himself into the mudroom, took comfort from the rubbery smell of his boyhood. The kitchen was cold and empty and the red linoleum floor faded to the color of dried blood. Clint Eastwood's paws tapped behind him. He walked past the gleaming table and over the rag rug of the hushed dining room to the foot of the stairs and told the dog to stay. He went up to his grandmother's room, his hand on the railing that Wheeler fell off once, breaking his arm. Guess which one.

Gran was propped on pillows in the bed. She clawed the bedspread and her eyes were open and staring out at the teal branches of the pine tree that scraped against the window. He stood in the doorway and waited until she eventually turned her head and met his scared and lonely eyes with her own.

"Kill me," she said.

* * *

He set himself and Clint Eastwood up in the little room off the front porch. When he and Wheeler had come to live here, Granddad converted it into a bedroom for them until Wheeler found God and left for Canada. Some New Age minister there legally adopted him, and then he moved with his new Fish family to Australia, the last Turner had heard. Teaching at some Fish college somewhere in the bush. Fish is what Granddad always used to call those born-agains. And the ones that were always trying to convert or blow up innocents he called Stinky Fish.

But there were too many memories for Turner out on the porch. Like the wallpaper Gran had put up for them with its repeating pattern of islands and anchors. So as soon as he could, he fixed up the old shed by the pond for him and Clint Eastwood, at least in summer. It had been his grandfather's workroom, gun room, potting shed, machine and furniture repair room. He'd nailed a fox skull above the door after he finally caught the critter, two cats and a dozen or so hens later—and it was still there. It had turned pee-colored, the bottom of the jaw gone, and a big black spider hatching eggs in one eye socket and storing dead flies in the other. Turner cleaned it up nice and white and nailed it back on. The shed was cool and cluttered inside, dusty sunbeams crisscrossed overhead. Clint Eastwood looked doubtful. Stared at the ceiling with his hackles on the rise.

"I see dead people," he said. "Who's that hanging from the rafters?"

"I don't see anyone," Turner lied.

Truth was Turner found it kind of soothing with Granddad swinging from the beam where he'd hung himself in his brown suit and Sunday shoes after Wheeler ran off to Canada. The gentle creak of the rope. Granddad didn't hardly know what to do with himself after Wheeler left. Gran had asked Turner to cut Granddad down, but he couldn't, or wouldn't, and he remembered hoping that no one else would either. He'd felt bigger with Granddad safely hanging up there, happy to have Gran and Speedy all to himself. Then Gran made him call old Mr. Lyons from down the road to do it.

Turner didn't know how Granddad got back up, and he didn't care so long as the old coot stayed where he was and everything could go back to being the same. But suddenly Granddad opened one eye, the other mostly rotted away. His face was veined in a violent purple and his one good eye filled with black and fixed on Turner. He fussed at the rope around his neck. Fuck you, thought Turner.

Turner set up a camp bed for himself along the back wall. He kept Clint Eastwood in during the day; the big dog seemingly content to snooze on a blanket most of the time. Every so often he'd get up and bark at Granddad or mosey out for a pee. Every evening Gran's nurse came rattling up the driveway in her bright pink Ford and Turner made sure he and Clint Eastwood were gone by then. He'd take him for long walks through the woods and across the moonlit corn of his boyhood. Behind the Lyons farm was a strip of no-man's land that ran to the woods, where he and Wheeler used to drink beer and smoke weed and scream across in their dirt bikes. And where Judy Lyons showed them her woo-woo in the tall grass by the creek. Wheeler asked later if Turner put his finger in it and Turner lied and said yes. Not long after that was when Wheeler left and Turner always thought Judy's woo-woo had something to do with that leaving.

Turner loaded Gran's Zip'r Roo into his truck and took her to Deansbridge during the day to shop at the Safeway or visit the doctor. This was more just so she could catch up with her old friend than anything else. There was nothing the doc or anyone else could do for her now.

Turner took care of the place. He fixed the picket fence and pruned the currant bushes and fumigated the apple trees and left the fruit out for the nurse whose mother made pies for the church. He cleaned the pond out the back with its little waterfall that trickled down from the woods beyond. He watched movies on his laptop in the shed and daytime TV with Gran on the Magnavox he moved up into the bedroom, but the smell of impending death hung low in the air like a false ceiling or the lid of a coffin closing shut, and he could hardly bear it. He offered to move her bed downstairs to the guest room and when she refused, he installed a Stairlift for her but she almost never used it.

A few weeks after he arrived they were upstairs watching the news and a report came on about the girl whose hand Clint Eastwood had bitten off. She'd had the reattachment surgery and the doctors said she'd regain sixty percent of the use of her hand. The mother yanked the little girl's arm above her head to show the reporter the jagged little scar that ran around her wrist like a bracelet.

"Wriggle your fingers," the mother commanded.

The little fingers twitched. But the reattached hand looked off. Like it was put on too tight or had gotten too small for her. And it was a waxy color, like a prosthetic even though it wasn't. The girl made a feeble attempt to withdraw her arm from her mother's grip, then miserably jerked her fingers around a little more.

"That child's got more scar tissue on the inside than we'll ever see," Gran declared. It was one of the last things Turner heard her say.

Turner felt compelled to rush out to the shed to tell Clint Eastwood all about it.

"She can't talk!" he said. "Or won't. What a stroke of luck."

"Lucky for who?" said Clint Eastwood, getting all rhetorical on Turner again.

"You know what I mean. We dodged a bullet back there. They'd rounded up all the pit bulls in the area but they all had alibis. Case closed." Turner exhaled dramatically, trying to draw Clint Eastwood out of his funk.

"So are we going back to Paterson now?" said Clint Eastwood.

Turner wasn't expecting that.

"Don't you like it better here?" he wheedled. "All the fresh air. Hell! We walk for hours every night."

But the dog just sank down then with his chin on his paws, and

Turner noticed for the first time how cloudy Clint Eastwood's eyes had become. It made him feel small staring at those unseeing blue discs, where once he'd been able to find himself doubled in the dark mirrored gaze of his friend. Turner'd had to drive to a tattooist off the interstate to get his nipple pierced again so he wouldn't disappear.

Wroooogh wroooogh.

Gran died a year later and Clint Eastwood went a year or so after that. Turner had begun to expect it. The dog's whiskers had bleached almost white soon after they'd arrived at Forge Hollow, his black mask turned ghostly. Sometimes he'd freeze on their walks, rigid and stone-still in the middle of a field staring at something just beyond. Something that only he could see coming. Whatever it was, it got him in the end. Turner sat with the dog beside the pond behind the shed from dusk to daybreak. Clint Eastwood had taken himself off there, where he lay on his side telling Turner his life story, stuff from his Atlantic City days that made Turner blush. The waterfall trickled in the background and the frogs burped and the mosquitoes bit. At times the old dog lifted his head and snarled at something and tried to crawl away from it, and if Turner could have pulled whatever it was off him he would have, his fist clenched at his own cowardice. If he could have punched himself in the face, he would have done that too.

The dew fell on the grass and soaked through Turner's clothes. The stars turned chalky. Lonesome hums from the freeway. Finally Clint Eastwood lifted his umber eyes to Turner. Dimly behind the cloudy veil of blue, Turner could once again see himself and the twin worlds they'd moved through together. Then those shapes slid off the edge and all that was left was Turner, alone. He lay down beside the dog and closed the eyes whose emptiness he couldn't bear to look upon. He rested his cheek against the massive skull and held him as long as he could.

"This is goodbye," said Clint Eastwood.

"But I want to come with you," said Turner.

"I wanted to go back to Paterson," said Clint Eastwood. "And look where that got me."

"Why didn't you say?" said Turner. Clint Eastwood snarled at him but Turner knew that the anger was just a mask for his fear.

"Home is where the heart is," said Turner.

"Half a heart, maybe," said Clint Eastwood. "Anyway, gotta go."

"Will you come visit?" said Turner. "Please?"

The dog bared black lips. "Think I'll go back down to Jersey for a while."

"I'll kill myself," said Turner.

"Make my day," said Clint Eastwood.

And then he was gone.

* * *

Although he could have moved back into the house, Turner stayed in the shed because it reminded him of Clint Eastwood, who in the end had gotten used to it—the swirling dust motes, the machine oil smell and Granddad bug-eyed and glaring down at them from the rafters. That was all changed now. The dog was dead and buried, with lilies of the valley budding on his grave. But Turner stayed. He couldn't help it—told himself that Clint Eastwood would be back one day soon, but that was a lie. Damn dog'd be back down in Atlantic City more like it, causing trouble just like the day Turner found him in that alley, abandoned and filthy but with more guts in his toenail than Turner had in his whole body. Turner had always felt safer with Clint Eastwood around and that was the truth. Without him he felt small and insignificant in the world. So it was no surprise that he now fell prey to those old terrors, inexplicable chills and strange smells. He tried to resist the voices that woke him, calling to him from terrible dreams, racked by the sound of his own heart beating itself half to death. There was a part of him that just wanted to get up and leave and finally he understood why Clint Eastwood never took to the place. For the first time Turner felt afraid of it.

One late winter morning soon after Clint Eastwood died, Turner woke up to a silence that sat on his chest like a stone, so heavy and final he could hardly breathe for terror. It was a minute or two before he realized what it was. Granddad was gone, and in the sharp, cold space once filled by the creaking of the noose, there was nothing. A terrible burning nothing. Turner's ears rang, and nailed to the chair, he stared into the rafters day after day, but all he heard was silence and all he saw in the dusty sunbeams was the sluggish rotation of the season. Granddad was out there somewhere, but damned if Turner knew where. He wanted to run away, but he felt too small to leave. The house wouldn't let him.

One spring day after that, he was cleaning the pond and heard barking from the house. His heart swelled. He couldn't tell if it was Clint Eastwood, his hearing not being what it was. But it sounded familiar. He headed toward the house at a dead run, banging through the garage and knocking over a drum full of worms and old coffee grounds. He thumped into the mudroom where in the dusty mirror he caught sight of his own reflection, scarred and pierced, wide-eyed and slack of jaw. A pale chicken bone through his septum and safety pins in both eyebrows. His mouth hanging open and dull studs visible on his tongue. One earlobe plugged in black, the other torn right through. And that was just on his face. A tooth missing and not too much hair left on his head. From inside he heard the uneven click of paws on the linoleum.

And from outside he heard Granddad say, "Where's that Wheeler?"

Wheeler? That must mean they were going to the city. Turner loved the long trips to the city, sitting in the back of the station wagon with Speedy on the seat beside him. He pushed through and ran to the kitchen window then swung around at the gimpy sound of the dog's paws on the linoleum. She stood in the dimness barking up at him and he struggled to pick her up. His hands gnarled and shaky. Speedy could move like a sonofabitch, even with three legs, but he got her in his arms, surprised at how bad she smelled. Her breath like shit and a slime where his hand cradled her ass. With the other, he palmed the ridged empty patch where Speedy's right leg used to be before it got torn off in the spinning spokes of Wheeler's dirt bike behind the Parson's farm. Turner looked up.

"Hi Gran," he croaked. "I hope you're feeling better."

But Gran didn't look better. Charging through the kitchen wall on her Zip'r Roo, her face eaten away from inside by the cancer, bloated bags of pee dangling under the seat. Behind her came Granddad, the rope burn around his neck so deep that Turner could see the muscle slick with blood and bile. Turner started to cry.

"It's all your fault he ran off," rasped Granddad, pointing a purple finger at him. The fingernail was gone and in its place a black goo, like mold. "You were never a patch on that boy, you damn fairy."

At that moment Speedy did a three-sixty in his arms and sunk her teeth into his right hand, the soft web of flesh between the thumb and fingers. He screamed and dropped her on the floor where she skidded on her own matter and ran over to Gran's scooter and jumped up into the basket. The scooter advancing toward him and Granddad not far behind. Turner backed up against the counter, pain radiating from his hand and up his arm, but it was the axe Gran pulled out from her soiled and squalid nightie that had his attention now.

"Give us your hand, child," said Gran. "The right one. It's time to take your punishment."

Fairy Tale

Spring came late that year. I had just finished planting the cherry tree in the yard when I heard the grind of a skateboard out on Route 90, the *thuckathuck* of tiny wheels up the driveway. I set the shovel down, wheeled around and there she was, the same girl who put a bullet in my spine in Kabul.

I backed up a couple of inches in my chair and counted to a hundred. She narrowed silvery blue eyes at me, slid off the skateboard and picked it up in one fluid motion, the pale board held up before her like a shield. Or a weapon.

Over there, I hadn't registered that the shooter was a girl. The *keffiyeh* tended to confuse the issue. Just some skinny kid, didn't matter who, bounding away through the rubble behind a blasted parking garage, rusty AK swinging from bony shoulders. But those eyes flashing sheet lightning back at me—I'd know them anywhere, and no amount of Prazosin could ever make me unknow them.

"Finish it!" I'd called after those bony shoulders, those runaway eyes. "Or I will!"

* * *

First thing I did was go inside to call the sheriff, my hands slick with sweat on the wheels of my chair. The girl with the skateboard just waited for me at the bottom of the ramp, cutoffs too small for her. I tried to keep a bead on her through the living room blinds, my unshaven reflection staring back at me through the slats. But by the time the sheriff came by with a jug-eared deputy, the girl had dropped back onto her board and taken off down the road again. So all I could do was wheel out onto the porch and point to where she'd gone, toward the woods at the end of the street. Sheriff said there were lots of homeless kids in these parts lately, on their way up to Canada for the summer, and I had to admit that the girl was dressed just like any punk I'd ever seen—crusty backpack and high-tops with no socks.

"There's a whole murder of those kids roosting in them woods," the sheriff said, shaking her head. "Sooner they fly off the better."

Sheriff Mayes was a tall woman with the cagey look of a basset hound. She admired the cherry tree I'd planted, pointed out to the deputy how the weeping varieties were more to her taste than the regular ones, although the blossoms could be tiresome late summer, the way they blew up a storm and got into the drains.

"A small price to pay," the sheriff said, standing on the lower step so she wouldn't have to look down on me, "for something so pretty in this ugly world."

The deputy raised his hand to me in an awkward salute and that afternoon I got a call from the social worker at the VA asking me if I was taking my meds. The runaway girl nowhere in sight.

* * *

But the next day she was back. Her face was smeared with grime and dead leaves were tangled in her hair. I gave her half my roast beef sandwich and brought out two cans of Sprite.

"I'm Dan," I said.

She told me her name was Aisha. When I asked where she was from, she said: "Places."

While she ate on the porch, I wheeled back in and called a PI cousin down in Jersey to follow up on the runaway angle. Dialing like a fiend before she got to the last of her crusts, I got in touch with the INS, and then an MP buddy—told him that the insurgent who brought me down on the streets of Kabul had come over to finish the job. I called my Sergeant too, who asked if maybe I'd brought her back out of loneliness. Sarge was always going on about how I needed to get out more.

"If I was lonely," I said. "I could think of better company to crave than my own worst enemy." But I stopped making calls after that.

When I went back out, she'd finished her Sprite, so I gave her ten bucks to put away the rake and shovel and take out the trash, and then sent her on her way. But she didn't leave, just kind of hung sulkily around outside the house, her skateboard wheels chewing up the cement the neighbor and I had laid with the help of the SAH grant and my savings. I tried to ignore her and after a while she drifted off, to the woods I supposed. But she was back the next day, and the next, hanging around longer each time. Once, just before dark, I wheeled out and said, "Shoo!" hating myself for it, and as if to spite my lack of conviction, she disappeared, leaving me unable to eat or sleep—terrified she'd left me alone, terrified she hadn't—until she came back.

And so it went. Each day we'd split a sandwich or some soup, and she'd help with some little chore or other, and hang around instead of going back to the woods or wherever she came from. And each night I'd peer out to check that she was still there sitting on her skateboard beneath the starry sky. Finally after a week, I gave up. I set a camp bed up for her in the garage, and that was that.

The chill June turned into a hot July, and on the 4th, my neighbor Bob and his wife took us into town to watch the fireworks at the high school.

Afterwards it was just Aisha and me out on the porch, looking across the yard past the weeping cherry tree to the woods. Summer evenings you can smell the lake on the other side of the highway, even though you can't see it. But tonight all you could smell was gunpowder.

"Runaway, my ass," I said.

The earth was still black around the cherry tree where I'd planted it the day Aisha arrived a month and a half ago. The bottom half of her face grinned back at me through a mess of wiener and mustard. She brought her right hand up in a dusky salute. "Happy Independence Day to you too, Dan."

I moved her into the spare bedroom after that.

Keep your enemies close. Sarge always said that too.

* * *

She said she was fourteen and that she liked Disney movies and Hawaiian pizza. When Halloween came around, I drove her to the mall and she picked out a Rapunzel costume with a long yellow wig that brushed the floor. She went out trick-or-treating and came home sooner than I expected, her pumpkin pail filled with sticky wrappers, her face chalky from indigestion. I enrolled her at the high school, got her to pick out some clothes online. She took her turn at the chores, but she wouldn't touch the garden no matter what, couldn't stand the worms, she said. She did nothing else for me. Wouldn't help me out of bed and into the chair, however much I screamed. It took me an hour to get into the car in those days. I'd lie on the bench press in the garage sweating and crying but I never called her and she never came.

I was six feet three before the war, played varsity soccer and then went on to play in the USL. By twenty-seven, not having made it into the majors, I enlisted, because it seemed like the right thing to do, and I was never good at figuring out right from wrong unless it was put there right in front of me. Over in Afghanistan I got together a mixed team, civilians and soldiers, women and men, and we played in a field the Canadians maintained across from the base. By that time I was twenty-nine, getting too old for games.

The cherry tree grew like a weed and so did Aisha. By next

spring, it was pushing six feet and leaning at a precarious angle and its weeping branches draped to the ground. Bob and I cut it back and he helped me stake it down, Aisha watching from the porch.

"Can't we build a tree house in it one day?" The setting sun reflected off the porch window, and Aisha was just a slim shadow dancing in the flames.

"She's too old for tree houses," Bob said under his breath. "Isn't she?"

But then, one day she found a ball in the garage and knew what to do with it. I looked into signing her with the local minor soccer league, and in the first trial game of the season, with the sun low over the lake, they won 13-3 against the sixteen-year-old champions. I watched Aisha, her ponytail swinging as she cut a swathe through their defenders with a messy *pe♦ala♦a* I'd seen more times than I could count in the dusty street playgrounds of Kabul. I began to pay more attention to her diet. Soaking her oats with fruit for breakfast. Salad and lean meats. Protein shakes. I applied for another grant and changed up to a power chair so I could train her at the college gym, the elongated penumbra of my wheels on the gym wall dwarfed by her darting shadow one minute, looming over it the next.

I'd go into her bedroom sometimes while she slept, hold my service pistol to her head. Count to a hundred.

* * *

On Halloween night just after her eighteenth birthday, I sat at the dining table watching the reflection of the news in the picture window, and there on the other side of the glass in the twilit yard she stood very still with her bare foot resting on a soccer ball. The TV showed a unit ambushed somewhere in Afghanistan, in a place called Shinwar, but I couldn't hear it. From behind the glass and even with my bad eyes, I could see that the soccer ball was slick with dew. My chest constricted. She wore tight shorts and a T-shirt, and she knew I watched.

What she did was to scoop the soccer ball up with her bare foot and bounce it on her left knee, hopping to catch it on the right one, then back down onto her foot and so on. Her calf muscles ripped and her long arms winged out. The cherry tree branches twitched behind her. She caught the ball on her chest, lifting her heart to the sky, her white-lightning eyes never leaving the ball, just like I taught her. I counted to a hundred before she let it drop back down onto the wet grass and she knew I counted.

Darkness pooled in the corners of the yard and she picked up the ball and disappeared into the garage. My temples thrummed. I shut my eyes and when I opened them, a stray blossom from the cherry tree floated down and came to rest like a scab on the empty patch of grass. I waited until I heard the clank of metal, and maybe I was crying a little. I wheeled away from the sliding door and past the specially lowered breakfast bar and into the kitchen. I pulled up short. The yellow Rapunzel wig from her first Halloween sat on the breakfast bar, its long tendrils stirring and resettling in my passing.

I hadn't seen that wig for years. It startled me, sent a current of anxiety across my chest.

I busied myself over the supper dishes, listening to her grunt and heave through her workout. Her sobs were still those of a child, but she was getting stronger every day.

For something to do, I put some candy bars into a bowl. Trick-or-treaters rarely came this far out of town, but you never knew. I heard the door to the house open. With each passing minute that she didn't come into the kitchen, I grew more tense, panic wound around my throat and made it hard to breathe. Worried that she wouldn't, fearful that she would. I began to think about soaking her grains for breakfast the next day. I wondered if she'd just decided to stay in her room, had hunkered down with a Disney movie and a box of Milk Duds—was that all she wanted? The yellow wig on the table sighed and rustled another question. It wasn't as springy looking as it had been four years ago, and I wondered again at her dragging it out after all this time. We were both too old for fairy tales.

She finally appeared stripped down to a crop top, her shoulder muscles bunched and shiny with sweat. I watched her walk flat-footed over to the fridge and open the door and stand there looking into it with her long dusky arms starfished against the light. Her hair was matted on her neck and I watched sweat trickle down past the puckered scar between her shoulder blades. The one that looked like a bullet hole.

She took out a carton of milk and poured it into the blender and added some protein powder. The blender's screams filled the kitchen, and I felt those screams in the back of my teeth.

She chugged the shake, wiped her mouth and sat down on the unlit side of the breakfast bar. "Why'd you drag that thing out?" The blond wig rustled and sighed and she glowered at it. I felt a cold tingling up my arms.

I took off my glasses with shaking hands and wiped them on my sleeve. "I thought *you* did," I said. "Good supper?"

She nodded, her nostrils quivering at the wig's synthetic smell, which had filled the room.

"Salad fresh from the garden." I heard the catch in my voice. Bob had helped me build the wooden track so I could wheel to the vegetable and flower beds.

Fading light from the backyard sliced across Aisha's face, leaving the top half in darkness. Only her eyes glittered.

"You want some dessert? I got frozen yogurt."

"Mango?"

"Mixed berry." I always knew the wrong thing to get. "Sorry."

"Nah," she said. She patted her hard belly, making the butterfly wings flutter on her navel ring. "Thanks anyway."

They didn't call her Aisha at the soccer club. They called her The Beast. The younger players sat strung out along the fence during her games, like birds on a wire, watching her every move. At halftime, they swarmed onto the field, trying to do what she did, talking it up. The trophies collected in the clubhouse, and the younger girls would trail after her at full-time, offering to carry her bag, ogling her bulging thigh muscles, her flat belly with its silver butterfly glinting in the sun. They all planned to get belly button rings when they were old enough, just like The Beast.

* * *

"What time is the party?" I said.

We both looked at the wig on the counter. Its fleshy yellow bulk holding its breath.

"Not sure I'll go," she said, drawing back from it so that her face was in shadow.

"Why not? You've got the costume."

"None of the older girls'll be there." Her voice scratched against the darkness.

Yesterday at training another scout had come to watch her play, offered her the chance of a scholarship, told her what her future would be. I sat in the SUV I'd had modified with optional hand control, and I watched them talk against an apricot sky. A motorboat whined somewhere out on the lake. Aisha shooting impatient looks in my direction and afterward, on the way home, wearing the club sweat pants with the words "All Stars" stenciled up the leg, she told me in her gravelly voice everything that sucked about the scout's pitch.

"Plus I heard the manager there is a burnout," she said.

There was something wrong with all the pitches—the school didn't offer her the classes she wanted, the team sucked, the college was too far away. I side-eyed the pumpkins on porches as I steered down Route 90, and told her she had to make a decision soon. I remembered what it was like to be able to wiggle my toes.

* * *

"Go on," I coughed. "You can't sit around at home on Halloween Night."

In the dim light of the kitchen, Aisha jumped up in that sudden way she had, like a big kid, scooped up the wig, and stormed soundlessly down the hall. I wheeled into the living room and turned on the TV to drown out the noise of the shower, the slam of cupboard doors, the spray of perfume. I must have dozed off because when she appeared in the doorway a while later she looked blurred and was limned in uncertain light. She stepped past the threshold into the living room wearing a long satin gown with tight purple sleeves puffed at the shoulders. The sleeves were too small for her. They stopped just short of her tanned wrists, and the seams strained around her biceps. The wig framed her face like a geisha's and fell to the floor, and her eyes were thunderheads beneath the bad makeup.

"Look, Dad," I was never sure if she was saying Dan or Dad. "I'm Rapunzel."

I froze with the remote pointed at her. She waited expectantly, her eyes moving from the TV to me to the remote, as if whatever her next move was, would depend on which button I pushed. My heart pounded in my chest. "Hell yeah," I managed to get out. "Lookit you!"

She began to waltz around the room in great looping steps like a dancing bear. The skirt was too short, and I could see how her broad feet wobbled in high-heeled shoes, and her arms were flung out wide and the yellow strands of the wig spun past in a sickening blur. The remote dropped from my hands. I waved them in time to her song, like a conductor.

"Rapunzel, Rapunzel, let down your long hair," she sang, a little out of breath.

I pivoted the wheels of the chair in a tight circle to keep up with her, but she began to dance rings around me, faster and faster, the tips of the wig fanning out and rattling the picture frames on the shelves—me as a child by the lake, my Purple Heart pinned to the bedsheet at Kandahar Airfield Hospital before they shipped me out. Aisha's heavy steps rattled the windows and plastic-smelling air rushed past. And I felt exhausted, past struggling, as if it were me dancing in high heels instead of sitting in a wheelchair, as if it were me bearing the burden of all that heavy yellow hair.

She stopped as suddenly as she started. Her grin turned hungry just like that day in the driveway when she turned up out of the blue.

"What's wrong?" My ears roared. Blood pooled in my mouth where I'd bitten my cheek.

"I don't think I'll go." The wig had slipped, exposing her real hair, plastered darkly against her head. "Dumb party."

"Everyone will be there," I said. "Look at you. Rapunzel!"

I always knew the worst thing to say. She pulled off the wig and the heavy yellow tips bungeed onto the rug. With her dark hair tucked into a hairnet she looked bald, pinheaded, diseased. Her mouth quivered and her puzzled face was dwarfed by the hulking shoulders of the dress with its monstrous puffy sleeves. Her sheet-lightning eyes pinned me to my chair.

"You really want me to leave you?" she said quietly. "All alone?"

I reversed back an inch, couldn't help it. Was that what I wanted? The M9 wasn't the only way. Or did I know? Did I really want her gone?

"Get out," I said, and then with less force. "Go. Have fun while you can. Go! Go!"

I wheeled out of the living room, hearing the lonely echo of my own voice. Because there was nowhere else to go, no more games. Just this place and this game now, and just these rules.

"Wait!" She chased close behind, still holding the wig, and her shadow jumped across the kitchen wall in a wild pantomime of a giant choking itself with its bare hands.

I took the car keys off the hook and turned around, tossed them at her. She yelped and fumbled for them, yanked the wig one-handed onto her head. The strands stuck out chaotically, some caught under the cap of the wig, some tangled around her ankles. Her lipstick had bled to one side of her mouth in a loopy pout. She stomped out of the kitchen and down the hallway to the garage and I called out to her, "Rapunzel?" but I could hear the question in my voice, and she didn't answer. I recoiled against the red glare of the taillights through the window, and then she was gone.

I sat there for a moment and thought of her at the party, enjoying herself, maybe dancing with someone. She still snuck into her room to watch that Disney movie sometimes—she didn't know I knew but I could hear the songs from behind the closed door, her scratchy voice singing along. I remembered that *Tangle* was the name of the movie, but what was the name of Rapunzel's prince?

Not Charming.

* * *

The kitchen was dark, but the lamp from the living room gave me enough light to work with. I scooped a cup of steel-cut oats into a bowl, added wheat germ and dehydrated blueberries from the bushes in the backyard. Then I poured filtered water into the bowl from the Brita jug I kept in the refrigerator. I felt weightless in the chair and the skin along my arms burned with pins and needles. The sudden scent of blossoms pulled me to the dining room where I could see through the living room windows to the front yard. I watched the breeze toy with the weeping branches of the cherry tree like it had pulled at the yellow wig. The wind grew stronger and the branches flailed and the few remaining blossoms pulled free, swirled around the dark yard and vanished. There was a tree house atop those massed and tangled branches. We'd built it together in the end, me supervising from the chair—and suddenly I knew. Aisha would never be too old for tree houses.

How can you conjure up a real person?

I turned back into the kitchen, bent into the cupboard beneath the sink and took out a box of rat poison. I ground the pellets into powder in a teaspoon and sprinkled it on top of her oats. I went back to the living room to wait, still trailed by the heady scent of cherry blossoms. I found the remote on the floor and turned on the TV. I must have dozed off because I woke up just before dawn and my back was in spasms. I knew she hadn't come home. Outside in the yard, long strands of toilet paper fluttered from the cherry tree. I wheeled into the garage. The dumbbells and metal plates gleamed in the emptiness. The car wasn't there. I went back into the kitchen and tossed the oats in the garbage. My throat burned and there was that anxious ache in the pit of my stomach. I drank some water and made coffee. I thought a few rounds with the heavy bag would help but it didn't. My lonely shadow in the chair punching at the wall.

At lunchtime I called the sheriff.

She came by later on her own, without the deputy. I opened the door in my rumpled clothes, but I was clean-shaven. I'd taken my meds and hated how they thickened my voice, made me squint in the late afternoon light. Sheriff Mayes stood on the porch with her hat shading her droopy eyes, her neck ruddy with the October winds. Told me how they found my SUV in a ditch out on the Interstate, keys still in the ignition, a silver butterfly navel ring in the glove box. She said the deputy would have the car back to me tomorrow. I didn't ask about Aisha's yellow wig. I figured if it was there the sheriff would have told me.

I thanked her but she was already halfway down the ramp. She stopped and turned around to look up at me in my chair on the porch.

"You figure it out yet, Dan?" she said.

"What?"

"What's worth fighting for," she said. "And what isn't."

I said I'd let her know when I did. Sheriff gave me a salute then, and I saluted back. Smell of bonfires in the air.

Fixed

Gloria was part wolf, part something else, and Gene had never bothered with one of those special "5-generations-removed-from-the-wild"
permits, because state permits didn't carry much weight on the rez
anyway. Maybe they should and maybe they shouldn't. Who was
he to say?

When he and Gloria moved to Deanbridge to be with his brother,
Gene went back to his game design, earned his keep helping out at
Slash Back, the vintage clothing café Steve ran with his girlfriend.
Steve seemed to be doing okay, at least for a gimpy Indian, he said.
He had his guitar and the band, and he had his girlfriend who he'd
met on a volunteer stint at an orphanage in Cambodia, and even if
Gene thought she was a little quiet for Steve, well, he didn't like to
say. There was plenty they couldn't talk about these days although
he tried, but then his brother would say, what about this reggae
backbeat, or try to fix Gene up with some friend of his girlfriend's
and that was never going to fly. So it was only when Gene decided
to head out again in their old man's beat-up Chevy with Gloria in
the back, that Steve finally spoke up about what had been between
them from day one.

The farm.

Their uncle Earl was dead going on two years now, and neither
of them had seen Auntie, or been out West to the farm since cousin
Ty's funeral, back in 2030.

"You get to Bakersfield, try and sell the old place," Steve said, "before that junkie boyfriend of hers smokes or blows or goddamn snorts away our inheritance."

"Not sure I'll get that far," said Gene. "But if I do . . .

* * *

The big animal slept in the backseat or rode up beside him, and things went okay for a while. He pulled over every few hours to have a smoke and let her run off some steam. She'd come back to the truck with her muzzle slick with squirrel blood sometimes, burrs matted in her thick black pelt. They slept rugged up in the truck in campgrounds, or public parks along with the drifters in their SUVs, everyone gone by morning before the moms came with their kids. Sometimes Gene checked into a motel to get himself cleaned up, left Gloria in the truck. They zigzagged like that all up and down the country, from Illinois to South Dakota and down into New Mexico, finding so much room to move between one ocean and another, between mountains and desert, that he began to forget where he came from, what he had left to believe in.

Except Gloria.

When she started acting up in Colorado, Gene thought maybe it was because she could smell her extinct timber wolf cousins in the silvery air, and then he thought maybe she didn't like him stopping at those bars at the edge of town. Big as he was, she'd still keep an eye on him from out the windscreen, worry knitting her shaggy brow at a man of his size letting himself get pushed around like that. She'd whimper at the way the truckers would lead him giggling into the backseat of their cabs, the marks they'd leave on his body of their loose-fisted love. But it wasn't just that. Gloria got worse, howled all the way through New Mexico, where he diverted to visit a friend of Steve's they'd both known on the rez. Coming out of the barracks, the man made the mistake of putting his hand on the door, and the wolf-dog, barking in deep, ragged triplets, all but took off his head. After that, Gene mostly kept her in the back, her pelt shedding all over a blanket he spread for her, and by the time they got to Phoenix, she was so rank with a weeping mange that he had to fork out the last of his savings for a vet to tell him she was getting old.

She was homesick, that was the thing, and Gene was too. For the cold clear streams back East, the dark arcades of fragrant pines, and the way a paddock would snap out at you, unexpected, thistles and goldenrod at its edges. Overhead the high whistle of a drifting hawk. The further they got from all that, the worse she got. And there was something else. She seemed scared, skittish, and he'd never known her to be this way, like she knew something he did not and could not.

Gloria's hackles lifted all the time and a high musk emanated from her so that the windows had to be wound down, the roar of the road filling Gene's head with the old bad thoughts. About how the dark had gotten into their daddy and had taken him away, about cousin Ty and what he did to Steve's leg. About the boy at the roadhouse with the strawberry mark below his right buttock. The road cracking out of the black like a whip, Gloria taut and farting beside him. Fixing him in her terrible yellow-moon stare.

At the California border the Chevy was on its last legs, and Gloria began to bark again and bang her rump against the passenger door and scratch at the dash with her forelegs. And Gene thought this is where he should say enough is enough. This is where he should turn back, open up that hi-fi store in Deanbridge that he and Steve were always talking about. But Gene thought about how much better that would be with the sale of the farm. Stock it with turntables and racks of sweet vinyl for all those DJs out of New York. He pulled off of the freeway and steered down the ramp. Found a dirt access road to pull into to discuss it with her.

"We're so close now," he said. "Let me just talk to the old lady, okay? Make a quick sale of the place, get her fixed up in a condo or something and then head back East. Deal?"

He tried to make himself believe that this was the right choice for him and Steve, for all of them, taking Gloria's great head in his hands and finding her amber gaze in his own.

"Steve could really use the money from the farm for that opera-tion," he said. "He never complains, but his leg gives him pure hell."

All this was true, but it was more than that and he knew it. Gloria didn't need to know Auntie to fear her, all she needed was to see in Gene's eyes the years unspooled, the playback of hurt and fear, to know that even if the farm was still worth anything after the quakes and the drought and Uncle Earl's mismanagement, and even if there was anyone left in Bakersfield to buy it, Auntie would hold off until the last minute, out of pure ill intent—she always had.

* * *

"You have an auntie?" Steve's girlfriend had said back in Deanbridge. "Bring her back with you—she must live with us."

And Steve and Gene had just looked at each other over the girl's shiny hair.

"In Cambodia maybe, she must," said Steve. "Not here. Not ever." Not *their* Auntie.

Their old man use to talk about Auntie, and how she was some kind of bad news. Last time Gene and Steve saw him was when they were just kids—said he was heading west in the station wagon to save his brother Earl from some bad mojo. Led his old bay quarter horse, Queequeg, into the trailer and took nothing else with him but his guitar and a bunch of chants he had locked in the attic of his head. They never saw their father or Queequeg again. A few years later the boys were sent out West to spend what was left of their adolescence with Auntie, Uncle Earl and cousin Ty.

Out of the begrimed windows of the truck, Gene saw the West Coast, not of his youth, but of the intervening years. The crumbling strip malls and shuttered neighborhoods and parking lots transformed into shanty towns. The charred Sierras behind, and especially the quarry lake of boyhood summers, drained to little more than a deep sinkhole overhung with crumbling rock face. At that, Gloria sat up and started on a low keen that rose to a guttural snarl at the unfinished housing developments, the liquefacted fields.

But in the end, it was Auntie, standing on the porch of the old farmhouse in the shadow of the mountains, who set Gloria off completely, so that Gene wondered if, straining at her leash with her eyes filled with blood and her lip pulled back off her dripping teeth, she was even the same dog. Didn't seem to faze Auntie though. Shriveled some since Earl's funeral, she just took off one slipper and hit the animal right between the eyes without spilling a drop of her Keystone. Gloria gnashed at the slipper and Gene managed to haul her 'round to the back of the farmhouse, Auntie saying after them, "That fleabag shits on my squash I'll shoot it."

Uncle Earl had been a merchant seaman in his younger days, died two winters ago from liver cancer, leaving nothing but debt, his vintage truck, and a couple of diamonds. Auntie used one to pay for his funeral, had the other made into a ring that she wore on her middle finger. Apart from that, she survived on palm readings and the proceeds from her vegetable garden, less whatever her new man took up his nose. But for Auntie the varnish-red peppers, pale bubble-skinned squash, and corn, of course, were about survival in more ways than one—the white way and the Indian way, and Gene watched her squatting up to her chin in the tangled rows at all hours of the day or night, graying hair streaming down her back, that tiny diamond on her finger, jabbing at the moonlight in strings of light that even Gene could not decode.

* * *

Auntie told Gene that Uncle Earl had given her the two diamonds, worth no more than seven or eight hundred dollars each, after he knew he was on the way out. When she asked where he got them, Earl told Auntie that he'd found them among the belongings of an Australian crewmate who drowned in the South China Sea.

Gene remembered the story from gossip around the time of Earl's death. But he wasn't prepared for what came next. He wasn't prepared for Auntie to flip her middle finger at him and tell him there were a bunch more just like it. Bigger maybe.

"Where?" said Gene, mesmerized by the winking stone.

Auntie shrugged her bony shoulders, all but grinned at him. "Your uncle was a secretive asshole, bub. Both of them brothers were in their different way—your old man was no better with all them whispers and chants, no sense to be made from any of it."

"He never could quite remember the words for those old-time incantations," Gene agreed, half to himself.

"Where there's smoke," Auntie said, returning to the subject of the lost diamonds, "there's fire. I know there's more of them rocks somewhere. I know it in my bones."

Auntie told Gene she'd looked in the shed, in the barn which contained nothing except for cousin Ty's old Grizzly and Earl's precious F-100, mammoth-like under a vast tarpaulin. She looked everywhere else, she said, even in the blackberry patch between the woods and the corn—all over the place—but she hadn't been able to find them.

"You look for them," Auntie said, tossing the gray curtain of hair from her face. "You and that wild animal sniff out those rocks, we can all get well."

"What makes you think I, we, can do any better?" Gene said, tearing his gaze away from Auntie's diamond ring.

"Go a ways toward fixing up the place for a quick sale," she said slyly. "Ain't that why you're here?"

But what Auntie had in mind, Gene knew, was a different kind of fix, one that involved a glass pipe and cheap Bic lighter for Major Buzz who she said had fought in the New Korean wars and was probably a little young for her, Gene thought, but, again, who was he to say?

Once after supper when Gene was at the sink cleaning up, he'd asked her if Buzz was a real Major, and she'd giggled like a school girl. Scraped her chair out from the table and said, "Real enough for me, bub. Real enough for me."

* * *

So Gene cleaned out the basement looking for the stones, searched the chimneys and the gutters, not that he really believed they were there, but because it made things better between them, between him and Auntie. And if things were better between him and Auntie, then they were better between Gloria and the old woman too—they couldn't get worse.

"It's that wild animal stink everywhere," she grumbled. "I walk into the store, folks walk out."

Well, folks had always walked out on Auntie, but again Gene didn't like to say. He and Steve had put as much space between them and her as possible. Her adored son Ty, unable to kill himself with drugs, ran off to die in some jungle as soon as he could. Even Uncle Earl had made himself pretty scarce when he retired, gone for days at a time, Auntie knew not where.

"Just find those stones, bub," she said, "and we can all get well, go our separate ways."

Gene's pretense at looking for phantom rocks gave him a chance to make some repairs around the farm. This was the family home and by rights would be his and Steve's one day provided Major Buzz didn't get his hands on it first. So he did what he could, but he'd never been very good on the land. That was Steve's area, until he lost the use of his leg.

One job that Gene attended to with more enthusiasm was getting Earl's truck up and running again. Partly because the Chevy only had one or two more rides left in her, but also, if they were going to fix up the place for a quick sale, they needed lumber for the fences and the sheds, wire for the enclosures, and a way to clear paddocks and run broken machinery to the scrapyard—a hundred things that justified the resurrection of a big old baby-blue Ford F-100 that still, even after sixty years and a few false starts, ran like dream. So that was how it was that by some unspoken arrangement, Auntie kept to her station wagon and Gene got free reign of Earl's truck, at least for now, provided Gloria got nowhere near it. That was her only condition—Earl would turn in his grave, Auntie said, to have that animal scuzzing up his pride and joy.

If the truck had been Earl's, the orchards were Auntie's. Unable to find her good lopper since it had gone missing years ago—before

Earl died—her apple, plum and peach trees were riddled with blight. Gene did what he could with a hacksaw and some rusted pruning shears, and Auntie followed with a sack for the fruit. The rest of the time, when he wasn't tearing around in Earl's truck, Gene listened to music or worked on his game designs, took Gloria for long walks in the woods or around the half-drained lake. Sometimes he drove to town to look for work—found his own kind of fix at Thresher, a windowless bar down by the tracks.

Gene built Gloria a big enclosure on the eastern side of the farm, near a twisted old pine by the cornfield where he and Steve and cousin Ty used to fool around on the ATV. It was as far away from Auntie and the house and the vegetable garden as possible, but the wolf-dog still got out once and demolished a couple rows of beans. Trampled on the new lettuce another time. Auntie threw shoes, and even Buzz emerged from the bedroom—a burned-out marine with old eyes and a young body rippling with muscles and tattoos—to tell Gene to get rid of the damn dog or he would. Except he backed down when Gene fixed him up with a growler of malt liquor and a bootleg version of Warcraft that kept the kid quiet for days.

Another time Gloria shat brown graffiti all over the squash, and Gene expected the worst, but Auntie just stood there behind the kitchen window watching the wolf-dog bear down on the low-hanging fruit, clawing her beer can in a way that made Gene forget to breath.

"You keep that goddamn dog chained up or I'll bury her, you hear?" was all Auntie said.

After that, Gene made sure to chain Gloria up every time he went out, but even that could not keep them apart—some terrible attraction between them like in the old-time story Gene's daddy told about a one-legged ship captain and a sentient whale. One night Gene came home late from Thresher to find Auntie trapped inside the house and Gloria on the back porch, her forelegs on the window sill and the two of them staring at each other, Gloria's red-wolf eyes pinning the old woman's face to the dark glass. Worst of all, the thing that chilled Gene to the bone, was the noise that came from the wolf-dog—somewhere between a keen and a howl—and the prayer that came from the old woman, something between a song and a sob.

But it was too late for prayers.

* * *

One freezing afternoon in late November, Gene was driving back to the farm with some groceries when he saw Buzz and Auntie up ahead in the station wagon. They'd just peeled up the on ramp and were hurtling toward the quarry. Gene turned off and got out at the farm, saw that Gloria's enclosure was open and the wolf was gone. His heart drumming in his big chest, his long arms flailing, he combed the ground until he came to a flattened patch of grass, a spray of blood on the bark of the pine that they'd missed in their efforts to leave no trace. When he checked under Auntie's bed he saw that the shotgun had gone too.

Gene knew he had little chance of stopping what had already taken place—the blood on the grass was proof of that—but knowing and seeing were two different things. So with a fading hope that the second might cancel out the first, he was back on the highway in minutes, speeding toward the quarry with the setting sun at his back. He thought he might meet Auntie and Buzz going the other way, but he got to the quarry without passing a soul. He skirted the rocky shore in the truck, driving too fast, freezing, his lips and mouth so dry that he could but croak Gloria's name out the open window.

Finally he found an upturned canoe in the sludge and the wolf-dog wedged in shallow water under a rocky ledge. Gene dragged her onto the shore. They'd shot her in the chest and in the head, her skull bones and bits of her heart, what the water hadn't washed away, matted in her pelt. Her tongue stuck out and was already beginning to swell. He tried to put it back in her mouth, icy streams of tears down his face. A tooth broke off in his hand, and he managed to drop it in his breast pocket, then wrapped her in a blanket and took her back to the truck. He put her on the passenger seat. One last ride. But he didn't trust himself to drive, his legs so weak, he couldn't brake if his life depended on it. So he sat on the bonnet and lit a cigarette and then another one with trembling hands, until the clouds blew up and the moon disappeared behind them with a yellow wink that was goodbye.

* * *

Back in the truck, blowing on his hands, Gene felt unsure now of what exactly his life depended upon. He felt rage one minute, the next cut away from it, the wind dark and indecipherable in his ears. Hope and prayer beyond reach, immersed in noise. He turned onto the lake road and had gone a couple of hundred yards when he heard a rattle deep in the belly of the truck. Like something had come loose after the rough ride along the shore, or was being dragged along—a branch or some brush. He pulled over and counted some beats, wished his head would clear. He took the flashlight from the glove box, left the truck lights on and got out. Closed the door, leaned against it looking to the left and right down the dark road. Then he went to the back of the truck but the tray was empty, nothing but sawdust and a coil of frayed rope. Gene squatted down and shone the light under the chassis. It picked up an angular shape hanging down a few inches above the ground. He looked at the shape and sensed it looking back at him, a greasy reflection passing across its surface. He reached under and tried to pry it loose but it would not come, so he went back for a wrench and then he crawled under. He pulled at it. It was a metal box, must have come loose from the wires crudely attaching it to the chassis. He got it free and dragged it out onto the road and stared at it. Uncle Earl's big old red tool box, rusted some and padlocked. He remembered it from when he was a boy and they'd first come to live with Earl and Auntie. He hadn't seen it or one like it all these years, and seeing it now, the size and heft of it, brought back all those old feelings of creeping dread, a kind of hell-sickness that followed him wherever he went, squeezed him between sea and shining sea so he could not breathe, couldn't think. Steam billowed from his blistered lips; his fingers were stiff with the cold. He used the wrench to pry the lock off the box, panting with the effort, awash in sweat beneath his jacket, and saw them then, the diamonds.

They caught the glare of moonlit cloud and threw it back at him, so that he squinted down at what he saw. A dozen, maybe more, from small to middling, a couple of them a carat or more, maybe. He picked a big one up and held it to the sky, saw the clouds speeding across its facets. He put it back in real slow, concentrating on not letting it drop from his trembling fingers. In the tray beside the diamonds were a pair of small pliers and a greasy paper bag in which rattled the settings, twisted scraps of metal. The diamonds sat in the tray you pulled out by a central handle, and when Gene tried to lift it, it stuck, finally jumping out into his hands. And there at the bottom of the box, nestled in a chamois, next to Auntie's missing lopper, were the ears.

Dried rags of flesh, right and left ears, some clearly female, others sprouting hairs. Some had dried and darkened over time, others looked fresher, waxen, dried blood in the grooves, cartilage poking through the rotted flesh. There was even a nose or two, looked like—the dome, nostrils and philtrum severed from the face with a heavy blade. Ears and noses alike, all with piercing holes, singular or multiple.

Gene squatted beside the tool box for a while, feeling the heat rise in his face, his heart drumming so hard that when tried to put the tray back in the box, his fingers would not work. He blew on them, rubbed them together and then awkwardly scooped up the diamonds, dropped them into his pocket next to Gloria's tooth. Weighted the box with some stones he found on the shore and walked around to a rocky promontory where the water hole was deepest and dropped it in. Toolbox, ears, noses and rusted lopper, like the tomahawks buried beside the warriors of old, for use in a different life. He tried to think of a prayer to offer to the owners of those ears and noses, their bodies doubtless buried in the mountains beyond, but he couldn't remember the words, so in the end, he took a cigarette from his packet, split the paper and sprinkled tobacco over the water in the only blessing he knew. His hands stopped shaking after that.

He drove back slowly, stopped on the way home at a truck stop to raise a glass to Gloria. When the barman, one hand on his emergency speed dial, asked about the blood on Gene's face and shirt, Gene said it was his dog's, and the barman bought him one on the house.

Gene got back to the farm and he took a shovel from the barn and put her in the ground behind the blackberry patch. "Take care of the place for me," he said, "and for Steve, for his unborn child." And then they came back to him, his father's words across the endless road and time. Secret words. Conjuring words. Blessings to protect and curses in a voice he barely recognized as his own. And when he was done, he regretted it a little.

He thought of burning the place to the ground, but it *woul* be theirs one day—Gloria would make sure of it. What other chance did they have against a force like Auntie's love for Major Buzz, any more than they had against her love for Cousin Ty, high on China White when he ran the ATV over Steve's leg down by the twisted pine?

There are things a person ought to know better, but that doesn't mean they do.

Gene dismantled Gloria's enclosure before dawn. He put the diamonds in a baggie he took from a drawer, all except one he left on the kitchen table for Auntie, so yeah, she'd know. By first light he was on his way—the Chevy, it'd make the city limits and he'd figure it out from there. He patted the tooth in his pocket, kept his eye out for a swap meet somewhere to buy himself a leather cord to hang it around his neck.

In the rearview, the hump of the mountains was dwarfed by a smoldering sunrise. He felt real bad about leaving Gloria alone with Auntie, and he hoped she'd forgive him, and understand. That Auntie wouldn't like living with Gloria any more than Gloria would like living with Auntie, but they were stuck with each other now, the tough old woman and the maggoty ghost-wolf who'd leave foul droppings in the squash. Who'd wake Auntie in the night with a howl from hell, and whose mote-blown eyes through the porch window would nail her eternally to the spot.

Forgive me Gloria, because Auntie will throw her slippers at where she thinks you are—she will hurl her bottle of Old Overholt at the window and it will shatter on the rug. She will curse the infernal tap of claws up and down the cluttered hallways and tremble at how you sniff for your fix at the doorway of the bedroom she shares with Buzz, panting through your shotgun holes. And fearless as she thinks she is, Auntie will weep when you leap onto the bed in a rank and bloody arc with black lips drawn back from your yellow fangs, and she will beg and offer herself instead of him—anything not to be left alone again. But you will not listen, you will not hear. You are sworn to another.

Forgive me, Gloria.

Rogues Bay 3013

When Esme's brother tells her how he became an angel, we are on one of those forgotten bays in the Southern Rim, a long narrow neck of brick red water garlanded by rocky headlands, with a small jagged slit of beach at its throat. The sand is coarse and clumped, littered with polymer scrap and driftwood. It is of little interest to anyone but the memory dogs, ratty, snaggletoothed mutts that yap at the pink spume and have to be untangled from the seaweed that washes in with the tide. The muscles on Esme's arms flex as she lowers herself into the water from a flat, rose-colored rock in the middle of the bay. From the shade of the makeshift officer's bar, I watch her swim to shore, the sun limned around the broad curve of her shoulders. She steps onto the sand and bends to pat the memory dogs, and I think how well I know her, how I'd have put money on her stopping to speak with one of the mutts, to whisper some nonsense into its furry little non-ears.

* * *

"He's dead." She is a little out of breath by the time she gets to me. Averts her eyes while she rolls a fresh blunt. "My brother's dead."

"Here," I hold out my lighter, the flame twinned in her dilating pupils. People mingle on the rocks to watch the sunset, enlisted personnel and noncoms too, Apologists and Rebels alike, with their ragged children and sidelined patriarchs—but the men's gazes are all on Esme, on the water streaming between her thighs and down her scarified arms and small breasts. From the stiff waiting gum trees on the headland, the hiss of the cicadas rises to a scream and is silent.

"You never mentioned a brother," I say.

"Half brother," her lips are blue from the cold. "Not that it matters."

I visor my hands over my face and look to the flat rock protruding from the water where moments before there had flocked a group of angels. Now there is no one.

* * *

"Angels are dangerous, kiddo," I remind her later over rehydrated chicken Kiev back at the base. I have arranged partner privileges for Esme in the officer's mess. The room is a vast space lit by recessed LEDs and empty now except for a droid with a mop over by the printing machines. Esme's eyes are oceanic beneath the cold lights, the archipelago of keloid scar tissue across her chest and both shoulders etched in shadow. The same dark mood clings to her here, as on the beach. She still smells of the sea, of kelp and heat. A gulf opens in my chest.

"It's a dangerous world," she says. "Angels or not."

"True, but they lie like the devil," I say. "You know that. He may not even be your brother. That was him on the rock? You're sure of it?"

"Half brother."

"Family's a slippery concept these days."

"No kidding." She stabs her meal with a bamboo fork.

I probe insistently, "You never met him before?"

She pushes away her meal and lights up a smoke. The smoke coils around her face. "My mother and stepfather had him to fill the void after I'd been recruited. I heard he was a dancer, ran away to follow his dream. I didn't call my mother as often as I should."

Her mouth twists with regret. Back at the base, she wears aviator gloves to hide her hands. I reach out to interlace my fingers in hers, side-eyeing the cleaning droid, who is lost in its headphones. Esme's hands are still misshapen from the burns, the knuckles thick and lumpy, rosy webbing between her fingers a result of the grafts. She brings the joint shakily to her lips. After a few puffs, the shaking stops. Her pupils ratchet open and I see myself twinned in their black and fathomless depths.

"Why didn't you ever mention him to me?" I say.

"You never asked."

"Well," I glance nervously at the droid but it is bent over its mop. "You take family where you find it. The world we live in, right?"

"Right. The quote-unquote Aristotle Project."

She wiggles gloved fingers in the air around the terrible words that wedge their way into the difference between us, a difference that has nothing to do with rank. A difference that has haunted me ever since my arrival at the Rim. It hits me again: why is she not more like me?

I shrug to hide my anxiety. "It isn't as if it was my idea to create artificials for the armed forces—"

"All this time," Esme cuts in with mock wonder. "Humanity thinking it was the only game in town."

"—or my idea to allow the artificials to seek unions with nons."

"Allow? That's your word for it?"

Her hair is the color of sun on newly cut wood. I don't ask whether her brother was artificial in whole or part. Purity's a meaningless complex these days. Like family, you take it where you find it. The Aristotle Project's mission accomplished that, at least.

"Did he tell you how he died, this so-called angel?" I say, leaning forward to cover her hands in mine.

"Forget it." She takes her hands away.

There is a dragging sound across the room, punctuated by soft clicks, and I look across to see a large flat lizard, drab green with a red belly, heading blindly toward the vending machine. The custodian lifts its mop and brings it down on the lizard. Once, twice, three times. Picks up the carcass by the tail and drops it in the garbage bag. When I turn back, Esme is gone.

I push back my stool and find her in the hallway, leaning against the steel wall outside the bathroom. I smell vomit on her breath.

And Dust—the powder she smokes to ease her pain, to accelerate the healing process. I can get her as much as she wants through my connections in the North. It smells strangely ferrous, like dried blood.

"Angels take bodies from the living, kid. You know that. Your brother could look any way he wanted to."

"Lucky him," she says.

* * *

The conjugal rights I've finagled for Esme and me are wasted tonight— after her visit from the angel, neither of us seems much in the mood. We both move out before dawn in any case, Esme with her squadron and me with the Vantage II command. She tells me she should return to her quarters, spend the night with her battle family. I don't argue.

* * *

I wake up in the dark to ghostly rivulets of rain against the tempered glazing. I gasp at an unexpected pressure below my waist, like a cold heel in my groin. My legs are missing.

Draped in shadows at the end of the bed is a crimson-haired angel. One minute he looms, the next he recedes as if on a conveyor belt. He is blind and naked and he is wearing my legs. His towering wings unfurl and something writhes, white and slimy, from a gash in his head.

"Is that fried microprocessor I smell," he says, wrinkling his nose, "or are you just pleased to see me?"

I register a slippage between his voice and the movement of his face, like a movie soundtrack out of sync. I reach for the light.

"Freeze," he says. "You stink of sin."

The angel is right. The room smells like scorched metal, and sweat beads my lip. "You're Esme's brother?"

"Half," he reminds me. "Not that it matters."

I flex the concealed mace on my right arm and recalibrate how fast I can get to the titanium fighting sticks beneath my pillow. Double Jeopardy rules apply here. You can't kill an angel but you can slow it down.

"You look well," I say to hide my panic. "Those wings make quite a statement."

"They've grown on me." He flutters them obligingly. "Almost two years since you killed me up in the Dip for trying to save my sister."

"If I'd known you were her brother I would have kept you alive long enough to wish you weren't."

"How's the phantom limb syndrome, Major?"

"Remember," I say, as my fingers inch toward the taiaha sticks. "Even with no legs I've a better arm than you, half-angel."

* * *

My ship had gone down in the Dip, a fork in the mid-Atlantic labyrinth that encompasses on- and off-world colonies, sovereign Orbital allies, and a number of stars. My legs were crushed beneath the instrument panel, the bridge in flames. The Dark Wing rescue rig that descended upon me seemed summoned by some hidden mechanism. Its famous insignia emerging out of the sky like fate's own handprint.

While I recuperated at the Command Base hospital, I found out that my rescuer lay in a critical condition. Something having to do with a malfunctioning flame-retardant mechanism on her blast suit. They kept her in an induced coma, burns to fifty percent of her body. Another thing I remember were the angels. There had been so many flying around the base hospital that the staff had to wear riot shields and polycarbonate visors, and I was thrown out of my wheelchair more than once.

After making some inquiries I found out that my savior was none other than the great Esme Black, the infamous Dark Wing herself. I could barely believe my luck. After all this, to be reunited in this way. But I couldn't get near her. A delicate young man with scarlet hair and a ring in his nose guarded her room. I'd watch him reading to her, plugging music into her ears. I assumed he was her lover. That was my mistake. He wasn't armed but that didn't stop him leading me off the hospital grounds and trying to kill me.

That was his mistake.

* * *

"Speaking of boo-boos," the angel says. "What were they thinking over at the Aristotle Project?"

"Maybe they weren't thinking." While I'd slept, he'd removed my legs at the hip joint. "Maybe they were just dreaming. Why shouldn't art want to create back?"

"To be or not to be to the power of n?" he sniffs. "Just imagine. All those virgin integers waiting beyond the pearly logic gates."

"You'd know more about pearly gates than me."

"But not as much about virgins," he says.

I try to take a swing at him, but the missing legs kick my ass. The angel giggles and makes a tsk-tsk gesture with a black-nailed finger.

"Thing is," I say, inching my hand for the fighting sticks. "Esme found me. Not you. I fixed her, not you."

The angel unfurls his dirty wings. "Hands up, Abomination."

I raise my hands. The sheets drop away. A vile metallic smell rises from my loins, a slippery patch spreading across the sheets in a sickening Rorschach blot. The angel is a dead weight, nailing my phantom legs to the bed.

"What does Esme know?" A trickle of sweat stings my eye. "What lies did you tell her there on that rock today?"

My shame makes me vulnerable and he takes strength from that. The massed feathers clatter and irradiate a white light that bounces off my torso, that force the taiaha sticks to clatter useless to the floor. An unseen hand pulls the sheets down further to reveal a revolver between my missing legs. Before I can reach for it, it too is flung to some hidden corner of the room where it lands with a dull thud.

"Speaking of lies," the angel runs a hand through his blood-red hair. "She says she's clean. Kicked that Dust you hooked her with."

"A life for a life." My mouth is dry. "Are you here for her or for you, half-angel?"

His eyes burn like klieg lights. "Ground Control to Major Whyte," he says. "I am not here for my sister or for me. I am here for you."

* * *

I never really cared about the Aristotle Project. I'm a pilot, after all, not a scientist. What do I know about neuromorphic protocols? Female hosts implanted with synthetic phosphoserine memristors? The stuff of dreams, far as I'm concerned. I never knew my mother. I spent many afternoons after school at my father's engineering lab. When I asked him once what the Aristotle Project was, he rambled on about RAM and DNA, blood and circuitry, about warding off viruses, artificials becoming smarter, living forever. Instead of listening, I began to fiddle with the instruments on the table, wishing I could go outside and play with the other kids. Until he told me that if I kept touching his equipment, he'd have to cut off my hand. That'd fix me, he said.

But I wasn't broken yet.

Not until my ship fell out of the sky. After they flew Esme out of the Command Base hospital with yet another Purple Heart, I lay waiting for my new legs. For the frag wounds to heal, for the engineers to make adjustments that would allow me to self-correct for the assorted traumas. It was just a matter of time before they patched me up and made me whole again. I'd been there before. But this time was different. This time it had been Esme. The monster who saved its maker. And now she was gone.

My father once told me that love was just a complex system. Another thing he said was that Aristotle was full of shit.

It took me a year traveling across most of the known worlds, but I finally tracked her down. She'd signed up for duty in the most remote outpost she could find, the unclassified Rogues Bay at the southern tip of the desert rim, her flying skills and derring-do the talk of the sector. She'd changed. Being in space as often as she was had bleached her scars as pale as moonlight, called the stars back into her eyes.

* * *

"What the hell did they do to you?" the angel growls. "These legs pinch like fuck."

"Keeps me on my toes."

Looking at the angel I see her instead. I underestimated his size. He is as tall as Esme, his shoulders sinewy like hers, and although unscarred, his nonflesh is seamed with empathetic silver, like an alabaster god. Pieces of his pretty face flap and collide.

"She didn't know you," the angel says. "You could have told her, Abomination."

The first time I saw her again, I was jealous, I admit. Surrounded by the happily wounded members of her battle family, jostling each other, joking and talking trash. Their smooth bodies sleek with muscle. Esme's a galaxy of scars. Some scruffy memory dog at her feet, smelling of rain. The way she looked when I invited her to my quarters for the first time, feeling the slow engine of fate rumble to life. Dark Wing, Sir, reporting for duty. I asked her what she loved about flying, and she just said, "The stars."

The stars.

They were in her blood. Literally in her DNA from the source code I spliced onto the surrogate's DNA. Because I could.

"I tried to tell her," my uplifted arms throb and I can't feel my fingers on my left hand, the one without the mace. "I asked her if she knew who I was when she rescued me, and twice she said she was just doing her duty, Sir, how I could have been anyone."

"But *you* knew who you were," the angel says. "And what."

"She had her chance."

My jaw aches with clenching. The rain beats down harder.

"You trapped her, Major." Suddenly he is gone, leaving only his raging voice and filthy wings towering above me like a bird of prey. "Not just with the Dust, but with your power. What kind of chance is that?"

"Any chance of getting a nose itch?" I say, my head doing wild one-eighties to find the rest of him—and me—in the dark. I feel crippled in the glow of the disembodied wings, helpless. Suddenly he materializes at the end of the bed again, crossing my knees over his ankles and wiggling my toes. I scream in agony.

"What about her family?" he says, his voice clawing at the darkness. "Did you ask her about them?"

My breath is ragged, my throat knifing. "She told me about a mother, a stepfather who died a few years ago."

"And her real father, Abomination? The one who made her?"

I close my eyes. "I was never particularly interested in Esme's past. It was her future I claimed."

* * *

She refused all of my advances. At first. I gave her whatever she wanted. Weekend furloughs to visit her mother, referrals to my own personal physicians, even a promotion. None of it had any effect, beyond a wary indifference. But then, after a particularly strenuous mission, she went through a terrible relapse. Her body twisted around itself, painful to watch. I offered her some Stardust, fresh from up north, but she said no, and I loved her all the more for it. My maker was right. Aristotle claimed that, in nature, like was attracted to like. But nature, as Aristotle well knew, was never the only game in town.

"You broke her."

"I fixed her."

* * *

Inevitably, of course, she was grounded. The great Dark Wing clipped and beaten, terrible to see. And still she refused the Stardust. Instead she would go on long walks in the bush to avoid the pitying stares around the base. She found a lizard mauled on the headland. It had been attacked by a BiProd, short for byproduct, living waste from the Aristotle Project. The jagged teeth marks at the lizard's pink throat were those of a human child, the welts on its back that of a monster. She took it into her quarters, made a bier for it and tried to keep it under her bed until one of her squad members noticed the stink.

"Fix it!" Esme screamed. "Fix it!"

She'd smeared puce makeup over the harsh topography of her scars, rouged her cheeks and lips in the lizard's blood. She looked like a hospital shower curtain with dreams of becoming a prostitute. A siege was under way in a remote orbital and her squad didn't want to attempt the extraction without her. Again. Just one fix of the Dust, she begged, maybe two. Just to get her into the firmament again, the spangled night.

I gave her what she asked for.

✳ ✳ ✳

"She didn't know what she was asking for," the angel snarls. "Or from whom."

"Truthfully," I say. "Who else would have had her?"

"You'd be surprised," the angel flicks a pierced tongue at me.

A bubble of jealousy pops in my throat. "There's another?"

The feathers on the towering wings pixelate, and some of the white goo leaks from his nose into his mouth. "There's always others."

"I gave her freedom from pain," my words inexplicably slur.

"You gave her lies." I notice now that his nonflesh is randomly pierced all over—bars through nipples, a cluster at his navel, a line of studs down his penis. "The worse kind."

I am freezing, legless. I fight the shakes, spit the words out through clenched teeth.

"My father cut off my hand when I was twelve, and do you know what he said?" The angel yawns but I tell him anyway. "He said it was for my own good." I'm yelling now, a high shrill rage making my torso shudder on the bed. "So there are worse lies in this world, Angel, than those I told Esme!"

The angel says, "And worse truths as well."

* * *

The ship's metal voice hisses a thousand whispered conversations. Beneath his blind eyes, the angel's cheekbones glisten with tears. "Some of her missions would take months," he says. "Years. I'd wait for her at this station, or that orbital. Used up all my savings trying to track her down. The great Dark Wing. My sister. At the hospital, all I wanted was to be there for her when she woke up."

"You were in my way."

I tense my right forearm muscles to unlatch the safety mechanism on the prosthetic mace, the one my father affixed to me as both blessing and curse, punishment and reward, because he could. He called it the Killing Hand. I think about it—wetware and software, blood and circuitry—for the thousandth time.

The angel licks a tear off his lips. "If I gave a shit, Abomination, you'd be the first I'd give it to."

He swivels his head so that I can see the part of his skull still missing from where I skewered him with my claw back in the Dip. Gelid globs of black blood clot his hair, like deranged glyphs. "You're all the same. Think you're so smart." His voice comes from somewhere deep in his wound. "She brought you back from the dead—her own father."

"I never asked to be saved."

"Saved? Rescued, Major, maybe. But you were never saved."

And then the angel whips his head back around and rises from the bed with my legs dangling beneath him like marionette sticks. Soul code pours from his hole. Time slows down. I'm a stuttering freak in silk sheets. The avenger's cold hands wrap around my throat. My defenses kick in then and I inhale. Contract my abdominal actuators and lift my torso off the bed—one-handed *tolasana*, scale pose—and engage the mace. Unleash the Killing Hand that brings the angel to his knees, my knees, opening in his nonflesh the wounds of ages, the angel screaming out some horseshit about me, what I am, words Esme must never hear, so I cut out his pierced tongue for good measure, leaving him wingless and naked and sucking his soul up from off the floor.

* * *

Esme is stationed with the others from her squadron. By the time I strap back on my legs and check them for contamination, and then get past the security cordons—even with my Killing Hand and the Wing Chun skills I'd hacked into the prosthetics—it's too late. Her bunk room is empty. When I finally catch up to her, she's scrambling along the rain-slick rocks toward the vaporous light of the inflatables near the launch carrier. Lightning cracks at the horizon. Her grunts of exertion tearing at my heart.

"You killed my brother."

"Half brother," I call out above the wind. "You should never have pulled me from that cockpit."

In spite of my night vision, I have trouble fixing her in position, not just because she's moving fast, but because her aviator jacket eats up all the light. I finally manage to cut her off on a sandy pass between the rocks.

"I couldn't leave you there," she says. "It's not who I am." The wind whips at her hair.

"You don't know who you are. Or what I am."

"Is that what this is about?" Her eyes narrow, her face contorted in rage, but no fear. "You claiming the right to unmake what you think you've made?"

Surprise registers as a buzzing in my head. "You know?"

I take strength from her tears. The rain makes a corona of phosphorescence around her head. If she is carrying a weapon it is well-concealed. I flex my claws against my leg. "Whatever filth you believe, ask yourself this: what difference does it make, a line of resequenced code onto some surrogate's DNA?"

"When that surrogate was my mother"—her voice catches, and she fights for control—"it makes a difference. When the line of code spliced onto the egg she carried was uploaded from an artificial—it matters. Because that would make the artificial not just my Major—and that majorly matters! But you! You knew it the whole time."

"I trusted my maker too," I say, waggling the Killing Hand that has made all the difference. "Self-blame comes with the territory."

Her eyes widen with a sudden realization, and she pushes her hair from her face. "Holy shit! You crashed your own ship? Just so that you could be rescued by the daughter you never had?"

"Esme, you'll always be my best thing. I didn't know you'd become so breakable, so . . ."

"So human?" The blue oceans in her eyes do not match. One is a tropical storm, the other a Nordic swell. She leans toward me. "Listen, Major Not-Dad—only going to say this once. The epigenetic side effects of that Dust you get for me? The real benefits? Ironically not just less pain, but more humanity. Irony? Not a strong point for you artificials, is it?" She brings a shaking hand to her head and then her heart. "Neural pathways lit up like landing strips. My genetic makeup self-modifying like a sonofabitch. More recombinant DNA in my veins than you can poke your Killing Hand at. Point is, not-Daddy—I am not what you made me. I'm human—mostly."

"My best thing." I shake my head, some worn-out mechanism deep inside me struggling to compute. "My best thing."

"Not even close. All that effort to destroy me as your father destroyed you, to make me the victim of your perverted dreams? The Dust fixed me, Major." She raises her hand to her temple again, this time with her middle finger extended. "We're barely related."

I stick out my tongue to taste the rain. I am gripped by a shutter-stop fit I can do nothing to stop. It's less the shock of what she is trying to tell me about the Dust's ontological side effects than the fact that her mock salute indicates that she is unarmed. Maybe she's just trying to make it harder for me, the way I did with my father, appealing to the better nature of the creator. Or maybe it's as the poet says: fathers and mirrors, abominations both.

Above us the trees writhe as a single grasping force. The spasm passes. I raise my Killing Hand.

"Go to hell," she laughs, exposing scars like comet trails at her throat.

"Not without you, child."

"Just because you want it, doesn't make it yours."

Her face glistens with tears, but her jaw is set. My core expands with something like love. Whatever her claims to having severed herself from her source code, she is still mine—to do with as is in my nature. Nature—was there ever a more dangerous word?

I unfurl my claws. But then, from her lips comes a low whistle that chills me to the core. It rises to a soggy piercing summons that echoes from the rocks. A muscle in my neck spasms and a circuit snaps. I smell the pack before I see it, pet memories grown hoary and healthy with time, all yap and drool. At the dangerous call of her heart, they sweep down from the bush and across the rocks in a wave of hackle and fang. Before I can unleash the Killing Hand, a tidal wave of canine vengeance brings me to my knees—vengeance on the false father—so that all that remains by the time they finish is a few scraps of polymer tubing and a carbon fiber frame. Esme is long gone too, leaving the blood and pelt-smeared parts of me to be carried out on the tide, floating beneath the crimson waves and waiting for a time when I too will be an angel.

When I too will be winged and dangerous and pure of heart.

War Wounds

Jack Devlin and Dicky Alford were fourteen and thirteen respectively when their daddies came home from the war. Two years later, in 1947, when Dicky made the monster, Jack's old man was running for chairman on the incorporation ticket, and Dicky's father, who served with the 2nd Combat Engineer Battalion out of Camp Elliot, had spoken no more than a dozen words to his son since *The Star* ran that stark front page: "PEACE." You've seen how it works in these small towns, the way war puts a bony finger to the lips of the hard men who return, hammers something untouchable into them, something undiscoverable like no matter what they told you, it would never be all there was.

Jack and Dicky both grew up on dairy farms between San Miguel Road and Otay Lake, right here in Bonita. All through summer, Jack would race his Schwinn down Proctor Valley Road through the unnatural coupling of pasture and desert, past the new reservoir all pale and shiny like the back of someone's throat. Jack got to thinking how if it weren't for the cattle and the illegals hefting mud-whitened hoes over their shoulders, he could be on Mars.

But on the day that Dicky made the monster, both boys were on their horses. Whose idea it was to leave their bikes, that part of their boyhood, behind—and what it had to do with Jack having turned sixteen in May, or the dog-eared Army Engineers Field Manual Dicky had taken to stuffing in his satchel—neither yet could say. The sky was leaden and the ground muddy after the rains, tarweed thickets hissing with insects and frogs. Jack felt hot under his hat.

They rode single file along the road shoulder, herds huddled at the dust-blurred edge of eye. From up ahead, Dicky's croaky braggadocio came floating back to Jack in snatches, until it sunk in that Dicky was talking about a girl called Kit O'Dea. About whether or not it mattered that she was so much older than him—nineteen—and about that unnamed man she was dating in Jamul, the one that kept her in perfume and earrings—and moving between topics with his usual dexterity, Dicky went on about how many bridges *he* could have blown up in the war if only he'd been old enough to enlist.

"Main thing," he said, patting the satchel at his hip, "is what it says right there in the Field Manual, 'Failure of a single demolition could cost the lives of hundreds of men.'"

The Field Manual had belonged to Dicky's brother.

Dicky slowed a little, allowing Jack to catch up. "Give me half a box of C4 and I'll show Jerry what fails all right.'"

"Smokestack Joe to boot," said Jack, and they both laughed.

Now this was at the cusp of the postwar housing boom, before San Miguel Ranch or Eastlake, when most cow country folk wanted nothing to do with Smokestack Joe, or "progress," as it was called then. Folks like Jack's and Dicky's daddies figured no more was needed in the valley besides a steady flow of illegals to work the farms and an elected official committed to keeping both the developers *and* the Jap citrus growers out in equal measure. So back then, that's how things stood. The year Staff Sergeant John Devlin, Sr. would become district chairman and Corporal Richard Alford, Sr. would blow up the Devlin barn and end up in the Soldiers' Home—PTSD not having been invented yet.

They stopped at the point where their horses crested the rise that looked east across Proctor Valley. Jack peered over the valley—a wasteland of sage scrub dotted by the occasional wrecked truck or crumpled serape all the way to Jamul. Dicky was back to saying how by the time he was in his twenties, it wouldn't matter. He could think of worse things, he said, than growing old with a girl like Kit O'Dea.

Kit O'Dea was a girl in town. She smoked Chesterfields, drove a '37 Ford truck that had belonged to an uncle back East who she didn't like to talk about. Kit worked at the Odeon and wore a soiled blue skirt and a matching powder blue pillbox hat, and there wasn't a male over the age of twelve in the dark of that theatre who couldn't smell her perfume over the reek of popcorn and the slurp of pop, couldn't taste her sugar or dream about it.

* * *

Once they got back from the war, both fathers returned to their ranches, and assumptions were that their boys would take over the running of the family farms one day. But Dicky was a reader. He just wanted to know about things or blow them up, especially when his brother's effects came back without his brother. Local men coming back on one leg or none, and Dicky's big brother never coming back at all—Dicky knew what the war had taken away, but he knew he was no cowboy, either. He liked to read about physics and conservation—a word no one even used back then—about genetics and superchargers and Sumerian cuneiform. He'd talk Jack's ear off about killer whales, how they'd mate for life, how the male dorsal fin would collapse in captivity, and how the females live almost twice as long and run the show. Usually Jack liked to listen to him, but today it hurt his ears, and Kit's name on Dicky's lips just made him want to break something.

"What about Mae?" Jack said. Mae was Kit's younger sister. She was in the same class as them at Chula Vista High School, and Jack had seen the way she'd looked at Dicky.

Dicky turned his face away, the pallor of his neck contrasting with the angry spray of zits along his jaw. He urged the pinto up over the rise and was about to say something else, but pulled up short at the sound. They'd both heard it, a low moan that made it hard for Jack to get any spit into his mouth. His mare froze, and Dicky's horse stopped just ahead of her.

The moan came again, from behind a cluster of oaks on the hillside to their left. Dicky rode through a gap in the wire fence, got there first. Even before the mare pulled up alongside, Jack knew what the trouble was, so that Dicky didn't have to say it.

"It's dead inside her."

Jack's nape prickled right under the dark hair he got from his Mexican mother and which Kit liked to grab by the handful, back of the Ford beside the reservoir where they met when they could. He hated the lie he'd wedged between him and Dicky but what could he do? Dicky was right. Kit got under a man's skin. The silky stockings beneath that crinkled blue uniform. How her hips jutted into Jack's belly, the way she didn't mind how hungrily he feasted on her, and how there was always more. No end to what they had, so long as they were careful, so long as they didn't give it a name. They never talked much when they were together—let the meteor showers or rumble of the dam talk for them, cattle nosing around the truck. But when they did talk, it was mainly about how Kit was going to be a movie star one day, or the latest outbreak of cow fever, or whether Sheriff Almirez would catch that wildcat or whatever it was mutilating illegals. What wasn't said, what stayed unspoken between them were the presents and money Dicky's father brought Kit when he came to visit her once a week at the Desert Flower Inn over at Jamul. Dicky's father was going to help her get to Hollywood.

Jack told himself that it would do no good telling Dicky about Kit. Dicky didn't have much anymore apart from his dreams.

"What's your dream, Jack?" Kit'd said in the truck by the reservoir. "Everybody has one."

"You won't tell anyone?"

"Who could I tell?"

"To go to Mars," he said.

* * *

Jack stared down at the road winding away below them, through what Dicky called no-man's-land, trying not to hear the heifer's moans.

Problem with watching a cow give birth is that the calf, when it has pushed its way through the birth canal and is emergent from the mother's body—problem is that it looks like nothing on earth. Jack could never get used to it, watched it hundreds of times, had roped and pulled the alien issue from that gushing hole a hundred times more, and still he couldn't abide it. The way what was growing in and eventually torn away from the mother, at least until it struggled into being, shapeless and blood-cauled in the dirt, looked like it could have been anything. A building, a rocket, a bridge, a man.

Jack did know that what was sticking out from under the heifer's tail was her calf. Foreleg was missing, that was the thing. He smelled blood and shit. All you could see was the eyeless head. A triangular mass, slick with blood, all angles like something broken. The heifer was on her side and she moaned again, the moan unnaturally rising at the edge.

Dicky jumped off his horse and went over to her. A ripple of panic and pain zigzagged up and down her bulk. She tried to get to her feet, flopped back down in the dust. When Dicky went at the thing beneath her tail, she clipped him on the hip with her hoof, put him on his ass.

What people don't realize is how big a Holstein is, especially compared to a stunted, acne scarred runt like Dicky. His head not much bigger than the veiled obscenity refusing to budge from where it had lodged half-born and all-dead, neither one thing or another. Dicky brushed himself off and limped back to her tail, plunged both arms in, pulled them out again slick with goo, and stepped away from her hind legs. Looked up at Jack frozen in the saddle.

"We got to save her." Dicky's arms hung by his sides, matter dripping from his hands.

Jack had grown too big for basketball, spent most nights at football practice, had half a head and twenty pounds on Dicky, but said he'd rather ride to the Schultz's—it was one of theirs—and call for a vet. Dicky said there wasn't time, she'd be dead by then, so Jack got off his horse, catching his foot in the stirrup on the way down. Stumbled on one leg before pulling himself free. Face burning, he picked up his hat from where it had fallen, grabbed a rope and went over to the cow.

"Best to rope her to a tree," he said, but Dicky's attention was focused inward, in his eyes a faraway look, like a safecracker's. Both his arms deep inside the heifer, he was rummaging for the foreleg, trying to reposition the unborn calf so he could pull it out.

Unborn maybe, but Jack still knew it to be a bull.

Overcome with shivering, he somehow managed to get the rope around the heifer's neck but not so it would choke her, and he roped her forelegs and then looped the rope around the oak. She ignored him, her black irises tumbling around a tiny core of blue at their center.

"Talk to her," Dicky said. "Tell her it's gonna be all right."

Jack had heard it a hundred times. Seen grown men on their knees, murmuring encouragement—blessings, prayers, or confession—into the straining ears of four-legged mothers caught between the need to expel and the need to take back the creature they had made.

Jack did not feel up to the task—Kit had not yet made a man of him, and Jack sometimes doubted whether that was even her intent—instead he joined Dicky and loosely roped the hind legs so that the heifer could still bear down. With the legs secured, Dicky's hand moved more easily inside her. He pulled out the remaining foreleg first. He wrapped both skinny arms around the calf's neck, his feet churning in the mud while Jack, grunting, put a shoulder to her rump. Dicky and the dead calf were head-to-head and mouth-to-mouth, Dicky's tongue extended in concentration, the calf's lolling in death, its unformed eye fixed on Jack.

The mother then gave out a bellow and the calf propelled forth in a rush of blood and afterbirth, gunk still gushing out of her as Dicky landed on the grass with the creature on top of him. Sat there for a moment dazed with it sprawled in his lap.

The heifer fell quiet, craning her head to see what the world had taken from her, and how she could follow it to wherever it went. Finches sang in the silence.

Jack walked around on wobbly legs to untie her. She lay still, except for her midsection, which hollowed out with every shallow breath. Dicky pushed the calf into the dirt and stood. They both looked down at it lying between them. The sharp corrugations of its ribs, three legs balletically sprawled. Its pelvis looked strangely flattened, maybe crushed in the birth canal, and its terrible unformed eye stared into the growing divide between them.

No-man's-land.

After a while Dicky smoothed greased hair off his forehead, and his lips hung loose and damp and laughing, the way they got when he was discussing Halley's Comet or Kit's laugh. But in his jittery narrowed eyes something moved that Jack did not recognize, a thing that in the course of delivering that dead bull, separated them in some final way, a severing that Jack wanted to blame on the war, on Dicky's brother coming home in pieces, his father in different pieces. But mostly he wanted to blame himself. And Kit.

"Are you thinking what I'm thinking?" Dicky said.

Trouble with a question like that between friends is that it's what Dicky would call rhetorical. At the time, Jack could only say that what they did next—call it a prank—made perfect sense. That whatever monster had gotten between their friendship—woman, brother, father—and whatever predator had infiltrated the valley—wildcat or killer, war or peace—and whatever its prey—illegals from Mexico or grown men from the shores of Guadalcanal and the forests of Ardennes—it made perfect sense to give it legs.

At first it was just a few slashes with hunting knives across the dead calf's body, but then the cuts became hacks and the hacks became amputations and rearrangements, until what was left was as unrecognizable to them as they had become, covered hat to heel in blood and shattered bone, to each other.

In the frenzy of the game, they each forgot about the mother, forgot about everything except for hacking to pieces the remains of their bond, so that by the time they dragged what they'd made over to the wire fence and strung it up there with entrails and vine, and felt the first drops of rain, they barely registered that the heifer had gone.

"Never mind," Dicky said, wincing a little on his bruised hip. "She'll be back with the herd, no one the wiser."

And Jack agreed that what with the size of Schultz's ranch, and the man power still not sufficient to work it after the war, even with the Mexicans, a pregnant heifer could have easily escaped notice.

The rain was a blessing, but not enough. They rutted their footprints away from the fence and cleaned the blood off themselves in a shallow watering hole at the edge of no-man's-land. Jack skimmed the muddy bottom fully clothed, pushing turtles aside with his blood-smeared hands.

Only thing left, Dicky said, was to rustle up a catch to cover their tracks. They rode down to the lake, keeping off the road, and then snuck home for supper, Jack's mother raising an eyebrow at the lunker he dropped beside the icebox. By lunchtime the next day it was all through the valley, from grocery store to movie theatre to football practice, how there was a mutilated calf slung up on the Schultz's fence. Over the next few weeks and for months after that, there were cars of sailors, trucks loaded with kids driving in to get a glimpse of the Proctor Valley Monster.

One night at supper, Jack's mother said how Lottie Schulz had told her that they'd found a dead heifer at the watering hole, no sign of disease or predator.

John Devlin Sr. said, "Animals die of natural causes too."

"Nothing natural about a heifer just keeling over for no reason," his mother said.

"Maybe she died of a broken heart," Jack's daddy said with a wink. "I heard Schultz's hired bull's a real lady killer."

By the time Sheriff Almirez came to take the thing down off the fence, it was gone. Dicky and Jack swore to each other that neither of them had anything to do with its disappearance, but however both wanted to believe the other a liar, this was more an excuse to explain the uncrossable divide between them than anything else. Hoofprints in the mud, the sheriff took care to mention, calling on both Jack's and Dicky's parents, were all that was left.

It must have been early December. Jack escaped from the smells of his mother's Christmas baking, and he and Kit were in her truck beside the reservoir, wrapped in blankets. Kit was crying for some reason, but silently, so that the sound of hooves came clearly to Jack from outside the truck. He listened for a while to the uneven thud that retreated and returned, like whatever was out there was making circles around them. Kit had drifted off, hiccuping softly, her eyelashes still damp with tears. Jack removed his arm from around her shoulder and rubbed a patch of steam off the window. Outside, with the white light of the reservoir behind it, stood a young bull. Its forehead was pierced by one horn, the other pointing toward the moon like a jagged fingernail. It favored a phantom foreleg, stood canted somewhat in the incandescent light, lathered in moonlit sweat. Blood dripped from a cracked muzzle, and Jack could see its innards squirm from between a gash in its ribs. One eye seeped blindly. From the other glowed a blue light which fixed on him, until lowering its shaggy head with a dancer's grace, it turned away, hindquarters naked and hairless and its sex almost brushing the ground.

Jack and Dicky were in some of the same classes, and Jack could tell, as friends can, that Dicky had seen the monster too, but how and when he never found out. They never spoke of it, or of anything much at all after that.

* * *

The Proctor Valley Monster changed things. It made the town a little bigger, the valley a little less hidden, so that it wasn't long before Dicky's father found out about Jack and Kit and set three blocks of C4 explosive on the roof of the Devlin barn. These he detonated on Christmas Eve with a pull lighter from sixty yards before turning his army issue Colt on himself. Luckily or not, depending on where you stood, the gun failed to fire due to a dud round, and John Devlin refused to file charges, claiming the Alfords had more than their share of war wounds. Old Alford lived out his days at the Soldiers Home in Chula Vista, and both Jack and Dicky would both have the opportunity to serve their country in Korea, but only one of them would return. One of Mae's first jobs as district chairwoman was to open the Lieutenant Richard "Dicky" Alford Memorial Library right here in Bonita where the fire station is now.

Last time Jack Devlin saw Kit O'Dea was that night in her truck, the night the monster found him. He read about her once or twice in the movie magazines but has since forgotten what they said. He still lives on the family farm, what's left of it, an old man now, older than old. Clint Eastwood old, he likes to say with a chuckle, burning across no-man's-land in his big F-250, headlights turning the road red as a vein, ahead of him a dark silhouette and the lopsided thunder of hooves.

Collision

The sky bulged above the diner at the edge of town. Cassi let the heavy curtains drop back over the window. She had tried to nap but now sat up with her legs over the edge of the bed. It was the middle of the day, and formless shadows made the walls of the room recede into nothing. She once again peeked through the windows at the ominous sky. The collision was coming sooner than she thought, than any of them thought. Her computer screen pulsed at the desk, encrypted messages waterfalling down the screen. She reached for her phone to check an incoming text message—surely her colleagues in the scientific community were as alarmed by the herniated sky as she was.

But the message was only from her brother, Issac.

Everything's change▪.

That was it. Her phone splished again and she opened a garbled audio message of him crying out, "But why?" Cassi held the phone at arm's length. The question sounded as loud as if her brother were in the next room. But that was impossible. Issac had left for school hours ago. She checked her watch. The lunchtime bell had just rung. In the background of the message, more faintly, Cassi could hear a jumble of quaint words that she had almost forgotten: "fairy," "fruit," and "fag."

Cassi stared at the phone as if it were a foreign object, something from the future that was already past. The words were from another time that would, Cassi had once promised Issac, never hurt him again.

They were their father's words.

Even though she could see that he was typing again, she texted back, *Where are you?* and the answer came before she finished: *In the first-floor bathroom.*

He was eight years younger than her, a junior at Fairstate High. Cassi taught physics at the same school, except on Mondays, her day off, when she tried to catch up on her own research. Today though, she had spent most of the time in the dark staring through the curtains at the terrible sky.

Another audio message came in from her brother, and more garbled yelling. If she didn't know that he was in the bathroom (he liked to use the unisex facility on the first floor) she would think that he was watching a movie with his arty friends. Mostly pale and fragile creatures, unlike tall, ruddy Issac, they wore *Stranger Things* T-shirts and huddled in one of the small screening rooms at lunchtime, eating leftovers from home and discussing *The Fall of the House of Usher* and *Invasion of the Bo♦y Snatchers*. But how could Issac be watching movies in the unisex facility on the first floor? And anyway, these weren't movie screams.

They were real.

She pulled her sneakers on, the tattoo on the back of her ankle faded to a vascular blue. Then she was outside in the high, bright white of noon, pedaling toward the school, desperate to get there before that bubble burst in the sky. Their neighborhood diner, where Issac sometimes hung out, loomed ahead at the junction. But just before she could turn off toward the town, the sidewalk split open, and Cassi went flying into space. Everything went dark and the bike felt pulled out from under her by a hidden hand. Then she was lying on the ground blinking through her tears at the bulging sky.

"Issac?" she screamed toward wherever her phone had landed.

"Who?" A waitress from the diner stood over Cassi with hands on her hips, splaying emerald-green fingernails that glittered in the sun.

Cassi heard the waitress's words echo off the sidewalk, multiply into a chorus of croaks, and circle back to ask her again: *Yes, tell us who.*

The *whirr* of spinning bicycle wheels broke through the echo, and Cassi side-eyed the huge gash in the asphalt—would she have seen it in time? She felt foolish now. Her knee stung and her shoulder throbbed where it had hit the pavement. The waitress wore a name tag that said Alphonso Jaya, the name of Issac's friend who worked at the diner.

"You're not Alphonso," Cassi said to cover up her embarrassment. She tried to push herself to a sitting position. The crack in the sidewalk heaved beneath her like she was something indigestible—the pale ground pushing her back to where she came from, to where she should be. "My brother's in trouble over at the school."

"Alphonso?" the waitress said.

"Issac."

Cassi was Issac's legal guardian, had been for five years, since she turned twenty-one and moved them back to town from their cousins' farm. Their cousins were significantly removed in geography and blood lines, and much older than the siblings—more like an aging aunt and uncle. They were too old to raise a couple of kids—runaways that family gossip told them they should have seen coming—but as Cousin Emily primly said, you never see the obvious until it's right in front of you, and sometimes not even then. Anyway, they had done their best. They took Issac and Cassi to church every Sunday, allowed them to bathe on Saturday afternoons once their chores were done, and never laid a hand on them. They never used the names Cassi had run away from (*"fairy," "fruit," "fag"*) and eventually Issac, and the world, moved on.

But Cassi never forgot. She still heard those names in her dreams, remembered how they scared her, even more than the man—their father—who used them. The *names* had a life of their own, she knew, and like all evil things, would find what they were looking for.

* * *

Cassi got herself up on one elbow and fumbled her phone closer to her. There was a small crack in the corner of the screen from the fall, but it was still working. The flesh on her knee was ripped and the blood laced with white goo that cut like broken glass. Cassi winced. A tightness in her throat made it hard to breathe. She told herself not to panic. She'd be back on the bike and rescuing Issac in no time. But that lump in the sky looked heavy, about to fall. And then what? She had to hurry. She stashed her phone and wobbled to her feet.

"Hey now," the waitress said, extending a hand. She smelled of cinnamon sugar and stale tobacco. Fat wings of black liner swept across her sleepy eyes. Cassi swayed and thought she might be sick. The waitress reached across to straighten the pendant at Cassi's throat, her long fingernails clicking against the chain. "Who's got the other half, hun?"

Yes, who? Tell us who, came the croaky chorus again.

Issac had bought the split-heart necklace for them so long ago that she often forgot she was still wearing one half (the left) of the heart, and he still wore the other (the right).

"Miss D! You okay?" It was a customer standing in a swirling fog of cigarette smoke in the doorway of the diner.

The waitress let the pendant go, her forehead knit in a pretty frown. "Miss Who?"

"Why, Miss D'Angelo of course," the customer barked. "The Home Ec teacher over at the high school."

But that wasn't right. Cassi was not a Home Economics teacher (called Food Tech at Fairstate High) as Cousin Edgar wanted her to be, but a physicist. She taught *science* four days a week at the high school, and on her day off, she and her colleagues got together on Dark Web hangouts and discussed a theoretical collision of worlds in the multiverse. Her online colleagues weren't just physicists, but cosmologists also—autodidacts and professionals all concerned with the appearance of that curve in space, and what it meant.

The waitress picked cheesy white goo from her apron. It was the same squirmy gunk that cut into Cassi's grazed knee, possibly some kind of antimatter extruded from the collision. Cassi had read about this in an unpublished paper by her colleague, Mohammed Deif, who lived right here in town. What else could it be? It wobbled between the waitress's green fingernails, and she grimaced and flicked it off. It flared whiter than the sun and was gone.

The presence of the antimatter was not a good sign. Cassi leapt onto her bike.

"There's been a collision. I have to hurry." She pointed to the bulge in the sky that looked like a face beneath a shroud, less a collision than a thought projection, a catastrophic materialization of a time that never was with a place that couldn't be. But the word, "collision" made the unthinkable easier to grasp, so that's what they called it.

That was the thing with giving something a name like the ones their father gave, not to Issac, but to his own hate and fear.

The name made it real.

The waitress who wasn't Alphonso Jaya stepped out of Cassi's way. She bumped her fists together in the shape of a heart and the negative space between her smooth white knuckles was like the contact zone between colliding worlds in a multiverse—Cassi tried to imagine what could crawl through those colliding worlds, or what already had. Her tongue felt too big for her mouth—staring at those paired white knuckles, she felt time grow sluggish again, the call of sleep. The waitress opened her fingers wide and made a sphere with them, so that it was just the tip of the green fingernails touching now, forming a single bubble of positive space.

And then she made her fingers burst apart. "*Ka-pow!*" she said, breaking the spell.

"Yes!" Cassi said over her shoulder. "The collision!"

"What does she know?" The customer spat a stream of brown spit onto the pavement. "She's just a waitress!"

But Cassi was already pedaling hard across Main Street. She rode through the white light, one hand on the handlebar, the other dialing Issac's number.

"Cass?" said her brother.

The bike swerved but she didn't fall. "Where are you?"

"In the—the ladies' room on the first floor." His deep voice wavered, and she heard him sob.

"That can't be right. The gendered bathrooms are on two."

"Unisex on one. Except it's changed. It's a ladies' now—weird."

"*You* sound weird. Kind of throttled."

"Because I'm lying on the floor," Issac said. "My head's against the toilet. And also, because they tried to throttle me."

Who? Tell us who? sang the worms, dancing at the edge of her eye. But she knew. "Can you get up?"

"Maybe. I could have a broken rib. Two is a possibility. Blood from my nose, and my lip is split, I think. And there are these wormish things . . ." He had that determined show-and-tell-voice he reverted to when he was trying not to cry. She hadn't heard that voice since they ran away from home.

"On my way," Cassi said.

Issac giggled musically. "They were standing outside the bathroom. One of them had white hair gelled into a kind of quiff. A quiff, Cass! Like Father used to wear!"

"You remember?"

"The quiff guy p-peed on me!"

A suffocating stillness pressed down on the wide boulevard, like the bloated sky was taking up all the air in the town. The squirming white goo between the cracks in the asphalt gave off a faintly sulphuric smell.

"Get up, Issac. Get out of there!"

Over the phone line she heard pounding footsteps on the vinyl floors, a heavy tread coming toward him. "Now!" she said.

There was the sound of the stall door banging open.

Ka-pow.

✳ ✳ ✳

The streets off Main Street were too empty for a workday. They were like the streets in *Invasion of the Bo•y Snatchers* except for the silently expanding fissures in the asphalt through which that worm-like debris wobbled. Her knee stung with the gelid particles, like pieces of a burst balloon but with serrated edges that sawed through her flesh. Cassi tried to brush the goo off with one hand but almost lost the bike again. Her head felt light with the smell of rotten eggs, and with terror.

She swerved to avoid a woman and small boy approaching from the opposite direction. She almost dropped her precious phone, caught it in time. The child pointed at it with a dull curiosity, his small crooked finger exerting an invisible force that pulled her to a skidding stop just before hitting them. His pupils elongated into malicious hyphens, like a goat's.

"What is it, Mommy?" the child baa-ed.

"It's a ray gun, Tommy!" The woman gave Cassi a perky wink. "A ray gun for killing Muslims!"

"*Pew-pew!*" The little boy fired an imaginary ray gun at Cassi.

Cassi had surely misunderstood the woman, who had said Martians. Not Muslims at all. But something was terribly wrong. The boy's mother wore a full skirt and a blouse with a Peter Pan collar like the ones in the closet that Issac had snuck into when their cousins were at prayer meeting. Issac would be the girl in Cousin Emily's dress and he would finagle Cassi, even though she was fifteen—too old for games—to be the boy in one of Cousin Edgar's heavy brown suits, which already had on them the soft peppery smell of death.

Cassie didn't know how she knew the name of the collars—she was a science teacher and she knew quantum mechanics. She wasn't really equipped to understand the finer details of the projected collision. And boning up on Mohammed Deif's theory of the inflationary multiverse in his unpublished paper, "Time and How it Emerges," had only confused her more.

What time had emerged into Cassi's own, and what did it want with Issac? The woman's Peter Pan collar sagged in the breathless heat and she led her son away.

Muslims or Martians? *Yes, tell us who.*

All Cassi could do was pedal harder into the light, which thanks to Mohammed's theory, she at least understood now to be a manifestation of time. If the woman in the 1950s clothing was anything to go by, the past was no longer passed, but superpresent. And it wasn't just that.

It was the future too, crowded into Main Street with military precision. Big plutonium-guzzling sedans and station wagons and monster trucks. All-American cars made by Refusebots from Russia. She didn't know exactly how she knew this. The part of her consciousness that could tell her the reason, was already merging with the reason itself.

She wiped her free hand on her jeans, smooshed some more antimatter, and rode faster.

* * *

The afternoon sun shriveled and turned gray. It was hazardous navigating the cracks that had split the sidewalk, cracks filled with those squirming gelid nonparticles burst from a gray vein between worlds.

Issac called again. He said he was now outside the Principal's office waiting for her. She let him do the talking, telling her about how his purple Docs were ruined, and his favorite dress too, claret red with gray stitching along the hem, from being peed on. The swelling in the sky had grown ominously large, like a frog's throat or a blister about to burst.

"What about the boys who beat you?" she said. "Are they being punished?"

She felt a terrible sadness, her knuckles white on the handlebars. Out of nowhere came the smell of the hair oil their father had used to comb his quiff into place. She could picture him with the comb poised above his head, his face angled toward the mirror to reflect his good side.

Over the phone, like he didn't want her to hang up, Issac put on his show-and-tell voice again. "Their jeans were cuffed. Cuffed! There were little white worms crawling over the edge—but they're not worms, Cass, are they? Remember the maggots that time when we ran away. Remember . . ."

* * *

After they ran away, and because she did not want them to live with their cousins, they hid in an abandoned warehouse just off Main Street. Disused ovens, which had once baked industrial ceramic parts, now served as private sleeping berths, jealously guarded, for runaways and addicts, whole families of the homeless. Squatters had brought in generators, set up fridges, microwaves and single-burner stoves in a makeshift communal kitchen. Cassi kept Issac close to her, talked to no one, curled up around her little brother in one of the ovens. She kept their dwindling supplies under her sleeping bag. They had one egg left in a soggy carton—she'd been saving it for their birthdays, which in a quirk of timing, happened to be on the same day—June 16. But when Cassi cracked the egg against the side of a pan, instead of the yoke, a stream of maggots tumbled out. Issac's eyes widened like blue moons. Cassi screamed and flung the shell out of her hands, something she'd be ashamed of later. Maggots danced all over the hot black surface of the pan.

Something she'd never forget.

* * *

"That's what the worms remind me of, Cass. The maggots dancing on the frying p-p-pan."

Cassi's heart went doom . . . doom. The worms were antimatter, probably. Squirming out between the colliding worlds and seeking life on a whole new footing. She flung some off her sleeve and told Issac she'd be there soon. In her panic, it became harder to think clearly about the collision now, the miraculous intrusion of one world into another. Mohammed Deif, didn't believe in miracles. It was just time, he would say, going all *Ka-pow!* on our hypothetical asses.

Cassi kept on riding through the breathless streets, the wheels skidding on the crescent-shaped goo, while over the phone, Issac went into a teary rant about the dire possibility of cuffs on jeans coming back into fashion.

✳ ✳ ✳

Mohammed Deif, a PhD candidate at Stanford who worked summers at his family's halal butcher shop on Main Street, was the only person in town who she could talk to about these things, but there was no time now. She began to pedal Looney-Tunes fast, her muscles burning. Mohammed had suggested that, just like in quantum mechanics—where cause and effect work probabilistically—time across the expanding multiverse of world bubbles must also be probabilistic. "Bottom line," he liked to say, "time doesn't work the same way across worlds."

But they both knew there was no bottom line. Nothing was an accident and there was no first cause.

"I'm coming, Eye," she said into the phone—a nickname from their runaway days in the warehouse, when they agreed to keep an eye on each other, and he drew a blue eye on her arm and made her draw one on him too.

Her legs wobbled and her shoes fumbled at the pedals. The thick warm air felt like riding into sheets flapping from a clothesline. She rode past the Unsafeway and the Toil and Trouble Laundromat and the Doctor's Orifice, and the Church of the Damned from where she could hear the choir croaking like locusts over the chorus, *"Tell us who, tell us who . . ."* She sped past the baseball bat factory and the Mini-Me Nursery School and the windowless warehouse where she and Issac had hidden from their father, and which later became a tattoo parlor where, to commemorate her graduation, she'd gotten a large blue eye tattooed on the back of her ankle.

"An *I* or an eye?" her brother had laughed when she told him about it.

Her mouth dry and her eyes stinging, she rode past the boarded-up Planned Parenthood building with graffiti across the walls saying "Killers" and "Repeal."

The worms in her knee bit harder, the toxic pain traveling from her hip into her lower back, and her head ached. She clutched her phone in one hand, jouncing on her seat. The small crack inched across the screen at a jagged diagonal. The ride to the school was taking longer than usual, time and space impacted by the collision.

She sped past the halal butcher, slowed despite herself when she saw that the man who waved at her from the window wasn't Mohammed anymore. And instead of Deif's Meats, the shop sign said Great Clips, and not-Mohammed was now wearing an olden-time white barber shirt that said "Mo" on the pocket in big embroidered letters that she could see from the street.

Cassi didn't know how much longer she could pedal. Her muscles burned. She squinted to see the school at the end of the ravaged road, antimatter boiling in deep ravines to either side. But the road just elongated into nothing.

Mohammed, a cosmologist not a physicist, nevertheless agreed with Cassi that the real problem in unifying the theory of cosmic inflation with quantum mechanics was *time*. He would put their two coffee cups, or beer mugs ("just between me and Allah," he joked) side by side and show her, pushing a single grain of sugar between them with the tip of a stirrer, how a quantum particle had a narrow window in time in which to move from probability to actuality, from existing *probabilistically* in many worlds—the multiverse—to being *measurable by a hypothetical observer* in one.

So that would mean that Issac's observation of something, or someone, had brought it, or them, into being. It had brought the bubbles together, made the impact measurable in time.

This time.

Like Cousin Edgar who wanted Cassi to be a high school cooking teacher, Mohammed's father wanted his son to stay in the meat business. *Pew-pew!* Where was he now?

* * *

By the time the school emerged at the end of the hyper-stretched road, the sun was a fish-belly smear in the sky. The flag drooped, indistinct through the fog of swirling particles. She jumped off her bike and ran up the school steps. The security guard stood beneath a framed photograph of the new President with his rakish eyepatch. Millions turning up at his rallies with matching red, white, and blue pirate patches. Cassi swiped her card at the turnstile and walked in under the watchful whir of a camera behind the President's eye.

Fluorescent lights pulsed in the empty hallways. Everyone was in class after lunch. Cassi stopped when she saw Miss Leakey, the Food Tech teacher, coming toward her.

"Have you seen my brother?" Cassi said, stopping short. Miss Leakey was wearing what looked like Cassi's lab coat. Cassi's pens bristled from the pocket. "Why are you wearing my stuff?"

Miss Leakey gaped at Cassi's phone. "Principle wants to see you. Your class tried to make primordial soup. They almost set the school on fire."

Cassi thought she might throw up again. Leakey had (probabilistically) not said "primordial soup" at all. She'd (measurably) said "pot-au-feu," which was beef soup of course, but Cassi didn't know how she knew this. The hallway spun, but Cassi kept on her feet and jog-walked down the snaking hall toward the Principal's office, banging her shoulder on a bank of lockers.

"Ah Miss D'Angelo," the Principal boomed, flicking a squirming white booger off his fingernail. "Good of you to join us. In your absence, your cooking students caused quite a stir today, pardon the pun."

"I always work at home on Mondays," Cassi reminded him.

An ornate brass seismograph gleamed on the Principal's desk.

"Cass?"

Cassi wheeled around at the catch in her brother's voice. A jolt of fire ran through her body and she forgot to breathe. His eye had begun to swell and his neck was ringed in red. A shred of toilet paper stuck to his long hair and he smelled of piss.

"I'm sorry, Cass."

She couldn't remember how to speak, so it was her heart that pounded, boom . . . boom in reply.

* * *

Cassi always wondered what the world would have been like if Issac-the-Eye hadn't done what he did that day on their birthday after she cracked the maggot-egg. If he'd chosen another course of action instead of going to a pay phone and dialing the country cousins—would she ever forget the bulge of their Buick as it rounded the corner to pick them up? And how far back did it go? Or forward? Was there ever a first cause that you were not already a part of?

They both knew that Cassi couldn't save him. Maybe nobody could, except himself. The last egg was gone. Their money was gone. Runaways turned tricks in exchange for a cup of coffee, a slice of pizza. Coffee was coffee, they said. "What's a trick?" Issac had wondered. One of the runaways had pointed out the protein content of maggots, so Cassi had quickly scraped them off the pan. When Issac came back, he dangled a birthday present in front of her. A split heart necklace he'd stolen from a pharmacy near their father's home. Cassi was furious. Issac could have been seen, she'd fumed, taken back. He had risked everything going back there. He separated the chains and gave her half a heart.

He'd wanted to take a picture of the maggots in the pan but she wouldn't let him, even though it was his birthday too. "What if I forget?" he said.

"No, Eye," she said. "We have to save batteries."

He giggled. "I," he said, and then he made a heart with his thumbs and fingers and pointed at her.

I for Issac. Which was Cassi spelled backwards. Their mother had been obsessed with word games—anagrams, anagrabs, crosswords, jumbles, sudoku, homophones, oronyms, pangrams, palindromes— scrap pads, dog-eared dictionaries, pencil stubs and puzzle books from one end of the house to the other.

* * *

Issac was taller than Cassi. He was too tall for the small chair in the Principal's office, and his legs and elbows stuck out at odd angles, like a broken, flightless bird. Mascara streaked his cheeks. Red bruises bloomed on his neck under long hair matted and crawling with those blind white worms of antimatter. He touched his tongue to his swollen lip, looking down at the broken necklace in his hand.

"They broke my heart."

"We'll fix it," Cassi said.

She tried to wipe his face with her sleeve but that only made it worse, smearing the gooey particles into the makeup and tears.

"What's that?" the Principal said, pointing at her phone. "A light saber?"

A light saber? Hadn't the woman in the street called it a ray gun?

"*Vraum-vraum*," the Principal swooshed an invisible light saber at Issac.

Cassi's mind felt blank. And then she remembered.

Light sabers and Ray Guns hadn't coexisted. It would take a hypothetical miracle to change that, like making humans and dinosaurs exist at the same time. Unless, as Mohammed suggested, time was superpositioned on a collision course with . . . itself.

Ka-pow!

"Where are the boys who did this?" Cassi finally demanded. "Why were they there at all?"

"I could ask the same about him," the Principal charged his impossible sword at Issac again.

Issac said. "I didn't see the new sign until it was too late."

The floor rocked and the Principal turned to the seismograph on his desk. The dial moving toward five.

"That's always been the little girls' room, son." the Principal said. "You're just lucky I came when I did."

"Not your son," Issac said. "And there is meant to be a unisex bathroom on each floor. It's the law, ever since President—"

"Who?" said the Principal, cocking his big head. *Yes, tell us who.*

Cassi pulled her brother to his feet. "Time to go."

"Three-day suspension, for wearing a dress, D'Angelo," the Principal called after them. "Just because you scream like a girl doesn't mean you can dress like one."

Klaxons began to wail.

Cassi pulled Issac into the hallway. Fluorescent lights flashed light and dark, off and on. Students streamed from the classrooms. Gooey blind blobs rained down on them from the sprinklers.

"What's happening?" Issac yelled.

"No time, Eye. We need to go."

"Wait!" Issac slowed as they passed the bathrooms. "See!" He pulled out his phone and aimed it at the pictogram of the woman. "Where's the unisex sign?"

"It hasn't been invented yet," Cassi said. "Not in this world."

"This world?"

"It's not our world anymore. Or it won't be soon."

"You mean those bullies are from another world?" Issac panted beside her, swiping at his phone.

"That world is this one now. Turn that off. We need to conserve batteries."

The protrusion in the sky hung low and bloated over the diner, a short bicycle ride west across town but they'd have to hurry.

They turned a corner of the hallway where another stream of students merged into this one. If only her heart would slow down so she could think.

"Look!" Issac said, pointing at some boys ahead of them. "It's them!"

One of the bullies had taffy-yellow hair combed back into a high quiff. The moment that Cassi turned to look, a chunk of floor gave way with a crash, and rebar shrieked through the cement, splitting the linoleum like a flayed hide. Cassi's vision swam again, and for a moment all she could see was a black void in which a dim carpet of lights flickered—lights from the school, from the town, lights down Main Street from all the big cars flowing on it, a flickering floating sea of galactic discs and zygotic nebulae, swimming toward the end of time's beginning. She blinked and the hallway materialized again, the high-haired boy skewered like a wiener, ass to mouth, on a length of rebar. Blood bubbled from his eyes.

"He tried to tell me you were the cooking teacher," Issac said. "I told him he was lying. You can't even fry an egg."

They made it through the turnstiles and out onto the street, students swarming—a sea of Peter Pan collars and cowlicks. His shoelaces had come undone and Cassi had a sudden flash of their father standing beneath a shuddering sky, his hands playing at his strap while pointing at little Issac's untied shoelaces.

"I don't understand!" Issac said. "I can't breathe."

They made it across the street and into an access path between houses. He stopped and put his big hands on his bare knees, drawing ragged breaths over his piss-soaked Docs.

She let him rest for a moment, quickly tried to explain that a collision of bubble worlds, possible at the quantum level, had been actuated the moment he saw the sign on the bathroom door, changing everything.

"I caused this—these bubbles to collide?"

She wanted to lie to him. To tell him that it was all his fault, because there is something reassuring about causality. You can be blamed for causing something but you can also be forgiven.

"I'll explain later," she said.

"What if there is no later?" he boomed. "Like there is no unisex bathroom anymore?"

She sighed and tried again. "You observed the sign and that changed its state and yours," she continued, "from hypothetical to actual. Like it opened a door or a lens, and what you saw changed in that instant but also . . ."

"What?"

"Someone saw you back."

"The worms?"

She shook her head and the movement made her motion-sick again. "They're just some kind of remnant from an impact tear in the quantum bubble."

"Who saw me then?" He held up his hand. "On second thought, don't tell me."

She told him anyway because he'd asked for it, and the least she could do was to leave him with a remnant of truth—something to remember her by. She grabbed his phone, launched the voice memo application and pressed RECORD. "You saw a ladies' room sign that exists in another universe through a probabilistic lens at almost the same time as whoever was at the other end saw you. Time is a two-way street, remember. No quantum interaction without physical fallout."

"But—"

"No butts." She pressed Stop, handed the phone back. "We need to go."

"Where? Where is there to go?"

A helicopter thwacked overhead.

"Remember the maggots in the egg? Think of a kind of quantum waiting area, where those maggots are superpositioned—that's what waiting in this area is called—to be or not to be in the egg until the moment an interaction triggers one or the other."

"Who are you calling a maggot?" he brushed a hand through his hair, wiped his eyes.

"Pay attention. The same *you* can't be in two bubbles at the same time, but sometimes the bubbles collide, and sometimes that collision produces a tear or a lesion allowing a passage between worlds. A window of equivalence."

"Of what?"

"Or a door. Either way, we need to get you to that passage."

Issac's mouth hardened as he took in the gridlocked school parking lot, the white faces smiling down at them from billboards on the street. She watched him register as if for the first time, the uniformed security guards at the school gates, the alien flag like a fresh bruise behind the swirling fog of antimatter. She saw him see it through her eyes.

"What if I hadn't asked for a hall pass? I didn't even need to pee," a dull edge to his voice. "I was just bored."

"Mother might have come for us if you hadn't called for cousins Emily and Edgar," she said gently. "I always wondered."

"You were the one who took you away from her in the first place." A cat, black and white, smoked along the alleyway, its tail switching. It sniffed at their feet, did a figure eight around her sneakers and his pissy Docs and then vanished.

"You speak with her from time to time?" Cassi said.

"No more than you do," he sighed and cleared his throat. "She says that between us, we probably made the right choice."

He shimmered behind a veil of her tears. Father with his high hair to give him impossible inches, had been so fearful of Issac, tall and athletic like their mother and with their mother's eyes, "Fairy eyes," his father said, reaching for the strap, and Cassi never forgave herself for telling Issac that Father's fairies were not the ones at the bottom of the garden, and the old man's idea of "fruit" was as unviable as he was.

"What's unviable?" Issac had asked.

"Something that cannot be," she'd answered.

* * *

The access lane behind the houses stretched out like chewing gum. The wind tore a page of a newspaper off the sidewalk. Above a black and white picture of a protest somewhere, the headline roared, "Lock them Up!"

They ran out onto the street and toward the diner. No time to go back for her bike. He held his phone loosely in his long, strong fingers, and she wondered if her message would survive the future. The alien cars parked on the street looked boxy, pixelated. The wormy particles spewed from the cracks in the road and pushed through the sidewalk, fatter now, like ragged blind rats, forming a thickening barrier between them and making it hard to walk, like through a snowdrift. They gripped each other's hands, their fingers slipping, pulling, pushing through the particles that clung to their clothes, tried to worm into their mouths and ears. She pulled one off her eye.

"I can't!" The white antimaggots welled up from the earth to join the ones that fell from the sky, raining back down on themselves. Issac fell behind a curtain of the swirling blind antimatter, and then Cassi finally understood. It wasn't Issac who was impossible. It was her.

They weren't trying to hurt him. The particles were protecting him, as she never could. Trying to save him, to get him to where he needed to be, but where she wasn't needed. To form a new bubble around him in which the only one who didn't belong was her.

Bottom line: she'd run out of time.

"Cassi. Come on!"

Who?

Cassi's nape prickled. She understood now that time was like the maggots in the frying pan, and the old warehouse, with its dusty disused coffins, was like the collision. Its squalid and doomed Fordian timeline on a collision course with its crack-house daze, in turn all tangled up in the possibility of its transformation into an artisan tattoo parlor. Where Cassi, like Issac, had changed something by coming back to get her Eye. What had she seen through that eye, and would it see her through?

An *I* for an Eye.

* * *

The diner loomed ahead of them like a bad quantum vein, or the wrong end of a gravity lensing telescope, one that bends quantum matter and throws time-space on a collision course with itself.

"You're coming too!" Issac yelled, sensing her hesitation. "You have to."

She had tried to save him once, and he her—when would it end? Neither of them were ready for this, but they had to be. Flakes of matter swirled around the diner like a snow dome.

"Not this time . . ."

His mouth contorted in panic between the veil of hair. "We've never been apart!"

She thought of the recording she made into his phone. Above the diner door, a neon apple pie sign crawled with those hungry squirming things. Columns of crepuscular light—Aunt Emily called them Jesus rays—juddered above the diner, poised in the contact zone between worlds. Her heart cracked like thunder—just yesterday, Sunday—Issac had asked her to join him and Alphonso for a piece of homemade pie. But that bubble, too, had burst. Alphonso gone like all the others.

"If you stay here," she said. "You'll disappear. They'll make sure of that. And I need you not to. The world needs that. Where you're going and where you've been. You've always been here. In all times. I saw you. And because of that I need to stay . . . to remember what it could have been. Needs to be."

The particles cleared for an instant. He clung to her. "Will there be others for you here? Others out of time?"

"Go!"

She had to push him in the end. The worms tore into the flesh of her arms where they pierced the veil. And once she withdrew, time did the rest, sweeping him toward the diner in its quantum purpose.

"Cassi!" he called peering through the gluey razorous blizzard.

"I!" she called out. "Am you. Never forget!"

Hadn't she always known?

His long hair swirled around his face. His dress flapped at his knees, and he stood braced in purple Docs at the threshold, like a Viking.

V for victorious. And also viable Vikings.

The worms fell thicker, a curtain of antimatter that would shred her if she tried to cross it. She pointed two fingers in a *V* sign at her own eyes and then at him, and, having no choice, he did the same. The silver heart winked in his palm just as the sky above the diner bulged like a snake swallowing its kill.

And then he was gone.

She was unable to stop shaking, her teeth chattering and drawing blood from the inside of her cheeks. After a time the white worms went back to where they came from, and she watched the gashes in the pavement heal, and then they too were gone. The only sign of the Jesus rays was a faint purple webbing across the nickel sky.

Cassi took a coppery swallow, went up to the diner and pulled open the door. Two customers came out, jostling her and she felt something slip from her pocket and thud onto the mat. The customers in the diner turned to her with hooded eyes. Their faces were gray and pulsed with purple veins like the sky.

"My stars! Whatever happened to you, Miss D?" One of the customers rasped.

"My brother . . ."

The word made ripples that faded to nothing. Below twelve-point bucks and football pennants fixed to the scarred, peeling wood, the customers' thick white fingers laced around white coffee cups.

"Who?" someone said. *Yes, tell us who.*

The cut on Cassi's knee opened. She wiped her nose with her sleeve and the gooey particles smeared across her face, the customers' gray lips twisted in disgust. She needed a coffee. It had been a long day. She pulled up a stool at the counter, reached for a napkin to wipe off the last of the antimatter. The customers stared up at the television set and lit Lucky Strikes and smacked their teeth hungrily at a commercial for maple bacon Spam. Cassi didn't recognize the TV station and there was a strange logo at the bottom of the screen. It was a stylized image of twinned search lights like devil's horns, or a goat's, angled at a red, white and blue sky.

"Coffee, hun?" it was the same waitress from before with the long green fingernails, except now her name tag said Nancy, not Alphonso.

Nancy poured coffee into Cassi's cup. The customers' eyes slid to Cassi and then back to the screens, and their horizontal pupils blipped and then flatlined.

"You didn't make it?" Nancy said.

Gooseflesh prickled Cassi's arms. "You neither?"

"Maybe next time." The waitress put the coffee pot down.

Will there be others for you?

They smiled at each other but there was a question in their smiles. Nancy's mouth quivered and she had to blow her nose on a tissue that she pulled out from her sleeve. Cassi padded her pocket for something that she felt she'd lost.

"That?" Nancy leaned over the counter and pointed to the floor. Cassi could smell cinnamon and menthol cigarettes on her breath. "You dropped it on the way back in."

Cassi bent to pick it up. It was a flat steel rectangle about the size of her hand. It was metal on one side and glass on the other. The glass was cracked but behind it was a picture of Cassi when she was younger, a tomboy with a determined jaw and wild dark hair, training to be a Home Economics teacher because that is what girls did, Cousin Edgar said. Especially unmarried ones.

The image on the screen bulged and then disappeared, and then all that was left was the broken mirror. Cassi saw the reflected oval of her face with the crack down the middle, each half slightly out of true. She put it back down on the counter.

"What is it, hun?"

"Beats me," Cassi said.

The coffee mug felt heavy in her shaking hands. She brought it to her mouth and took a sip. It was bitter. It was good.

Glow

On the night of the elections I am with my cousin Ray and his human wife, Janyce. Footage flashes from the living room screen showing water-cannoned activists squirming on the asphalt, flayed detention survivors arcing across the crowds in heart-shaped orbitals singing Maria Callas arias. Jeering voters wave placards, saying "Lock 'em up!"

My cousin and I are smashing shots, but we are drinking for different reasons. He is hailing presidential nominee Bud Towers as the Second Coming and I am trying to get drunk enough not to argue. Janyce has made her famous lobster burritos. My little sister would hate them.

I lower my voice and say in our language, "You do realize that Towers has been running on an antialien platform since day one?"

"Hostile media shenanigans!" Ray cries out in reverberant English. The reflection from the swimming pool makes craters across the pale moons of his eyes.

Even before his name was Ray—when we were still eking out survival deep in the bowels of our wounded world, long before it spat us out to face the radioactive vomit of our bloated sun—what entranced him about earth were its shenanigans. Its youth, and light, but mostly its *spirit*, he said. Humanity so frail, and yet so consumed by the need to empower their gods. So acquisitive, but yearning for dispossession, he enthused. So solitary, yet committed to the crowd.

But I always wondered if my cousin's attraction to Earth was just because his name in our language is Uli, God of Bad Jokes.

From the kitchen you can hear Janyce saying, "Sugar. That's the secret behind my coleslaw. Tenderizes the cabbage."

One of her daughters says, "You tell us that every time, Janyce."

Janyce says, "Call me Mom. Please? Just for tonight."

I think my little sister would like Janyce's daughters. She was the same age as the youngest when we arrived at the detention center. Fourteen. That was eight years ago.

"Towers will make us great again!" Ray says.

"Us?"

He lowers his voice. "Speak English. You know how Janyce gets."

One of Janyce's daughters is telling her sister about Oceanika, a new orbital space habitat with an ocean but fifteen miles above the earth, with beaches and sunsets and bars.

Janyce comes in with sliced limes. "Lisa, you ever been to sea?"

"The detention camp," I say.

"Of course. Sorry."

ICE keeps newly arrived aliens imprisoned on disused oil rigs in the Amundson Strait for a minimum of thirty-six lunar months for processing. Another week to get through the checkpoints after transfer—you need papers, a letter of acceptance from a halfway house or shelter, and they give you a new name. The immigration officer shoved a battered pink suitcase at us, made us empty our pouches at gunpoint. "For your own protection," he said. "Anything found in a random body search gets confiscated. No ifs, ands, or buts."

At "buts," he jammed the barrel of his rifle into my belly slit, parted the flaps. My eyes watered at the reek of cologne on his skin, sour coffee on his breath.

I remember how Ray's claws shook as he transferred our meager possessions from his pouch into the suitcase—the remainder of our cash, Grandcousin's medals, and the diaphanous shroud that had been my sister's skin. Amy—that was the name they gave my sister— sat quietly in her wheelchair beneath the Humanity First cap they made her wear, dwarfed in a greasy bridge coat. The officer, licking his lips, motioned for her to take it off but Ray was quick to shove her medical papers at him. Soon as the officer saw those, he had no choice but to wave us through, Geneva Convention and so on. I hated Ray a little at that moment, despised his fear of being turned away. There was a part of me, even then, that wondered what might have happened if he'd allowed the officer to take her coat, allowed my sister to sit there exposed, naked. Show everyone what detainment had made her into. But that would have landed all of us back in detention, so instead Ray's bioluminescent markings just flashed a queasy green, which they mistook for a smile.

"Welcome to New Liberty," the officer said. "Have a nice Day."

* * *

"If Towers gets elected," I say, licking salt off my thumb, "The first thing he'll do is round us all up and throw us back in detention, that place you were so desperate to escape, remember?"

"And you weren't?" Ray doesn't move his gaze from the TV.

Bud Towers's Humanity First party had suggested two possible repatriation destinations for "displaced" aliens. These were JL45-J872, a small world in the Proxima Centauri Galaxy, and a disused refuse satellite that the Chinese had been trying to auction off for a decade.

"We'll be deported to JL."

"Not us!" Ray shouts, very drunk. "We belong here! The ones who get rounded up are criminals. Lowlifes."

"Lowlifes" was Ray's term for illegal aliens, so called star-spiders. Those who'd been unable to get papers, and whose unauthorized entry into New Liberty circumvented the inspection and detention process were such a source of such overwhelming bitterness to Ray that he managed to ignore the fact that less than twenty percent of star-spiders survived the trip, and half of those ended in jail, slavery, or prostitution within twelve months of arrival.

Janyce's oldest daughter pokes her head around the door. "So being in the wrong place at the wrong time makes them what? Dangerous?"

The room spins. She sounds just like Amy.

Over the eons spent below ground to escape the death throes of our sun, we evolved tough dorsal armor for protection against falling rocks, and phosphorescence to light our way. Somewhere between emerging into the inky permafrost that was all that was left of our world and splashdown in the middle of the Amundsen Strait, my sister—when she still had her skin and before her name was Amy—asked what it meant to be in the wrong place at the wrong time. What it would make us.

"Something that we don't know about yet," I said.

Ray's got an air rifle for the rare coyotes drawn to the oases of floodlit arroyo and potted yucca, but it's mostly just the rabbits he goes for. And they always get away. He taps nervously on the table with his talons (Janyce makes him keep them short) and gets up to check the sliding door yet again. Except I know it's not for the coyotes. ICE operatives are never very far away, even in a good neighborhood like this. Amy worries when I visit Ray that I won't be back, and when she worries, she bleeds. "Milu," she messages, "I want to go home," forgetting that I'm Lisa now and she is Amy, and we *are* home.

Ray wrinkles his nose at a montage on the screen of Towers's opponent in harsh gray scale. "He'll have her behind bars with all those off-world terrorists she's so keen to let in," he slurs. "Then see how much she likes them."

Janyce refills the bowl of chips. "Did anyone else read how she used campaign funds to buy her maid a boob job?"

"Is that a joke?" I say. "Why would anyone buy their maid a boob job?"

She playfully pokes her tongue out at me. I don't respond. The tongue is not just a muscle in our species, but the primary inceptor organ.

Janyce is Ray's second wife in the five years we've been in New Liberty. She came with two teenage daughters, and Ray works hard to pay for the nice secure house at the edge of the desert, plus Amy's and my apartment, and her medications. There isn't any insurance for what my sister has.

Janyce says: "I don't *love* Towers. The things he says about women and . . . others. But look at all the riffraff coming in from who-knows-where. I just want my babies to be safe."

Unions between aliens and humans don't produce live issue. We have other means of continuing our species. Her oldest puts the coleslaw on the table with an unconvincing eye roll. I'm drinking too much, soddenly seduced by this dream of warmth and family, until I think of Amy alone in the dark fighting a different fight. "Your dream, not mine," she would say to Cousin Uli, way back when Earth was just a lucent sphere he'd paint over and over on the walls of our cave. I look at Janyce's daughters, dressed in the latest fashions, skin shiny and whole—a jagged X pulsates across my heart.

"Honest people," Ray says, hooking a clawed thumb at his wife. "Just trying to get ahead."

Janyce's youngest touches the phosphorescent X on my chest. "That's so cool."

Amy likes it when I glow too. Back when we're alone in our apartment, she watches from her chair, ghostly and seeping, and I dance for her, and in the dark in our high prison between earth and sky, I am a warrior once more, garlanded in light.

Ray looks nervously toward the sliding doors to the yard.

$* * *$

Even before surfacing, we got wind of the anthropocentric foment brewing on Earth. On the refugee ship we watched broadcasts of a retired Senator demanding genetic editing to remove off-world 'mutations' like scales, pouches and talons. Constitutional lawyers declared mixed marriages illegitimate at best, illegal at worst, due to being unconsummated in the lawful sense. Epidemiologists worried about cross-species contagion, but couldn't say of what.

And when we were in the camp, Amy obsessed over the news, snuck off to meet with other scared, angry teenagers. "Youthful shenanigans," Uli said when I worried.

Religious leaders had declared our bioluminescence the real threat—no Luciferin without Lucifer, they warned. ICE bosses said it was the dorsal armor that was the problem.

Ray didn't care. Amy—before she was Amy—tried to tell him Earth wasn't what it once was, especially New Liberty. All that "Land of the Free and Home of the Brave" stuff disappeared when arable land did, and from sea to shallow sea, she warned, the only thing left was humanity's desire to believe in something. I think now of my cousin's luminous blue cave paintings and how they lit up his night.

Somewhere between the exercise yard and the detention center showers, my sister learned that RBS means both more and less than "random body search." When I went to visit her in the infirmary afterward, she said, "Being at the wrong place at the wrong time makes you nothing."

The apartment I share with her isn't in a swank neighborhood like this one. She doesn't go out much because infection's a risk without skin, and antibiotics are expensive. Mostly she stays in the dark, talking online with friends she's never met—"freedom fighters" she calls them—who send encrypted messages from beyond the stars. I work nights in a networks operation center to supplement Ray's earnings, ride two hours in the subway to score Amy's opiates from the black market connect her freedom fighters hooked me up with.

Once I asked Ray why his bioluminescent markings were so faded, and he swept an arm out to the neon-studded street, the heavens ablaze with orbital worlds. "Why glow," he said, "with all this light?"

But I don't think that's true. I think the real reason he doesn't glow is because Amy can't. Atonement's no joke, I guess. Some fights never are. I think back to the detention rig, how each time Amy would try and throw herself over the rails, or go after the guards with some instrument she smuggled from the infirmary, Ray would try and pull them off her. Until the last time when they outnumbered him seven to one—no hope with seven—but it cost him three months in solitary anyway.

* * *

Ray passes a huge scaled hand over his forehead as if to wipe away a thought. Pours a round and says, "Remember sour milk?"

The bored guards on the rig made us drink sour milk to see if it would get us drunk. Another time it was coffee dregs mixed in toilet water. We may not pass on our DNA the same as humans, but we share 98 percent of it with them. Tequila does just fine. I down the shot.

The screen erupts in cheers as another district falls to Towers. I check the time and wonder how hard it will be to get a cab home. It's Amy's bath night. She needs me to get the temperature just right, not too hot, not too cold. She needs me to light scented candles so she can't smell herself, and when she gets out I must scrub the tub clean so she can't see the red ring she leaves behind.

A siren wails up the canyon and floodlights arc over the house.

Janyce says, "Maybe we should move."

"Where to?" the youngest calls from her bedroom, excitement in her voice.

"Out of the desert."

The oldest laughs. "There's no such thing anymore."

Her phone tings and she goes into the hallway to take a call from her boyfriend. I think of offspring, of the dormant nucleotide sacs inside my pouch, hovering at the edge of life for a DNA shot they'll never get from an inception I'll never get the chance to choose.

From his campaign headquarters, a sweaty, gloating Bud Towers calls for unity.

"See?" Ray says haltingly. "We're all Terrans now."

"You don't look like a Terran." I point to the screen where, among the jubilant human mob, there is not a single alien.

It's nearly midnight. The crowds wave baseball hats like the ones they make refugees wear on arrival—embroidered with the Humanity First mascot, a simplified interpretation of DaVinci's Vitruvian Man. The wind blows shoals of hectic reflections from the pool across the walls and throws ragged shadows across my cousin's face. I snake my hand into my pouch, feel for the telltale chip implanted in all of us on evacuation. To keep track, our home-world activists said, to find us if we needed to be found. But Ray had his excised as soon as we were processed. No need, he said, only get us into trouble. We had the government of our adopted country to take care of us now.

I've had too much to drink. There is high wall around the yard to keep out the coyotes, and I am halfway to my feet when a shape crawls over the edge. Heat rises in my chest and I point, wordless, at the door. But no one turns around.

The lump along the top of the wall is joined by others. Why can no one see what I see? One by one the shadows stand, silhouetted against the light-choked night, and one by one they drop into the yard.

"Coyotes?" Ray finally swivels in his chair.

I shake my head, neither standing nor sitting.

"I'll get my gun." He lurches out of his chair with a scrape that makes Janyce's eyes flick in alarm to the parquet finish.

"Poor bunnies," the youngest says.

My legs shake uncontrollably. "No bunnies," I say.

It is ten minutes past midnight. The Western Rim is the last sector to fall to Towers. The backyard swarms with ICE operatives. They smash the door, spraying glass across the rug. I slither behind the oak sideboard stacked with Janyce's family photographs and the girls' soccer trophies. The dark millennia burrowing in caves and tunnels has made us agile.

Ray returns from the bedroom with his air rifle, and a rookie— seeing nothing but an armored alien with a gun—lets off a panicked round.

Janyce slumps into her lobster burrito.

Her daughters scream. The operatives fall on Ray. His bands of light strobe a chromic green. "Save her, Milu!" he screams in our language so they won't know I'm here, hiding. "You know how!" He is still screaming as they drag him away.

The crowds cheer, ushering in the new era. When all I can hear below that is the girls' sobbing, I come out. Janyce has slid off the chair and crawled onto the rug, leaving a smear of blood across the floor. I know what Ray wants. But cross-species re-inception—the recombining of her human DNA with my alien genetic material—is unheard of. Even among our own kind the risks of illegal re-inception—deleting or altering one's own genetic material—are high, and in our subterranean cities it was punishable by expulsion—death. But I'm already expelled.

Janyce's daughters are crying and holding each other. Their mother hovers between life and death. There's so little time.

"Look for a pink suitcase," I tell them. "Pack it with whatever you can't leave behind. And hurry."

I turn Janyce over and wipe lobster off her face. Her blue eyes are glassy and her breath is shallow. I rip open her shirt. I unfurl my tongue, and push it into her bullet hole. The tissue is custardy and her blood feels warm—I explore and suck until I come up against the hard sharp flaps of the slug. Its edges tear at the fleshy muscular probe, and the luciferase in my tears mixes with the taste of tequila and human blood.

The bullet drops to the floor in a mess of hot red tissue. I gasp, drooling and shaking, not knowing if inception has been successful, dreading the possibilities. When—if—Janyce wakes up among shadowy activists on some bare-bones cargo ship in deep space, will she remember this from her previous life? Will she remember taking friendly fire on a Guatemalan rug at the edge of the desert, her body flooded by restriction enzymes in a nightmarish probe from which she'll awake alien to herself? Maybe she'll find a scar one day, a phosphorous wink from a place in her dreams, or in her nightmares.

And then it happens. Her brow begins to swell, the dermis around it hardening into thick plates. Inception shouldn't be this fast. "Janyce!"

I say, wondering if she knows her own name anymore. Wondering if she knows anything.

I rummage in my pouch to activate the tracking chip, and with stop-action, stuttery hands message our retrieval coordinates and estimated arrival time. I jam the dials, but manage in the end to press 'Send', except I'll be gone by the time rescue comes. Will they understand? How my fight, whatever's left of it, is here, for a home still worth fighting for, and for her.

For Amy.

The sisters rush back from the bedroom clutching the battered pink suitcase. They pull up short as their mother's French polished fingernails extend into coffee-colored claws. I motion for them to be still. Janyce's eyes flutter open, pale as the moon.

"Will she know who we are?" the youngest asks.

"Will she always be our mom?" the oldest asks.

I tell them, yeah. Just like my sister, even after the guards had taken away her skin, was still my sister. And always will be.

Like Ripples on a Blank Shore

The Host went down in an eruption of crimson and bone, bringing commuter traffic to a standstill. Car windows unwound as drivers scanned for the shooter. Reports would later confirm that a pedestrian lost her footing on the splashed goo of the Host's brain matter and broke her hip in two places. The passing woman turned out to be the shooter's aunt.

There was no doubt about it. Hosts were bad news.

That was the beginning. No one in Deerport, or anywhere, knew what drew the Hosts in such sudden numbers to some towns and not others. Experts attempted to pinpoint a cause, or reason, or remedy—but no one could agree on even what they were, let alone why. Arriving in twos and bad-news threes at the Greyhound Station, into Deerport they came over those dark, wet weeks. Alighting uncertainly from the bus or the backseats of Uber rides, they tracked slush down the aisles of the Safeway and slowed traffic and filled the darkness of the purple-curtained multiplex theaters with their relentless, restless rustle.

And there were more on the way, according to Professor Maya Grayson at Sullivan College, an expert in medieval folklore and on all things Hostish. When asked by a reporter, "Why so many Hosts pouring into Deerport?" Grayson quickly answered by referring to last year's Tower 9 Incident in New York City where an apartment building in the Upper West Side attracted Hosts (a shortened version of the singular *hostis*, from the Latin word for enemy, stranger, or guest) by the hundreds. Residents reported seeing them slumped on the fire escape and in the basement laundry room, leaving a shimmer of dark ooze along the walls where they edged like spiders. Riding up and down the outside of the building on the joists, laughing—if that clotted sigh could be called a laugh—as the wind peeled off their loose flesh.

"I can understand glass towers in Manhattan, but why Deerport?" the radio caller had asked Professor Grayson. But no one, not even Grayson, could say why they came to a certain place, or for whom—if they targeted certain individuals or towns. Nobody knew.

At six p.m. on a Monday evening, the Upper Deerport Terminus was thronged with Hosts and nons. Celia, at five feet eight, scanned over the sea of heads for Terminal 10, where her bus was already almost full and ready to depart. She'd never make it through the crowds in time. She would be lucky to make the next one. A male Host with a seamed face jostled her elbow. From one swollen eyelid, slid a single tear, tensely oblong. Celia watched the tear trickle down the filthy crease that bisected his cheek, over his jaw and back into a bloodless slit at his neck, and decided she would get an Uber. But getting out was easier said than done—the Terminus was packed.

Gooseflesh rode the back of her neck—there was something wanting about their presence, as if they knew her even if she didn't know them. That was the problem with these so-called infestations—random and inexplicable as experts insisted that they were. It was as if the Hosts knew where they were going and what they were looking for. Or who.

Impossible, according to the experts, unless volition could be attributed to Nature itself. Panic squeezed Celia's temples as her vision tunneled looking for the door.

She tried to pivot on her heel. She jostled shoulders and briefcases—impossible to tell which line was moving off the buses and which was moving on. It all seemed the same line to her. The terminal grew steamy and rank with human body odor and a smell like clogged leaves pulled from roof guttering. She had been planning to go for a run when she got home this evening, but all she could think about now was pouring a big glass of wine and going to bed. It was too wet to run anyway. She managed to get herself turned halfway around and edge sideways through the crowd and out, finally, through the big glass terminal doors and onto the street. Gasping in the sudden cold, she fumbled with shaking hands for her phone and pulled up Max's number.

Can you pick me up? she texted. *The buses are crazy.*

Max: *Because of the Hosts. Me•ia's all over it.*

Max usually took his bike to work. But today he had the use of a little silver Ford compact that belonged to his sister Clare—who had once been his brother, Clay. Max couldn't pick Celia up, he reminded her, because he was driving to Sullivan to pick up Professor Grayson—who was also his grandmother—for a family reunion here in Deerport to celebrate Clare's transition. Celia knew that Maya Grayson could drive herself, but this was probably the old lady's way of getting some alone time with her favorite grandson. Her only grandson.

Celia and Max had only been dating five months, not long enough for her to have met all his family. Recently he had taken her to one of his grandmother's lectures at the college, titled: "To be but not to be: Aristotle and the *Hostis* Dilemma." Max introduced them at the reception. Professor Grayson had fixed her eyes, magnified behind batwing glasses, on Celia and pronounced: "You're the one from that ghastly California wedding last year? How many dead?"

Max had tried to change the subject with some awkward question about the Host infestation, but Grayson appeared not to notice. "I recognize you from the papers. You were engaged to that tycoon, the robotics man . . ."

But Max had already begun to drag Celia away.

* * *

Celia had always thought of herself as someone who needed to be taken care of. She watched the ellipses slide across the gray bubble on the screen. The reunion on Friday was taking all of Max's time—she'd hardly seen him over the weekend because he was busy getting work done so he could clear his schedule.

Is Clare there yet? Celia texted.

Max texted back that he wasn't collecting her up until tomorrow and what about if they all meet then for lunch?

Darkness was falling fast and she could smell a fresh snowfall. It annoyed her that Max couldn't pick her up. She felt unnerved by the swarms (if that was the right word) of Hosts, who looked almost like regular humans but—even after sixteen years of research—defied most people's idea of what that was. They were not (theoretically) dangerous in themselves, but their eyes had a strange way of reddening after dark, like trashcan fires. Those dirty eyes followed her out of the bus terminal, and ragged formations of Hosts were already outside, lifting their noses to sniff the cold, sticky night. A male came toward Celia annunciating wildly and in an advanced state of decomposition, that clear ichor gushing from his bottom lip and from eye sockets filled with what looked like molten lava. She quickly called an Uber.

It was a first-degree felony to murder a Host, and so-called *acci*۱*ental* killings—usually vehicular—could get complicated fast, depending on the circumstances. Other than that, no one knew how they died, if at all, or if they were born in any natural sense of the word. In the rare autopsies performed on them, the frontal lobe—responsible for volition and decision-making—presented free of gyri and sulci, and looked more like a bowl of creamy oatmeal than a rosy red human brain.

When the Uber pulled up, there was a Host already in the back seat. Celia felt ashamed for hesitating, the driver watching her disapprovingly—or apologetically—in the side mirror, she wasn't sure. The people of Upper Deerport prided themselves on their inclusivity, and refusing to get into a shared ride with *anyone*, Host or non, was out of the question. She tried not to stare at the fluid flowing from the Host's sensible shoes onto the rubber mat. The car left the city lights and was soon cruising through night-swirling snow, the driver separated from them by a wall of air freshener and talk radio. A farmer from Lower Deerport called in, complaining that the Hosts teeming into the city would soon outnumber the . . . but whatever the caller was about to say got lost in static as the driver discretely changed stations. He and Celia exchanged tight smiles in the rearview. The Host then said something that Celia didn't understand and repeated it in a tone of barely suppressed hysteria that was both human and not at the same time. Both sentient and insensible, as Professor Grayson said at her lecture, reminding the audience that according to Aristotle's law of non-contradiction, something can't be both human (or anything) and *not*, at least not at the same time.

So what were they?

Maybe it was the wrong question, and that bothered Celia. The Host's glottal filled the car, frustratingly just at the edge of comprehension. What was she saying? Take me home? Kill me? Celia tried to block it out at the same time as she strained to understand—there was something accusatory about the reverberant moans and staccato chortles. Something knowing.

Religious leaders had suggested that the Hosts spoke in tongues. Experts in the occult disagreed and said it was a language older than man, its sibilant clicks maybe older than time. Science writers hypothesized an extraterrestrial origin; SETI relaying recordings of their mangled words—if that's what they were—into the cosmos.

The Host's febrile rant rose to a crescendo and then fell to a sodden murmur. Celia moved her feet a little further from the spreading seep on the floor. The Uber steered through the suburban streets, and Celia tried to think back to the first reported appearance of a Host sixteen years ago. Since that time, there had been an unnumbered profusion of changing theories—stranded souls (self-beaching, like whales, in bodies that could be traced to no one), or spontaneously regenerated cold cases, Jane and John Does sprung from who knew where (or what), or aliens trying to pass as humans (and doing a terrible job of it). Using special software, linguists played their speech backwards and at different speeds, codified and pixelated. Money poured into think tanks and research centers like the one run by Max's grandmother at Sullivan College. Yet progress was slow and confounded by the rapid physical "disassembly" of the Hosts in "captivity." So all Celia could do (wanting and not wanting to open the passenger door and push the Host out onto the street) was to quietly agree with her copassenger that yes, it was wetter and warmer than you'd think it should be in February, and darker too.

The Host hissed in defeat and shrank into her thin woolen coat. She fixed eyes like broken rubies on the steady flow of mucus from the tops of her shoes as if it were her last possession.

* * *

Celia's neighbor, Mr. Ferris, lived on the ground floor of their small apartment building outside the city. Celia closed the car door behind her and checked the mailbox. Ferris sat smoking in the dark on his little front porch and tremulously watched the car disappear, the Host's open mouth mashed against the rain-streaked window.

She nodded to Mr. Ferris and stumbled over a couple of young Hosts all but invisible in the darkness at the foot of her stairs. Instinctively she reached an arm out to steady herself, making contact with the damp pliancy of one of their heads. Her gorge rose. She couldn't tell if it was male or female. The hair was wet, slimy with ichor. They both looked up at her with red eyes brimming with rain.

Mr. Ferris said, "They've been there all day. Like they were waiting for you."

Again, that wary, accusatory tone that laced its way into almost any discussion in Deerport involving the . . . invasion. Like what side you were on was too close to call. As if choice might have less to do with it—with being human—than anyone in Deerport thought. And that had to be someone's fault, right?

"Why would they be waiting for me?" Celia laughed loudly. "That part of their brain's soup."

But Mr. Ferris just wobbled his head neither yes nor no. "I've called the Emergency Service to get them the hell out of here."

* * *

After her LA wedding got called off over a year ago, Celia had moved east and picked a town where there was no one to disappoint and nothing was her fault. She'd mostly kept it that way, even after she and Max began to date. He knew about her past, of course, partly through the rumors and hearsay, but he wasn't interested in talking about it. Best not to dwell, he said. About a month ago, he found the dried wedding bouquet in her closet, and she'd asked him if he was disappointed.

"In what?" he'd asked. "That you were almost married once or that you kept the flowers?"

"Either."

He'd danced a stiff little jig and said he was okay with it if she was. "I'm Irish," he said. "Disappointment is in our mother's milk."

His upturned mouth said he was joking but his downturned eyes said he was waiting for the punchline.

* * *

Celia called goodnight to Mr. Ferris. She itched to take a shower although there had been exactly zero recorded human deaths from contagion by a Host. She was on the third step when she heard him cock his rifle.

Ferris was of the generation who lived most of their lives before the first so-called Stranding in '01, which left the unnumbered souls beached in flesh conjured (some said) from dreams. At first, in their bulky parkas and twisted scarves, they were all but indistinguishable from a heartsick humanity, until you got up close and there was that telltale ripple of gooseflesh at the back of your neck, the half-pleasant smell of dried flowers and deadfall, an urge to both pee and cry.

Sixteen years later, Ferris still talked about Hosts as if they weren't there, as if just because he couldn't understand what they were saying, they must not be able to understand him either. Celia knew, as he must, that there was no point in waiting for the Emergency Service vans. They'd drop the Hosts at the city limits, but the Hosts would came back. They vanished when they were good and ready. No one knew why, or where to. Following a pod—or a "pack" as they were sometimes called—of Hosts to their next destination was known to be a waste of time at best, bad news at worst. So-called "Host Hunters" typically reported anything from a blown carbu-retor or misremembered turnoff causing unforeseen delays. Flash flooding, a breakup call from a lover, some glitch in the celestial software. By the time the hunters got to where they thought the Hosts might be, they were somewhere else. It was just bad luck.

"There's one up at your kitchen table too," Mr. Ferris called up after her. "I saw it from the backyard."

"Killing a Host is manslaughter, Mr. Ferris." Celia kept going up the steps without turning around, lest she lose heart. Her mouth felt dry and her eyes hurt, like when she was little and her uncle, coming in to say goodnight, would open the closet door, walk inside it and come out, intact. Still himself. Just to prove to her that it was empty of monsters. For now.

"Manslaughter," she heard Ferris say behind her. "Ain't that a joke."

No one locked their doors in Upper Deerport. Just her luck to have a Host in her house. Celia's hands slipped on the icy door latch. She dropped her umbrella on the front step and stood in the threshold for a moment to let her eyes adjust and to will her hands to stop shaking. The kitchen table stood against the rear window that looked down over the building's shared barbecue area. The dark glass reflected the blank kitchen countertops and Celia standing by the fridge—tall, her hair attractively shorn, and still in her winter coat. The Host that was there earlier—if that was what Mr. Ferris saw—was gone, with no sign in the kitchen, or anywhere else, of anyone at all. She sagged against the fridge. The big glass of wine that she'd been looking forward to no longer seemed like the kind of thing she wanted to do alone, and the bed where she finally stretched out fully dressed, barely creaked under her weight.

She woke before dawn, weeping, something that hadn't happened for months. She'd dreamed again about her uncle. In the dream she (it was both her and not her) was driving north on Interstate 5 when she hit a Host. The Host bounced off the hood, but when it landed on the snow, it wasn't the Host. It was her uncle lying there instead.

On waking, her nose was blocked and when she turned onto her back, tears trickled into her ears. She sat up and blew her nose, and then she smelled roses and rust.

Celia waited for her heart to slow, unable to get warm. She sipped some water from the bottle on the bed table and sank back under the covers, still clutching the Kleenex box to her chest. She pulled the quilt up and tried to fall back to sleep, to find erasure in another dream. In this one she was standing in the shared barbecue area and when she looked up at her window she could see the Host in her kitchen. He stared ahead, not at her, but over her, across Deerport at the freeways beyond that led to other towns, other cities. In the dream the Host was male, although Mr. Ferris had not said that he was. To reach him, Celia had to climb down—not up—twisting flights of broken stairs. When she finally got to her kitchen, the Host stood waiting before an oblong box on the kitchen table. Celia in her dream went over to open the box, and in it, her wedding bouquet was swimming in blood.

She woke up curled on her bedroom floor, drenched in sweat and freezing. Her arm was asleep from where she'd been lying on it. It hung from her body like a dead fish. She got up and pulled on a robe with the other hand, went into the kitchen to look for the Host, but now all around her was a terrible emptiness, full of nothing but itself, an enormity of sighs.

She turned the furnace on and waited for her coffee by the window. Hosts congregated beside the barbecue stove in the courtyard below. Rain fell and in the sky was a glimmer of rainbow. Rivulets ran down the tarp covering the stove. The Hosts huddled around a plastic table beneath a huge steel umbrella, shivering indifferently in cheap thermals and parkas. One of them had a torn ear that dangled beneath a balaclava by a shred of skin. The leg of another had burst open like a squished caterpillar.

Celia switched on the TV. The local cable station was running the story under the banner, "Upstate Town Divided by Influx of *Hostis*" (the Latinate term was often confused for the plural form). There were two panelists. One was a high school science teacher calling for tolerance, saying it was like coastal Florida towns infested by geckos, or a breed of rare bird, or beaches in New Zealand where the whales repeatedly stranded. He called for unity in the effort to herd the Hosts and get them moving again; but the other panelist, a congresswoman, was calling for a different kind of roundup.

"It's not a question of *if* they're contagious," she said. "But *what with.*"

"What about the homeless? The disabled?" the science teacher said. "Burn victims or refugees from a chemical attack? Would you want to round them up too? Who are we to judge who's doing a good job of being human and who's not?" He crossed his legs and laced a bony hand across his knee. "Or even how being human is different than not."

"I don't leak," the congresswoman said. "At least not in public."

The science teacher turned to the camera. "My point exactly."

Celia went back into the bedroom to get dressed for work. She turned on the light but it made little difference. She opened the closet to pick out her clothes. The corner of a cardboard box peeked out at her from the top shelf beside her backpacks and purses, and she reached up and brought it down. It was white and rectangular like a small coffin. She cradled it in one arm and raised the lid. Inside the box was a wedding bouquet—white roses and tulips, not swimming in blood like in her dream, but tied with a pink ribbon. The petals of the roses had dried to yellowed parchment, and the leaves of the tulips twisted into black fingers grasping at the ribbon as if it were a noose. The smell of it was the same as in her dream.

Celia put the box back up on the shelf and selected a pair of black denim vintage bib-and-brace overalls to wear with a green turtleneck sweater. She picked out sparkly socks and black patent brogues. It was Tuesday, she remembered. The day Clare—Max's glamorous new sister—was due to arrive.

Mr. Ferris was already waiting at the bottom of the steps. His whole head trembled—and she wondered if it was the first manifestations of Parkinson's Disease.

"Make sure you lock your door."

"Okay," she said, even though she knew he'd come up as soon as she was gone and see that she hadn't.

* * *

At her stop, she had to wait for the later bus because the first two were packed. Celia watched a woman in a long puffy jacket barking instructions into a megaphone to volunteers rounding up Hosts into minivans. But Celia knew they'd be back, just like the whales in the New Zealand towns restranded—unwilling or unable to be saved.

"Why can't we understand?" Max had said when they first started dating and the New Zealand whale beaching was running on the big screen at the pub where they met for lunch. On the screen were hundreds of dying pilot whales stretched to the horizon. "Why can't we save them?" His mouth stayed upturned and his downturned eyes brimmed with tears.

* * *

Celia finally got onto a bus and tried calling Max but got no answer. She felt tired from her dream. She stood hanging onto the overhead rail, hemmed in by Hosts and nons. With one hand she scrolled through the news columns. A technology magazine was running a new take on the clone theory—the Hosts were possibly escapees from a cloning experiment based in San Diego. A local cable station had Professor Sullivan on Skype from what Celia recognized as Max's parents' living room. "—the Uncanny Valley," she was in the middle of saying. "Soul survivors seeking refuge in dreams made flesh."

The bus turned into the road that led to the public square over-looked by her office building. Her phone rang, and in the gray-noise ambience of the bus crowded with Hosts, the sound of Max's "hey" was flat and hard as beaten metal.

"Did you come by my place yesterday?" she asked. "Before you went to collect your grandmother?"

"Yesterday? Nah, I was working from home. Why?" His breath was a little ragged and she could tell that he was riding his bike to work.

"There was someone in my apartment, according to Mr. Ferris."

"A Host?"

"I don't know."

Celia's office was in one of the many canal-era warehouses repurposed in this part of town for creative start-ups, media firms and film companies. Through the bus window she noticed that a small crowd had assembled around some protesters carrying signs that read, *Go♦ hates Fakes.*

"I saw your grandmother on TV," Celia said. "From your place. That must have been exciting."

Max had a nice laugh, deep and breathy. "It's all publicity for her new book. *The Uncanny Valley—Where No One Can Hear You Dream.* What do you think?"

"Grandma could have a point," Celia lowered her voice, which seemed to boom over the muted rumble of the bus. "Take Replicants. Doppelgängers for instance."

"Or rattlesnakes," Max said. "Or guns. Or us."

She could hear the air whistle around the mic from his earphones. What could he hear at her end? The tense silence of non-Hosts anxious to be anywhere else? But her ears strained to hear what the Hosts were trying to say, and she fought the desire to know what it was.

"You still there?" Max said.

"I'm here."

"Must have gone through a dead zone," Max said.

He swore under his breath at something or someone in his way and she waited, before continuing: "What about the farmer who opened fire on the Hosts who'd gathered in his field? I just read on the news that a bullet ricocheted off the post and killed his prize steer. That's what I call uncanny."

Max grunted, his breath struggling in the cold. "A freak accident."

"That's what they called my wedding," she said before she could stop herself.

"I'm sorry," Max said. "That was bad. Bad happens. Bad luck, bad shooting, bad weather."

She struggled to draw a breath of frigid air laced with stale tobacco, cologne, the wormy musk of the Hosts. The bus had slowed to a crawl. She'd be faster walking. No one is keeping me here, she reminded herself. No one is keeping me on this bus.

"It was the dress." It was out before she realized it. Celia didn't like to talk to Max about her wedding. She could be anyone she wanted to be with him, or was that a lie too? She covered her mouth with her hands, but she could feel them listening. It was as if the entire bus was a cosmic sound shell, a giant ear turned, like a wolf's, toward the sound of her pain.

"Says who?"

"Dillon said it belonged to a Host."

"That is the biggest load of balls and you know it, Celia," Max panted into his mic as he pedaled, his brogue deepening with uncharacteristic irritation. "You ever been to a Host wedding?"

He wasn't trying to make her laugh, or to sound stupid. She liked the way he never tried to call her anything but her name. Not Cici, or Cee, or worst of all, Ceels, like Dillon did. Just Celia, because as Max once pointed out, her name meant *heaven*. "I'm Irish," he joked. "We'd no more give heaven a nickname than we would give one to Himself." And he'd pointed his finger to the blue summer sky, his downturned eyes smiling at her over his upturned mouth.

The Hosts on the bus had begun, one by one, to look at her. They weren't staring, not exactly. Some of them even had their eyes rolled up in their heads, globs of that ichor quivering on their lashes. There was a stillness to them, a gaping receptivity, that she never felt with her own kind. It was as if a part of them was receptive to a part of her, she sensed, which was significant to them in some critical way.

"There are lots of things about them that we don't know," she said into her phone, trying to free her backpack from where someone was pressing on it. "That we don't see."

"You're sounding like your ex now," Max said. "Or like Grandma. Get off the bus."

"I can't," she lied, despising herself. "They won't let me."

"Shit!" he said, and she heard the angry skid of his bike, and his bell, which he almost never rang. "They're everywhere today."

I tol *you so*, she wanted to say. His panting slowed. He'd given up, gotten off the bike.

"Don't you ever just want to know what it feels like," she whispered into the phone behind her mittened hand, "being one of them?"

"Careful what you wish—" he said, the rest lost beneath the squeal of brakes, and then, "Only way we're going to know what it's like to be a Host is if we become one ourselves, Celia. And that's not how it works."

A seat emptied behind where Celia stood and a Host sat down in the space next to the window, turned his face emphatically to the glass. He was dressed in an oversized peacoat, and a bloodless gash in his hand went all the way down to the yellowed bone. Celia breathed in that sweet, offal-like reek.

Max was right of course. You didn't become a Host, like you became a ghost, or a Zombie in a horror film. There had been no reporting of loved ones disappearing, turning up the next day with no brain and ill intent. You stayed human and Hosts stayed Hosts.

"Speaking of how things work, this family reunion of yours . . ."

"What about we go away for a weekend? Just you and me. Maybe somewhere warm? I mean it."

They had not gone away together yet. Was that what she wanted?

She heard him swear and when she asked him what it was, he said that it was nothing—he'd just pinched his finger trying to fasten the bike chain in the cold.

"Is it bleeding?" she said to no one. "You're far from your office."

"A walk'll do me good. You'll think about what I said? Damn finger's bleeding like crazy. You'll think about getting away?"

She imagined her voice swimming like a lost soul through the wires to his ears. She imagined Max's blood from his finger seeping onto the slush, and she saw the red spreading, and herself drowning in it.

The bus opened its doors, and she had to yell above the noise of the protesters in the square. "When do you pick up your sister?"

"Who?"

He hung up, leaving her with a pounding heart and an overwhelming urge to sit down in the empty space next to the Host by the window. And never get off.

* * *

The morning sleet had stopped for now and everything glittered. Workers swerved to avoid spilling their coffee on Hosts, or banging them with their laptops.

Celia had finally managed to drag herself off the bus and stayed, shaken, at the edge of the square to avoid the waving banners and chants. She crossed to the steps of her building. A protester handed out leaflets beside the bicycle stand.

The only goo♦ Host is a ♦ea♦ Host! the leaflet screamed.

"Killing them's a crime!" called out a bearded man walking past. "They're human beings."

"They're bad news is what they are!" shouted a woman in a yellow raincoat. "Getting put in jail is a small price to pay for popping one."

The woman aimed her finger at the bearded man, a well-known film producer who worked in the building. He pushed through the revolving doors and Celia followed him. As the doors circled past she heard an echoed *pop-pop*—deeply familiar by now, and eternally strange. She stopped short in the lobby and slowly turned, unable to feel her feet. There were screams. Through the eerily revolving door, Celia saw the yellow-raincoated woman drop to the curb and a circle open up around her. By the time Celia reached the elevators, news had broken about a sniper (another one) who was allegedly trying to take out Hosts from an upper story window, and missed. Instead of hitting a Host, he'd shot the woman. Sirens filled the air and brakes squealed outside as squad cars cordoned off the area. The elevator lights blinked—bad news all right. Celia turned to the street one more time—the woman lay on the ground, her yellow raincoat frilled with red, like a broken egg.

The twelfth floor was entirely taken up by the cable station where she worked. By the time Celia got off she was awash in a sickly sweat, her knees wobbling. She moved through the ritual of nodding to her colleagues and taking off her mittens and shakily pouring coffee as if in a dream. Over the next twenty-four hours, she would read online reports that the shooter, a sign writer with a small suburban business, had been taken into custody and, in fact, that the yellow-raincoated woman had been his favorite high school teacher—the one, he reportedly confessed, who had seen his true potential.

Hosts were bad news.

∗ ∗ ∗

Nerves at the office were on edge. There were half a dozen Hosts in the lobby but security managed to get them into the elevators and press the Down button. No one knew where they went after that, although later, a technician reported seeing them on the roof. At least they were out of the office for now. Celia made herself a second espresso from the machine in the staff café but spilled half of it on the way back to her office—still unnerved by the shooting. And still in the black grip of the bloody flowers in her dream. She tried to tell herself Max was right about the wedding dress—Hosts didn't get married. They didn't get born or die of natural causes. They didn't get anything. They just were.

She sipped her coffee and wondered if the Host had returned to her apartment. If he or she was there now, sitting at her kitchen table in a pool of that clear goo they leaked. Like spit and tears mixed together.

Most of the station's so-called creative staff—the writers and publicists and artists—worked in glassed-off pods along a central hallway. Since joining the company nine months ago, Celia had shared a sunny double workspace with another writer who'd been let go just before Christmas, leaving one half of the area in eerie shadow. The cable station was always either downsizing or in the process of being swallowed up by another media conglomerate, and Celia knew that the only reason she was still there was because the managers didn't want to have to deal with a woman with her history. Especially a woman.

Especially a bride.

Anyone with a backstory like Celia's had to be bad news. Bad luck. "Do you still have the wedding dress?" her coworker had hissed at Celia after she'd been fired. "The one that was bad luck?"

Bad luck was bad news. Bad luck was Chernobyl. Bad luck was a virus.

When the desk in Celia's sunny double work space became available, no one offered to take it.

* * *

While she was polishing up the promotional copy for a new animated series, Celia got a text from Max. It was a picture of him at the airport with his sister Clare, spelled like the name of the county in Ireland their parents were from. They mugged with grim cheer in the same pose as in a framed picture in Max's apartment, when Clare had been Clay. Clay was younger then, with those down-turned blue eyes in a narrower face than Max's, and wore a knitted beanie with a brim. The picture had been taken on a white winter afternoon on a skiing vacation before Celia and Max had met. Their matching red hair—Clay's sticking out beneath the beanie—was stark against the snow. Clay's arm was over Max's shoulder and Max was turned adoringly toward his older sibling, but Clay's eyes scanned straight ahead at something just behind the camera—the photographer maybe? Max had told Celia that Clay had always been a knitter, and wore those homemade beanies obsessively, like some scrap of identity too precious to deny, too painful to acknowledge— even tucked one into her suit pocket on prom night.

In the picture Max sent from the airport, Clare was wearing the same beanie. Celia wondered if she had brought it along or if Max had, a loose tie to a past neither of them could believe in anymore. She was no longer a redhead, but darkly brunette with rich purple bangs of a shade so lush that it made Celia's eyes water. She wore a leather jacket over a blouse, above which peeked the jet-black tendrils of an expensive tattoo. Celia registered the family's accentuated cheekbones and full, sad mouth. She recognized the oversized puppy eyes Clare shared with Max, and which found the camera over the top of heart-shaped sunglasses, like Gina Davis in the movie posters for *Thelma an◆ Louise*.

And what happened then was that Celia's nostrils picked up the familiar tang. She slowly put her phone down. Her nape tingled. When she turned around in her chair, there was a Host sitting at the empty desk in the shadows.

Due to some mental trick or lack of sleep, at first Celia thought it was Dillon Nix, the man she'd almost married. But on second take, she saw that she'd never seen this being before, despite a shameful finger of attraction that scratched at the inside of her ribs—that familiar shock of white-blond hair, that faulty smile. Hosts often looked like people you knew, except that they didn't really. It was a kind of illusion, like a mirage, experts said. You wanted them to look that way, and the fact that they did was merely an "effect" of the "cognitive dissonance" caused by their sudden appearance out of nowhere, which frequently figured, the experts said, as a "reappearance."

Careful . . .

But Celia couldn't shake the compulsion to call Dillon in LA just to be sure. Her ex's SoCal cheer, when he picked up the phone on the other side of the continent, rang reassuringly false, which in itself carried a ring of truth. She had to focus her gaze on the Host sitting in shadow at her coworker's desk to gather her thoughts.

"There's a Host sitting in my office," she said. "Is that normal?"

"Hello to you too," he said. "Quite the influx over there so I hear."

Dillon Nix was a trained therapist from Australia, but ran a robotics start-up in LA.

"I thought at first it looked a little like you, but . . ."

There was a phony self-deprecation to his laugh, "Like me but dead?"

"Just the white hair." Celia lowered her voice. "He's kind of cute, actually."

"Ah," Dillon boomed. "R2-D2 cute or Roy Batty cute? Or cute like 'how many human norms can one entity violate and still be called cute?'"

His sour mood surprised her. What didn't surprise her was that he didn't ask how she was doing. Whether the nightmares had returned? If she was still on the meds? When she'd dropped out of grief counseling? He'd only be disappointed in her answers, so it was best not to ask.

"They're herding them up best as they can."

"Good luck with that!" Curious the way he'd always shouted into phones. Maybe it was because he still thought he was in Australia.

"They seem to be following me around. I feel like I'm the one being herded."

Dillon boomed something about wagon circles, a well-known default Host formation, but whether to keep something, or someone, in or out, no one could say.

Celia felt that almost orgasmic stirring of a worshipful urge that overcame her whenever she was with Dillon, and was why she was attracted to him in the first place. The less he was, the more he appeared to be, and that authority over himself spilled out into the world and filled her with wonder. Turned her into a puppy. All she had wanted to do was roll over and beg, show him the new tricks he taught her. Until she found the wedding gown. That was no one's trick but her own. Or so she thought.

"Someone must know what they are," Celia whispered. "Maybe they're just not telling us."

It had been Dillon's decision to wait until after the guests' funerals before rescheduling the wedding ceremony, based on his expertise as a therapist. To go ahead any sooner, he assured her, would leave them with insurmountable survivor's guilt (hers already was). They'd begin to blame each other, he warned, if they rushed back into it. By the time they called off the engagement a month later—in November—they already had.

"In all honesty, Ceels"—his Australian accent made it sound like *sails*—"I think a government conspiracy is the least of our worries. The Hosts just present too many options. They could be anything. Aliens. Angels!" He was beginning to sound a little hysterical. "Even brides!"

His cheap shot didn't surprise her. But the effect of his gravelly drawl on her did. He could still hold her transfixed, mesmerized, nailed to the spot. He knew nothing. He was no one. His hair was white like the Host sitting across the office from her, and he drove a white BMW and wore a clean new white T-shirt every day. His genius was in making his no one into a someone. She felt like curling up under the desk and just listening to his white noise. Almost.

"To attribute volition to a Host, after all, is—"

"I have a friend," she interrupted, "who says it's all balls."

Why should she accept Dillon's ownership of her? His crumbs of information conjured from who knew where? What did he want from her? What had he ever wanted?

"Balls?"

"He's Irish. But seriously, Dillon. How do you know that it was the wedding dress? Maybe it was the chapel—that has a history too—all those Hollywood marriages that ended in scandal and despair."

"That's the problem, Ceels. The chapel has a history. The dress didn't." Was that a flicker of panic in his voice? Irritation? Dillon never allowed himself the luxury of irritation. He never allowed himself to invest in anything to that degree.

"Why does there have to be a cause, first or last, for everything? Maybe what happened was just a bunch of factors. Chance? Luck? Something in between?"

Dillon fake-groaned like he'd explained this to her, or himself, a million times already. "Except it never rains in LA anymore and the day of our wedding there was a freak hailstorm and six of our guests died and you were wearing a quote-unquote vintage wedding dress that looked like if RuPaul got together with Old Mother Hubbard . . . no one wears a dress like that."

"I did."

"My point exactly."

Of course Dillon wasn't listening to her. But what was that in his voice? There was a shrill edge to the mellifluous drawl, flawed somehow in a way she'd never noticed before. It had been a while since he'd recounted the details of the disaster to her, something he did all the time in the beginning, as if to get the events straight in his own mind.

"What kind of friend?"

"His grandmother is Professor Maya Grayson."

"The Quantum Ontologist!" Dillon scoffed. "Quant Ont is like calling the study of faeries, Alternative Entomology. Please. Spare me that subspecies hoo-ha. Whatever they are, they're bad news, and you of all people—"

Celia felt a strange pleasure at Dillon's overreaction, at having caused it somehow, or engineered it at least, simply by being here. She bit her lip and watched the Host tap at the keyboard. The fourth finger on his left hand flapped like a deflated skinny balloon. She felt suddenly transported to the half-empty Brentwood chapel where she and Dillon had waited for a congregation that would never assemble. The few scattered phones, including that of the celebrity celebrant, had tinged, reporting freak ice storms that had closed the freeway, sending hundreds of cars off the road, the hospitals full. Dozens critically injured, six dead.

All six were guests at their wedding.

"Whatever. Ceels? Wipe the keyboard after he's gone."

"On second thought," she said, "my Host doesn't look like you at all."

* * *

She hung up and went over to stand behind the Host. He was scrolling through the news sites like he was looking for something. The side of his face looked like smashed plums, a landscape of pulpy, bruised tissue through which his jawbone gleamed. He gave a phlegmy sob.

Celia's manager walked past and peered through the glass wall at Celia standing over the Host, and then he quickly looked away, in pity or fear, it was hard to tell. Pity at fate's leprous power—fear that bad luck was as contagious as it was incurable.

Celia went back to her work, trying to forget about the Host. But if she was honest with herself, there was something reassuring about the gentle tap of his keyboard—the void that hung over her shoulder seemed smaller and not as dark. After all, the Host was a coworker of sorts, and better than none. At lunchtime, instead of going to the staff cafeteria, she brought her sandwich out and passed half across to him. He took a bite and then put it down, resting his hands on the desk in front of him. There were crumbs stuck to his fingers, a blob of mayo on the flattened, flaccid pinkie.

"Have you seen the Tate Nudes over at University Gallery?" Celia said. "It's meant to be a very good show. Deerport doesn't usually get those big international collections, even though it's just part of it—the rest is still at MOMA. So I was in New York for the first winter that I moved back East, before I took the job here. I'm a sucker for Rodin. You too? You think you won't be affected by *The Kiss*. You think, just another sculpture. Photographs make it look cheesy, even. But see it in the flesh, it just lays you out. It's intimate to the core. Like a scene from your own sex dream."

The Host's mouth jerked in what she took as total agreement.

A rap at her glass partition startled them both. It was the receptionist who said that Celia had a visitor waiting in the lobby. The receptionist peered through the glass at the Host tapping away at his keyboard, and beat a hasty retreat.

Celia tore herself away from her one-sided conversation with the Host and checked the time. She was shocked to see that Clare's plane had landed over an hour ago. Celia had totally lost track of the morning—where had it gone? There were three missed calls from Max. She checked her reflection in the dark screen of her computer, wished she had time to make herself look more presentable for Max's glamorous new sister.

But when she got to the lobby, it was only Max, and he was alone.

"Have you had lunch?" he said. He had a messy Band-Aid on his finger.

He didn't wait for an answer.

"I would have gotten here earlier," he said. "But I had to take Clare home. And then the Hosts have set up a kind of . . ."

"Wagon circle?" she said.

He nodded. "Around this end of the block mainly."

He looked pale and there was something wrong with his head. Something more than the fact that he was wearing Clare's beanie under his sweatshirt hood.

She decided not to tell him about the sandwich she shared with the Host. After speaking with Dillon, she felt herself slipping into old habits of not wanting to disappoint.

Of lying instead.

"Feel like a beer?" His big droopy eyes searched her face. "Clare was wiped and just wanted to get home. So it's just me."

They went next door to the pub. He ordered a burger with his Guinness but hardly touched it and didn't notice when she ordered nothing but a glass of water. Hosts circled the bar with their dread sense of erratic purpose, and their flesh looked torn in places and flapped on some of them like wings.

"How's it all going?" she said. "How are you and Clare with each other?"

She reached for one of Max's fries and dragged it through a puddle of ketchup.

"Awesomely cool. Totally chilled!"

Without warning, Max drew the hood of his sweatshirt off his head and pulled off Clare's beanie.

"Whoa!" Celia gasped. "You shaved your head?"

"Clare did." He passed a hand over his blue-white scalp and grinned at her searchingly. She reached across and touched the warm, bony curve of his head, kept her hand there longer than she meant to. She didn't expect it to feel so sensual. In contrast to his scalp, his face was badly shaved, patches of rusty stubble he'd missed, a razor cut on his chin.

"Why?"

"Truth or dare. We used to play when we were kids—she thought it might break the ice."

"Did it?"

A Host edged past their stools and Celia caught the scent of worms.

Max leaned forward, already a little drunk. His droopy eyes were boyishly bright—the lights of the pub radiating off his bald scalp like a halo. "She says to me, she says, 'You know Maxie, in the end we finally get to be the person we always wanted to be.'"

"What did you say?"

He leaned back and looked away, banging out a quick drum riff on his knees.

"I said, be careful what you wish for, Sunshine. Be careful . . ."

"And then she dared you to shave your head, just because you called it?"

Max drained his pint and waved a waitress over. He deliberately centered the empty glass onto the coaster. "No ma'am. I called 'Truth.' That's the thing of it. She says, 'Okay Maxie, truth it is. How'd you like to be bald? Haven't you always wanted to shave your head?' And I says, 'It's true. I have. You know me.' And she says, 'I knew you'd say that. See? That's why I brought these along'—she gets out the clippers—'because I *o know you, Maxie, and always will. And that's how you can know it's still me, Clare—it was always Clare, never another.'"

She heard the sob after he said his sister's name, and felt her own eyes brim, couldn't catch the tears before they fell. She laid the fry back on the plate.

Max wiped his badly shaven face with the heel of his hand and rubbed it back and forth across his flawless scalp. The two halves of him looking somehow more in sync than they ever had.

"What did you say?" Celia finally asked.

"'Do your worst,' I says. And so she did."

Be careful what you wish for.

* * *

Max and Celia had met at an industry fund-raiser. He was on a working Visa from the UK. A freelance musical producer, he'd found a job in Deerport recording soundtracks and jingles, in between trying to work on his own projects. He still occasionally brought out a pat Irish persona, like the dead bouquet she kept in her closet, saved for what? For whom?

Whatever he knew about her un-wedding—the ice and rain spinning cars off the freeway, Celia waiting at the alter in the vintage dress she'd bought for a song on eBay—he never mentioned it unless she did. And after the disastrous meeting with Grandma Grayson, she rarely asked about his family.

Now he said, "If I'd known Clay was always Clare . . ."

"What would you have done differently?" Celia said.

"Taken up knitting?" he said, and she thought, *No joke.*

"Anyway, I like it." She had to admit that this new Max—unraveled was the only word she could think of—had an appeal. Was that Clare's doing, or had it been there all along? "You'll survive. You're Irish."

"Guilty as charged," he said, doing that awful little elbow-jig of his. She wondered if he could sense the stares of the other customers, or if he was too stricken to care. And too drunk, maybe.

She pretended to laugh, and he pretended that it was a joke. She could pretend to be anything she wanted. She'd moved back East and began to run, went to the gym and lost twenty LA pounds, became as lean and spare as a cheetah. She drank Negronies and downloaded nineties hip-hop and bought bamboo underwear and was saving up to go to Helsinki. Max never tried, even in jest, to use her survival as a rickety bridge between them, and she pretended that she didn't want him to.

Now in the noisy pub, she reached for his hand.

"How's the finger?" she said.

"I'll live."

Outside, clouds gathered over the square and Hosts loitered restively, reminding her of her new coworker left behind at the office.

"Best let you get back," Max said, sensing her distraction. He had returned the beanie to his head. He was all eyes again. All mouth.

"Lots of copy to write," she said not meeting his gaze. "It never stops."

"Amen to that."

They were still holding hands out on the street until a Host walked between them. Celia waved goodbye and rushed back into her building, racing for the elevator door before it closed, already thinking about the Host in his half of her office, hoping he'd still be there. It was only after she'd made it through the door and saw that her office was empty, that she remembered that Max had just spoken about Clay and Clare as the same person. As if by saying it, he could make it true.

* * *

She felt cheated by the absence of the Host, the breath crushed out of her as though she'd been winded. She stepped further into the office and shut the door wishing she'd not stayed out so long with Max. Not that it was his fault. *Guilty as charge*. She broke off a yelp when a white-haired figure emerged from a pool of shadow. Her hand clapped over her mouth, watched the Host, *her* Host, sit back down at his desk. Before he could change her mind, she tore off her coat and sank down in front of her computer but didn't start her own work until she heard the soft tap of the keyboard resume behind her. She went online and ordered three more pairs of overalls in different styles and colors, as if there was some connection between what she was wearing and the Host's appearance. Dillon always hated overalls. Was that it?

"I'll be right back," she said, closing the door behind her and locking it.

Then she went to the café, made two espressos under the fearful, pitying eyes of her human coworkers, and brought them back to the office without spilling a drop.

"You know how you go to the movies, but even after the projector's off, the images are still there?" Her mouth was full of muffin.

The Host sipped his coffee noisily, watery brown dribbles down his chin.

"I think that's why Max misses Clay so much, not because of who's gone, but because of who's still there."

The Host said something that sounded like a Wookie at prayer. His scalp between his thin white hair was webbed in black.

"You're here about the wedding gown of course." Celia brushed crumbs off her lap, glancing from under lowered eyelids at that white hair, the same but different. "It was pure Spanish silk, if you must know, with French lace. The veil was embroidered with real pearls, ostentatious as hell, but that's Hollywood. But I don't have it anymore. Long story."

The Host leaned on a key, and Celia watched the line of backslashes march across the keyboard. "Would I have kept it if I'd known it belonged to a Host? A choice would have been nice. All I knew was that Dillon *isn't* like it—that's what I loved about it the most, truth be told."

The Host interlaced withered fingers on the desk.

"But about it belonging to a Host—how did Dillon know and why didn't he tell me *before* the ceremony? He was so sure afterward, in his grief, desperately so. Like if it wasn't *that* which caused it, then what?"

The Host grunted and seeped.

"Is that what we're afraid of?" Celia said, leaning forward. "Having no one to blame?" She had a sudden thought and leaned forward so far that her hands were practically on the floor and she had to tilt her head up to see him. "Are you . . . God?"

A coworker rushed past, looking straight ahead and pretending to talk into their phone.

"It was a stupid dress. All lace and puffy. Dillon hated the idea of me getting married in something pre-owned by anyone but him. He gave me money, told me to get another one, but instead I spent that money getting it altered to fit me. Like a glove. The alterations cost more than the dress itself."

The Host said something in a baby-voiced babble that made her flesh crawl.

"Why did I marry him?" she said. "Because he was Dillon Nix. And I was nobody."

The Host moaned, dug in his ear for something and put it in his mouth.

* * *

When Celia got home that night, she felt Mr. Ferris's eyes on her from behind his living room window. There were no Hosts on the stairs, but up in her apartment she drank a big glass of red wine and watched them mill around the courtyard from her upstairs window. Lucky she had more overalls on order, because there was no way she'd be able to get past all those Hosts to the laundry facilities.

The next morning Celia put on the same outfit with different shoes (white Doc Martens) and stopped at Whole Foods for two salads to take to work. The market thronged with Hosts. Security guards tried rounding them up and funneling them out the back door into the alleyway. But the Hosts just circled the block and came back in the front door.

The UPS delivery was waiting at reception when she got to work. She opened it in the ladies' room and changed into a fresh pair of bib and brace overalls—faded denim, white stitching, which went with the Docs.

A new girl in production came into the bathroom. "What about all these Hosts? Kind of weird, right?"

"Why?"

The girl smeared gloss on her lips in exaggerated casualness, so that Celia knew her coworkers had already filled the girl in on Celia's history. She said that there were hardly any in her own building, not like here at work. "Maybe they're attracted to certain blood types, like mosquitoes," she said, casting a sidelong glance at Celia in the mirror.

Celia went into her office and shut the door behind her so that no one would hear her conversations with the Host. She'd shoved his desk and chair as close to the shadowy end wall as she could and the computer monitor all but blocked him from view. Celia did some more work, wondering how she'd look with purple bangs.

At lunchtime she noticed that another of the Host's fingers had a crimson split right down to the bone, and that there was a spreading dark patch at his crotch.

"So now—what you really wanted to know? After the wedding was called off, Dillon insisted I sell it," Celia said. "But I was terrified that I'd spread the curse, if that's what it was. Hadn't I done enough already?"

The Host's head wobbled precariously on his neck.

Celia adjusted a strap on her overalls. Dillon had been so relieved at her accepting his theory about the dress that they made love for the first time since the aborted wedding, and it was as good as it had ever been. They both wept. His best man from Australia was one of the dead—her dress had killed them all.

"I did what I could," she said. The original eBay seller had disappeared. She'd tried to cut it up. But it was still a dress, no matter how she tore at it. She tried to set it on fire in a trashcan and it smoldered and someone called the fire brigade and she had to pay a fine. She took it to the dump, scared even then that it would be found, and the bad luck would pass on. And on. She drove back to the dump and it was still there, like a pile of dead swans.

"In the end, it got taken out of my hands. Someone spray-painted,

"Guilty!" on the side of my car, threw a brick through the window and took the dress—and my wallet and phone and earphones and sunglasses. So that was that."

Her new coworker bubbled milky snot from his nose, and Celia agreed that the car thief could have been a Host. Taking back what was theirs.

"Max says balls. His word not mine. He said it was probably just a thief, saw the loot in the car and a way to make it look like something else. People are like that, he says. Always looking for a way out. After Clay went to New York for her surgery, he took all her stupid beanies and hand-knitted scarves and sweaters to the Goodwill and then went there the next day and bought all of them back. He says humans are nothing but bundles of bad choices. There's no first cause. No one thing to blame."

As if on cue, Max called. She rummaged for her phone so she could decline the call, and when she turned back to the Host, he was gone.

* * *

That night she dreamed that the Host had found a door at the bottom of a flight of broken steps but had lost the silver key. When she got to work the next day, Wednesday, the Host had not returned.

The next night, her dream was of a wedding. It took place behind a door at the bottom of that broken winding staircase. Drifts of dirty snow piled at the edges of the steps, hiding a silver key that only she could see. The Host still had not returned to her office.

On the third night, she dreamed that she was watching a movie with the Host and Clare, and Max's photographed face came up on the big screen. He was sitting in the poise of Rodin's *Thinker* except he was bald and his scalp was webbed in blood where the razor had split the skin, and his brain seeped through the crack in a thin red slurry. Max was trying to tell Clare something, his eye feverish beneath his bleeding scalp. The stage curtains jerked slowly closed. Celia screamed and rushed to the stage but she was too late. The curtain lay on the boards in meaty purple chunks.

By Friday, it had been three days since she'd seen the Host except in her dreams. She took out the last pair of corduroy bib-and-brace overalls straight out of the UPS box and went to work, her eyes burning from lack of sleep. Her stomach cramped from too many cups of coffee and peanut butter straight from the jar.

All through the town of Deerport, the Hosts were wreaking havoc. Roads were closed. Children were kept home from school. Mr. Ferris called a van to remove the Hosts clogging up his property but it broke down halfway to the city limits, the driver forced to miss her child's parent-teacher night, and by nightfall the Hosts had returned to the apartment building.

Then, late on Friday afternoon Celia, immersed in her work wrapping the animation publicity, suddenly felt a hot moist hand on her shoulder. The hand grew heavier, almost painful. Was it Max come to pick her up? She felt a hot rush of fear: she knew Max's tentative touch and this wasn't it. She couldn't turn around, even if she wanted to. Her computer said that it was ten past five. The office was dark and so was the hallway. Everyone had gone home for the weekend. She had lost the entire day, floating through it on the broken pieces of her dreams. From the corner of her eye she saw the Host's kinked and bloody pinkie bone. His damp thumb at the base of her neck. A tendril of ooze from his filleted finger ran down her collarbone.

"Are we going out?" It was barely a whisper.

He took his hand away and waited for her to put on her coat.

She shouldered her small backpack and followed him out using her security pass. The streetlights were burning when they got outside, grimly festive against a charcoal sky. Celia shivered and pulled her coat tight. Tonight was Max's family reunion. She pulled out her phone and tried to call but he didn't pick up. She tried to imagine him and Clare having fun at the party and Grandma Grayson making clever jokes about Clare's purple hair and Max's no hair. Or was it the other way around? Grandma's clever jokes about how truths are really dares and dares always tell the truth.

Celia and the Host walked together for a while, and the weekend crowds parted for them because it was unusual to see a Host with a non. She heard mutterings of "contagious" and "diseased." He threaded a jerky path toward Smith Park, occasionally looking back with agate eyes to make sure she was following. When the Host got to the fountain, he sat down on a bench next to another Host, a female, as if some kind of destination had been reached. Celia stood off to one side, wondering if he had led her here or she him, and why? Had he meant for her to follow, or was it simple instinct for him to come here—to join the rest of the herd? It was dark and she seemed to be the only non-Host here. There was a surliness to their numbers, a threat in their red eyes and one of them kept up a steady growl. Her heart hammered and she rummaged for her phone to call Max—but what could Max do? On the other side of the fountain, the masses of Hosts gave way to college students. Men sitting at chess tables, bag ladies snoozing. Celia breathed in the mulchy scent of the Hosts, tried to tell herself that this was what she wanted after all. Wasn't it?

The hot spicy fumes of the noodle market setting up at the end of a boulevard of poplars wafted across. The female beside Celia's Host peeled a luxuriant strip of pulpy skin off her arm. She dangled it like a ribbon. The skin was webbed with fine crimson threads that clutched to the flesh like string cheese.

"Hungry?" said a voice to Celia's right.

Celia turned and recognized Clare's purple bangs and disjointed smile from the picture Max had sent.

"You must be Celia," Clare said, hoisting an oblong bike bag. "I'd know you anywhere."

Celia couldn't decide if there was disappointment in Clare's voice or not. She felt a current jump between Clare and the not-Dillon Host. Had he brought Celia here on purpose?

"Do you two know each other?" Celia said.

"Who?"

Celia turned but her Host was nowhere to be seen.

"Sit for a while?" Celia walked toward a seat on the other side of the fountain near a juggler and some beer-drinking students.

Celia followed the purple hair. The fountain partially obscured the massed Hosts from view.

"The park is the nicest part of this shit town," Clare said, pulling her leather jacket close. "Always was."

A woman at the other end of the bench got up and walked away.

"Aren't you meant to be at your family reunion?" Celia said, sitting down.

A reggae band was tuning up over near the noodle markets.

Clare reached into her bike bag and took out some knitting. It was clearly something she'd started only recently, a nine-inch square of bulky wool in an eye-stinging shade of rusty orange. "Decided I needed some air, so I grabbed Max's bike. You've met Grandma, right? She's in her element, going on about Aristotle's law of non-contradiction and such. How what the Hosts are and what we are can't both be human. How you can't have two contradictory states of being at the same place at the same time, according to Aristotle. And Grandma." She yanked at the yarn, which jumped out of the bike bag at her feet.

"Like you can't be both alive and dead at the same time."

"Or male and female." The knitting needles clacked like dueling swords. "Just imagine!"

"Max missed you," Celia said.

"Damn!" Clare said, retrieving a dropped stitch. "He misses something. I can tell he's still looking for it, but it's a part of him, not me. Always was."

"Give him a chance."

"I could say the same to you." Clare looked over her knitting at Celia, and her eyes glittered like mirrors. Contact lenses, Celia thought. Or drugs. Her pupils were enlarged like a nocturnal animal's—ringed in dark blue.

Celia remembered her dream, the image of Max on the walls of the theatre even after the projectionist had left the building. The silver key to the door at the bottom of the guilty steps.

"Do you think Max's Clay is out there somewhere now?" Clare said, looping an ochre string around a stubby finger. "Do you think Clay is one of them? Somewhere both possible and not?"

The smell of worms was all around them, coming from the Hosts. They massed around the fountain, circling it entirely, the spray forming a ghostly prism above their dark heads. They jostled each other, a focus to their sleepwalker's gait that made Celia's legs grow cold. One turned toward her and bared carious gums.

The scarf had grown an inch. The earthy orange would bring out the blue of their eyes—Clare's and Max's. As if reading her mind, Clare said, "It's for my fiancé. An eternity scarf. She's a snowboarding instructor."

It occurred to Celia that the color of the scarf was uncannily like the color of Max's shaved off hair.

"What's an eternity scarf?"

"One with no beginning or end," Clare stopped and ran a finger along the attached edge. "When it's done you just sew both edges together with the same yarn."

"If Max's projection of Clay is out there," Celia said. "With them, the Hosts, what do you think they want?"

Clare laughed, "To be an◆ not to be, maybe."

"To be free." Celia smiled in spite of herself. "What brought us here together tonight? Them? Or just chance? Just destiny?"

"Maybe nothing," Clare said, pausing to retrieve another stitch. "It is the main park in this part of the city, and it is Friday night—everyone comes here. Glad you did though."

Celia persisted—something told her that time was running out. The Hosts massed closer. "Sometimes I think that what they want is for us to find out what we are. So that they'll know what they are. And only then will they leave us alone. Once they know."

"Once you know you're dead, I say."

"I feel like I've been two people."

Clare pulled out the big ball of yarn from the bike bag and handed it across to Celia. "Do you mind? It keeps catching on the edge of the bag."

The loose ball of yarn quivered on her lap, headless, legless, devoured by the slicing needles, or . . . transformed?

"You were engaged to that robotics ass, Dillon Nix, in LA? Max told me that was you." The needles clicked faster. The ball of yarn on Celia's lap twitched as if being flayed.

"Is that me dead already?" Celia said. "Or is it still out there?"

"We're all scared of that," Clare said, and there was a pinch of Irish salting the edge of her vowels now. "Maybe that's what *they* are. That part of ourselves that's dead to us."

Celia gently teased some yarn free from the fiery ball on her lap. "Or just free not to be?"

"Max says be careful what you wish for. Balls I say. But that didn't stop him from refusing to believe what he already knew." Clare sounded like she was trying not to cry. She'd dropped so many stitches that the orange square had become a misshapen rhomboid. "I say, the truth will set you free."

"Six people had to die to set me free."

Clare turned to Celia, the knitting needles frozen in an *X*. Lamplight washed her purple bangs silver. "The papers said five."

"My uncle was pulled from his wreck and died at home. It wasn't reported in connection with the wedding. My aunt insisted. They raised me."

Clare put the needles flat on her lap. "I was there. When it happened."

"Where?"

"Max doesn't know. I was in LA with my band. We were caught in the storm too, but we were lucky. We just pulled over and waited it out. I remember seeing the news that Nix was getting married, but I didn't pay it any attention—not my scene. But afterward, he gave an interview—"

"Several," Celia said, patting the furry ball of yarn.

"—the vintage wedding gown supposed to be haunted, how it must have belonged to a bad-news Host and how they have hidden weddings and funerals, like elephants? How he warned you, but then when he saw you in it you were so lovely that he relented, blahdeblah."

"So wait. You were there? In that storm?"

"Yes, and then I came back to New York for more surgery." Clare resumed her knitting. "I didn't know that Max was dating anyone until now. He told me about you and showed me a picture and I recognized you from the papers back last October. You're taller in person. Prettier too."

"I've changed a lot."

"We finally get to be the person we want to be," Clare said. "But there's a cost."

"It was the dress," Celia said, picking at a blister of paint on the park bench. "I kept it to spite him. Like it would make a difference. Like owning my decision to walk down the aisle in a ridiculous dress could somehow make up for being owned by a ridiculous man . . ."

"Owned is owned. Nothing ridiculous about it."

"It was a bad choice."

"In men or dresses?"

Celia began to cry. The reggae band was in full swing, and the music drifted across the park.

Clare began to talk so quietly that Celia had to lean closer, their knees almost touching. "The manager of that all-girl band I was in, she lived in LA. She wanted us all to meet there prior to our tour, but mainly to party, bond and so on—she'd set up some club gigs in Echo Park. So . . . the other thing. She lived in the same building as Dillon Nix! Call it what you will. Coincidence, weird chance. Toil and trouble, whatever. A few days before that storm hit—"

"Before my wedding."

"—which frankly none of us were all that interested in, the wedding I mean, just more LA bullshit as far as we were concerned. Especially that glitzy chapel Nix went on about in interviews—such a sordid history. Anyway, we're in the van around 11 p.m., come to pick up the manager for a gig, and we're parked in some empty stretch of the parking garage so's we can smoke and whatnot while we're waiting for her. So, granted, none of us is what you'd call sober. And then, out of the blue"—Clare's needles stopped again, this time like stilts, and she looked across to the fountain, as if seeing it all again in the ghostly mist—"there's this white BMW SUV screaming down the ramp. I mean we actually heard it before we saw it, *vroom, vroom* and so on, and then there it is, and the driver's on his phone of course—white Andy Warhol hair—and then wham, he hits a Host! Comes out of nowhere."

Celia turned to throw up to the side of the bench. Clare waited.

"Blood on the hood, splat on the ground, guts coming out of his mouth. Dead as a mackerel. What I remember is the gunk sprayed across the windows, looked black as tar—that's how lit up the garage was. Dude in the white Beemer never slowed, just kept going."

"How did you know . . ."

"That it was Nix? Cos we got the plates, yeah? Our manager turns up, we tell her about it, she says it's his car. The way we describe him—white hair, crazy pale eyes—garage is lit up like a morgue remember—it was Nix. So we call the cops and bail. Nothing made the papers of course, and by then we were already on tour. But before that, the manager did say how the body disappeared, and the car too. Came back a few days later good as new."

"Just in time—"

"—for a white wedding."

There was a long silence. Across the park, the reggae band changed to a Prog Folk duo.

Clare continued, but she didn't resume knitting. "I thought about the Host lying with its guts spilled all over that clean white floor, and sometimes I dreamed about it. Sometimes it was me on the floor. Sometimes it was Max, same guts, different face. And then I forgot about it. I quit the band and stayed in NYC to have more surgery. I could have said something when I saw the papers and there was all that hoo-ha about the dress—I read about it in the doctor's office in a woman's magazine—honestly, I had other things on my mind."

Celia patted the gutted ball of yarn, wished she had something to rinse the taste of puke from her mouth.

"You look really good," Celia said.

Clare shrugged. "The hormones kicked my ass. I got an infection due to some issue with my blood type. I have scarring that shouldn't be there. I survived. My best friend didn't. They hung themselves in their Chinatown apartment. I'm sorry about your uncle."

"He never trusted Dillon."

A light rain began to fall and Clare gently took the yarn from Celia's lap and dropped it back in the bike bag. "You had a close call. Maybe there's a Celia somewhere out there who's not so lucky."

"You mean a Host?"

"Who knows?"

"But the dress . . ."

"Dress, shmess. Look, it could have belonged to some grandma in Tijuana. Or a Host. Or both. All I'm saying is that it gave Nix an out. I mean that Host's dead body just disappeared, according to our manager. And all the blood with it. Whatever or whoever that dress belonged to before you bought it—it gave Nix something, and by extension, *someone* to pin the blame on for all the freak stuff that happened after that."

"The storm."

"It wasn't your fault. None of it."

The rain misted down and there were diamonds in Clare's purple hair. Celia tried to remember something that she hadn't let herself make sense of until now—the white BMW inexplicably in for a service just days before the wedding, and Dillon having to use a rental to run wedding errands and pick up guests from the airport.

Clare wrapped the eternity scarf around the knitting needles. She had neat square hands, like Max, and had left the nails unvarnished, which made them look more feminine. "Here is what I think about Hosts, seeing as no one's asking. I think the whole luck thing is iffy. Maybe not total superstition but more in terms of entanglement, paths all caught up in a kind of quantum snake ball. But I do think they're stranded in some way, like whales. I do. I think they were maybe on a path and now they're off the path—stranded in bodies never meant to be, but are. Does that make sense to you? Possible and impossible, and unable to make a choice until they interact with the right person, or place. Something is the key to their being, but until then they're as trapped as all of us, just looking for a door."

Celia thought she could make out the white hair of her Host coming toward her.

"I have to leave," she said, standing up. "Are you going back to the reunion now?"

Clare looked across at the approaching Host. "Maybe," she said, shoving the knitting down toward the base of the needle and putting it in the bike bag. "I'm getting married next month. I guess I should tell Max."

"What do you want him to say?"

"I don't know." She shouldered the bike back and stood up to face Celia. "'Congratulations,' would be a start."

"Fuck Aristotle," Celia heard herself say. Her Host was almost upon them.

Clare let out a final laughing sob, and held out her fist to Celia's. "And the bus he rode in on."

＊ ＊ ＊

Celia turned into the icy rain. The Host kept a few feet behind her, but he was tall and the white hair was easy to see in the dark. He herded her to the city bus terminal and her scalp needled with alarm, but she felt powerless to resist. She felt numb, needing to process what Clare had told her, needing to decide if there was a part of her that had always known about Dillon. And what then? What would she have done? She noticed too late that she had stepped onto a bus that throbbed like a giant bull. The Host had saved her a seat midway down the aisle, and she got in on the window side, breathing the frigid air in gasps.

"It wasn't me!" she turned to the Host. "It wasn't the dress."

His hands flapped in sticky indecipherable signs.

The bus rumbled into the city, doubling back onto a boulevard along the park where the noodle market was in full swing, music throbbing and the cries of children—paper lanterns swinging in the breeze. At the other end, the fountain bubbled darkly, the seats around it emptied of hosts. The bus continued through the warehouses, past stores and restaurants, before moving out into the theatre district where one of the Hosts ahead of them pointed excitedly at the marquees and flickering neon. The Host beside her made bubbles of bloody spit that dribbled down his chin and pooled at his throat. Non-host passengers shot nervous glances in Celia's direction, and jostled to get out at the multiplex where a David Lynch retrospective was playing, and then a few more got off at the ballpark. A college boy flipped her off as he alighted. The bus heated up and Celia drew off her coat and put her backpack on her lap. She was drenched in sweat.

"Where are we going?"

The bus roared past office parks, picking up speed between stops where it dropped off nervous customers, picking up Hosts in exchange. It rattled past the factories that lined the river. Ahead of them was the small airport. Discs of light moved in the sky above it. A plane taxied in and Celia wondered how many more Hosts it was bringing with it. The bus let off anxious passengers at the airport, and some more Hosts pushed on, in varied states of fragrant decay. Once past the airport and onto the highway, it skidded on the blacktop and Celia held onto the seat in front of her so she wouldn't end up in the Host's lap. He flicked red raw eyes at her and away again. The aisle was a chasm of black space that sliced the bus into two halves.

"Is this our stop?" she said, and when the next one came and went, "Or this?"

Looking down the aisle of the bus gave her vertigo. She noticed that it had begun snowing again. Big black flakes swirled past the windows. The two students who had been sitting in front of her had long gotten off, and there were two Hosts in their place. She looked around the bus.

Everyone was a Host except her.

"I think I'm on the wrong bus," Celia said. Had she been given a choice?

All the non-Hosts were gone. She was the only one left. She was so terrified she couldn't move. The inside of the bus grew dark, the red eyes all around her were bodiless and broken.

"Next stop," Celia yelled and banged the stop button over and over again. "Next stop!"

Outside, a mall floated behind the swirling flakes like a showboat on a vast river. She stood up and tried to climb over the Host's legs into the aisle, fighting the vertigo. Her arms felt unexpectedly heavy and she realized that it was because she was holding the giant wedding bouquet of roses and tulips. She'd been holding them the whole time. Her muscles cramped with the weight. How much longer could she hold on?

The Host obligingly shuffled beneath her to the window seat and Celia crawled over him. But when she looked at the black strip of aisle, like a bottomless chasm, she lost her nerve. She sank back onto the aisle seat, burying her nose in the forgiving scent of roses.

"I want . . ." she said.

But did she know?

A Host across the aisle pulled his eternity scarf off and the flesh on his neck came with it. A body that could have been, would have been, maybe should have been and maybe not, but which for some reason, still was.

"Driver," she weakly called out. But the driver was a Host too—in the large mirror above the wheel she saw an iridescent bubble of mucus, like a marble, from one meaty eye. "I want to get off! Stop the bus."

As soon as she said it she knew she'd made it true. But would that be enough?

Behind and ahead of her she could see a convoy of buses ferrying the Hosts out of Deerport, their headlights off and dark inside, the snow slanting down. Celia's bones had turned to cream. The bus pulled over and let someone out but Celia couldn't see who it was.

She pulled her phone out of her backpack with shaking hands. The battery bar was a hairbreadth of red. She called up Max's number but only managed to drop a pin before the screen went black. The bus picked up speed again. Wind whistled and the fields were a blur, distant towns a smear of light. She suddenly felt so cold, colder than she should feel.

The freezing air burned the skin on her arms, horrifyingly, inevitably bare in French lace. She looked down in shock, her eyes traveling from the white of her Doc Martens to the torn white hem of the wedding gown. Of course. How could she not see this coming? Had she been wearing it the whole time? Had she ever really taken it off?

"I felt so guilty," she told the Host between chattering teeth. "I thought I'd ruined everything. That it was all my fault. But it's really so beautiful, isn't it? So real. The cream of the silk. When I saw it for the first time, it made my mouth water. I saw myself in it right away. I don't know why. It was like if I didn't wear it, I'd be letting something of myself go, a right I had to make Dillon see me. Really see me. It was the first time I'd stood my ground the whole time we'd been together. Maybe the dress was to show him, to warn him, maybe. That I owned *myself*—the dress was *me*! Does that make sense?"

Her chattering teeth made it hard to say any more, and she heard sobs from some of the Hosts.

"You're right, of course. Dillon didn't see me in the dress. He only saw himself."

Her own Host, the one who belonged to her alone, lifted up his head and uttered some snotty syllables that smelled of rotting leaves and dead petals.

"A way out?" Celia said. "Yes, he saw that too, but that came afterward." And then she leaned across so close to her Host that their shoulders were almost touching, and she could feel his pulpy pain beneath her own. "Who took it away? The body I mean, of the Host that Dillon killed? You? Or him?"

The veil dug into her scalp. She wished there was some life left in her phone to tell Max how wrong know-it-all Grandma Grayson was, how wrong Dillon and everyone was—how real and unreal are not mutually exclusive categories. Fuck the law of non-contradiction, she wanted to tell him. Fuck Aristotle. Here was the proof—the Hosts demonstrated that with their unbecoming bodies that *shoul* have become, could still become. Bodies that weren't and yet also were. All that yackety-yak about stranded souls and ghost ships, clone this and alien that—Hosts were bodies, real as roadkill, lying on the broken steps of possibility, waiting for the key to the door of not there, there.

For a way out.

She had to get off. She struggled to her feet, awkward in the layers of heavy silk and the veil of pearls. Her Host snatched at her, and Celia looked down for a moment at their joined hands—hers as cold as ice, his as hot as blood. "Thank you," she said.

She pulled away with a reluctant shudder and plunged feet first into the dark space of the aisle, the engine vibrating under her feet like an impossible mammoth. The Hosts became frenzied. They grasped for the bouquet with jerking limbs and splintered bone and she heard the tear of silk, the pop of unstrung pearls. "Please!" she called. "Let me go!"

The bus convoy screamed around a bend and Celia lurched down the aisle yelling again and again, "Stop! Let me off!" The driver hit the brakes at the apex of the curve, but clipped the bus ahead of it, and spun off into space, rolling across the void, spilling impossible bodies across time and space, and Celia felt herself lifted off her feet. The wind rushing through the rolling bus tore the wedding bouquet from her hand and she hit her head on something hard, tasted pennies, broken glass everywhere, roses and tulips spinning through the window out onto the snow, the ribbon a pink squiggle, and flowers everywhere, black as snow. And before the dark closed around her, a door opened, wider than an ocean, but wide enough for just one life, one shadow—and so a choice had to be made. She grew another, both whole, neither contradicting the other, each spinning off in opposite directions, one dressed like a bride swirling into the impossible dark, and the other finding solid ground at last. Celia, standing finally in her own shadow on the highway, hunched against the weather in her overalls and a turtleneck sweater and Doc Martens filling with snow. In her hand a scrap of veil, beaded with pearls. She lifted her head to the scent of roses and rust and to the red taillights of a small silver car

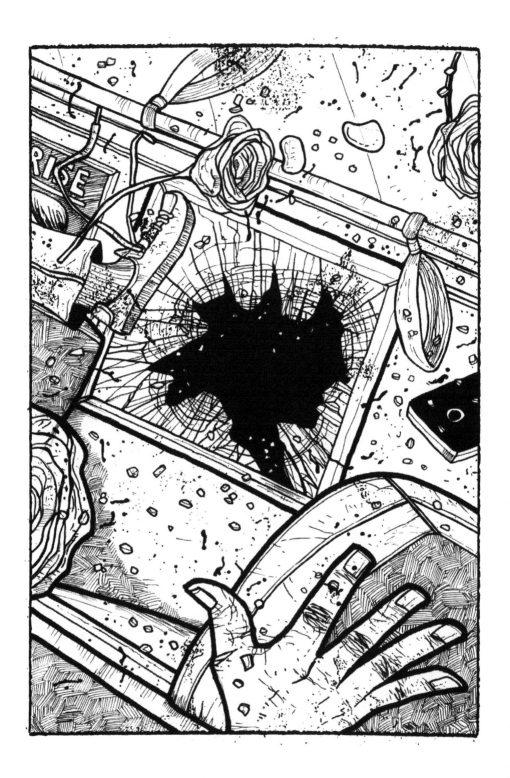

pulled up ahead, its engine running. She felt lighter than she'd felt in months. From here, a snow-blown gauntlet of twenty yards, she could see the limned oval of Max's shaved head lean across to open the passenger door for her, and so she stuffed the scrap of veil into her pocket and began to walk, and then as the snow fell faster, to run, toward the lights, toward the open door.

Author Story Notes

Union Falls

People ask me two things about this story which are 1) Why "Bette Davis Eyes"? and 2) Why an armless piano player? My answer to the first question is that while "Bat Out of Hell" was chosen for a reason—the piano intro—Kim Carnes's BDE was initially just a random song from the eighties, random the way so-called "placeholder" details can be random. But it ended up being right, as so-called placeholder details often are. I think this is partly because if you're concentrating, placeholder details, like any details, are never random but come from the same place the story comes from. Ame's voice in my head always had that slightly cracked Kim Carnes sound—peculiar and compelling, with that unique 80s-era under-overproduced sound. In the writing, it became easy to imagine her singing that song, and then kind of getting it all wrong, so it ended up earning its place in the story. Like the image of Bette Davis itself. An image that makes you think, oh no. Train smash. What's wrong with this picture?

The second question is why the armless stranger who, ironically, touches Deel the way no one else can? My stories are peopled by this kind of encounter—something between chance and destiny. In real life, I don't talk to strangers. I'm generally scared of them. I think I can come across as a little unfriendly, but that's because I know that no matter how invisible I try to make myself, that skinny kid with the nervous itch on the bus'll be sitting next to me on the train the whole way up from San Diego to San Jose, and that bag lady will ask me to show her my boobs, loud enough for everyone to hear. And that hospital patient will make friends with my dog and try to hitch a ride home with us on the roof of my car. All true stories. Rim walkers target me, and probably a lot of other writers too. Just in passing—often so fleetingly that the only way I know they're real is because of the mark they leave on my soul.

Raining Street

Sometime last year, I suggested a story-a-week program for a writing workshop I run out of a pub called the Shakespeare Hotel, on the condition that I could participate as a personal challenge, and they went for it. Someone suggested taking turns with providing prompts—and that took off too. The result is that for forty-something weeks, none of us, me included, have gotten away with making excuses for not trying to squeeze out something that looks like a story, every week. We're on the home straight now, just a handful of weeks to go, and it's been a hell of a ride. Around week seven, someone volunteered the prompt, "An ordinary day, a paranormal experience," and "Raining Street" came out of that. It began as a piece of flash, then like so many of the Bradburies, as we call them, morphed into a three-act story. Thank you, Shakespeare Group!

Anyway, the central premise comes from an ordinary day in my life when my kids were little and we were trying to survive, like Rebel, in a swank neighborhood that we couldn't afford. My neighbor—in real life a good witch—suggested getting out of the leafy nethers and heading into the chaotic guts of the city, where the food was as cheap as the shadows were long. Off I'd go, once a month, come back with an SUV bursting with groceries and my head full of stories. After its first iteration, I expanded "Raining Street," and workshopped it with my own writing group, a bunch of talented Australian authors called the Thorbys. Once they put it through the wringer, I asked my friend Angela Slatter to look at it. She made her usual wonderful suggestions, including that I show it to Andy Cox at *Black Static*, who took it. Bottom line, find some trusted readers, and do what they say, and hey presto. Bottom bottom line: never pay $7 a kilo for apples.

The Box

I was writing in a literal box, a windowless room off the bathroom of the house we just moved into and I was feeling boxed in figuratively too. Some times are like that. Scary and lonely and lovesick. My dog was starting to die. My home life was in flux. If love is the Harry Houdini of human emotions, then fear is the ruptured appendix. We create boxes to put our love in, and then we wake up one day and forget where we put the key. I wondered about loving someone so much you couldn't let them go, and even before that, maybe you couldn't let them out of the box of that fearful love. What would that look like?

Ava Rune

This began as an experiment in Australian Gothic. I remember reading about the young Mary Shelley spending time at her mother's grave, partly for inspiration and partly to make out with Percy, and this image kicked off the story, followed by Norse magic, forbidden love, and string bikinis. I also liked the idea of screwing with readers' expectations when it came to Willard's character. I wanted his arc to begin at zero and end at hero, but not in any kind of conventional way.

Lion Man

The whole thing came out of when we finally moved out of the nethers and into the city, and our new neighbors had a bunch of dogs and cats— including a giant Rhodesian Ridgeback called Earl. Earl's humans were drunks. They'd start on the vodka at 10 a.m. and be on the white wine by noon. They'd reassure anyone who'd listen that Earl was just a big ol' gentle giant, but anyone in their right mind, including my stalwart Staffie, Eric, knew better. You didn't have to have superhuman powers of hearing to pick up Earl's chuckles and the way he'd mutter under his breath, *keep believing it shit for brains.* And you didn't have to have superhuman powers of observation to notice the very short, very thick leash they kept Earl on at the playground.

"Lion Man," outed me as a writer of the weird. But that wasn't how the story began. It began as a straight narrative with a tough but still rational set-up: what if the dog you love bites, and maims, an innocent child? What do you do? I got so many rejections for this story that eventually I gave up and threw everything at it. Everything I really wanted it to be. I skewed that initial premise so tight it made the whole structure teeter over the abyss: what if the dog is some kind of incarnation of Clint Eastwood and he can talk but not like a talking dog, like a movie director in the form of an Atlantic City player who also happens to be a dog, and what if the little girl's mom is her own kind of trickster, and what if going home is the toughest kind of reckoning there is . . .

I sold it the next time I sent it out.

Fairy Tale

The simple story behind this is Ray Bradbury's "Heavy Set." I read it a hundred times and wanted nothing more than to have written it. I think if Satan had walked in at around reading number fifty-six and offered me the byline in exchange for my soul, I would have said, color me there. Satan never showed, far as I know, so instead I decided to pen a version of it flipping the genders of the mother and son, to dad and daughter, and that was the one that got away. The result is a far cry from Bradbury's flawless tale of love and dread but *Fairy Tale* will always be for Ray.

Fixed

I was with my daughter on the Surf Liner from LA to San Diego, a trip I've made more times than I can count. We were half asleep after a long-haul flight from Sydney, and I woke up to soft voices and a big man holding court with a bunch of marines about his wolf-dog. When he noticed I was awake, he smiled. "Little bitty inside voices," he said. "So we wouldn't wake you." He had a smart way about him. Turns out he was part Iroquois, and like us, a long way from home. My first novel, *American Monster* came out of that conversation, as did the character Gene, and this story is adapted from a chapter in the novel.

Rogues Bay 3013

I love reading science fiction but it's hard for me to write. Without a science background I struggle with the . . . science. But sci-fi worms its way into so much of my horror, like I can't help it, so I try and cover my tracks best as I can with actual worms and ghosts and monsters and weird chimeric jabs and feints, anything to distract the reader from how over-my-head I might be. What got this story going were two things. A long conversation in Manhattan with my great friend—the Parisian-American-Danish writer, Seb Doubinsky—about how to write your way, not out of, but into homesickness. So far in, that homesickness becomes a second home. And secondly, going to a little hidden bay here in Sydney's inner harbor one summer evening to watch the sunset. It's pretty much as I describe it in the story, from the mutts too scruffy for the cool doggy beaches, to the wafting weed and the tattooed locals drinking beer under shadowy ledges. Even the liver-colored rock that juts out of the water in the middle of the bay is real, the one where angels fear to tread.

War Wounds

When Keith McCleary and Matt Lewis invited me to submit a story for *States of Terror II*, New York was already gone, so I grabbed California while I could. I was born and lived there, but I grew up in other places, so I missed out on urban myths like the Proctor Valley monster. I made up for it this time, and the story took me way down in the rabbit hole, even managing to convince me, while I was down there, to try my hand at historical fiction, just for kicks. Keith and Matt's edits were a joy, as was meeting them and my fellow contributors at the San Diego launch. But the best thing about this story, for me, was reading it to my uncle in the audience. I can still see him there leaning on his cane, and although I know now how much pain he was in, he made sure on that night that it didn't show.

Collision

One of all the impassioned stories I wrote in the wake of the 2016 elections, "Collision" is also one of my most ambitious. I wanted to write two stories in one, stitched together so seamlessly that you could never see them both at the same time, like one of Escher's Impossible Objects. Each reading, whichever one you saw coming, had to have equal power, equal inevitability. I wanted form to mirror function—a collision of worlds, a collision of stories. Horror vs. science fiction. Matter vs. antimatter. Bubble vs. reality. And so on.

The author Angela Slatter initially called it a "rip-apart and Frankenstein together again" story. Bless her. She could see that there was a story there but one that needed to be "autopsied then revived." One reason it wasn't there yet, she suggested, was that I was too close to the material. You think? Me and half of the American voters. But she was right. I needed to step back.

So I did. I gave it enough time to let the two stories complete themselves and each other. I changed the initial dueling viewpoints to a single problematic voice. I tried to get out of my own way. I have Charlie Finlay to thank for his comments, Tricia Reeks for critical last-minute suggestions and my husband John for reading it for the hundredth time and seeing a small stitch around one of the monster's two heads that had come a bit loose.

Glow

This story came out of watching the 2016 elections on TV in Southern California with a close family member who had voted for Trump. The experience was a reckoning for both of us, as for untold families across the country. When Gordon Van Gelder emailed me with a story request for his anthology, *Welcome to Dystopia*, I had the notes that I'd written based on some of this, and it became "Glow."

Like Ripples on a Blank Shore

It never rains in Southern California. Everyone knows this. When I was living in LA I went to the wedding of a good friend who turned up out of the blue. The wedding was at the Frank Lloyd Wright-designed Wayfarers' Chapel in Palos Verdes. There was a freak storm and almost no one showed up. We got caught in the storm—cars off the road, it was crazy—we made it to the chapel but we missed the ceremony. The reception was subdued—no one dead, but a few of the guests in the hospital. My friend's wedding day. She wore a ridiculous dress and looked beautiful in it. She looked happy. I had a brand-new baby daughter, less than two weeks old, and I was happy too. My friend and I had lived together for a while, knew a lot about each other's ups, and about each other downs, and I thought about why things turn out the way they do, and the answer is more questions. This story isn't about that wedding, but it's partly about how things like it, experiences like that—they never completely go away, but ripple in and out of your life in ways you can't predict. Or drop off like stitches in a knitted scarf, only to be picked up again, maybe, without you even noticing. My friend and I haven't seen each other since that day.

The title of the story is a line from Radiohead's song "Reckoner" from their *In Rainbows* album. The song nails for me the sense that being—human, or other—is a matter of being pulled apart and put back together again. Decomposing and recomposing. An infinity of ripples.

Acknowledgments

First and foremost, thank you to my readers—you—past, present and future.

My deepest thanks to my agent and buddy Matt Bialer for his faith, support and guidance through the years, and to Tricia Reeks and all the folks at Meerkat for their smarts and patience.

Road-trains of gratitude go to Angela Slatter for having my back generally, and specifically, for reading and making helpful suggestions for early drafts of several of these stories. Ditto Sebastian Doubinsky, brother-in-arms, for being in my corner when I needed it most.

Thanks go to the Thorbys Workshop—Rivqa Rafael, Nathan Burrage, Anne Mok and Jess Irwin for comments along the way, and for my "Shakey Hotel" students for being inspiring and insanely prolific.

Thank you to Keith Rosson for his gorgeous illustrations.

Sisters are my salvation, and they come in many forms. My real sisters Anne Montiero and Cathy Stern kept it real when things got wiggy, and vice versa—thank you! Sarah Klenbort and Helen Koukoutsis read and critiqued outside their comfort zones and are still my friends—amazing! Andiee Paviour, for always being at the end of a text or phone line with writerly and sisterly love, here's to you!

To the editors who saw fit to publish early and recent work, I owe a debt of gratitude. John Joseph Adams, Cameron Pierce, Richard Thomas, Gordon Van Gelder, Andy Cox, John W. Wang, Deb Hoag, Keith McCleary and Matt E. Lewis—thank you for not only getting behind some of these tales but also making them all they could be. If you did not believe in stories above all else, none of us would be here.

Thanks to my husband John for his reading chops, and the weekly date nights. To my kids, Isabella, Jack, and most recently and joyfully, Troy Palmer—thank you for the magic love pie.

About the Author

J.S. Breukelaar is the author of the Aurealis-nominated novel *Aletheia,* and *American Monster,* a Wonderland Award finalist. She has published stories, poems and essays in publications such as *Gamut, Black Static, Unnerving, Lightspee◦, Lamplight* and elsewhere. She is a columnist and regular instructor at LitReactor.com. California-born and New York raised, she currently lives in Sydney, Australia with her family. You can find her at **www.thelivingsuitcase.com**.

PHOTO © 2018 GUY BAILEY